Soul

By Fiona Angwin

twf
Publishing

Soul-Scars

Published in the UK by:
The Writer's Forum Publishing
www.thewritersforum.org.uk

ISBN: 978-0-9564436-9-4

Text, Cover Photo Copyright © 2017 Fiona Angwin
Cover Design © 2017 Peter Jeffery

All Rights Reserved.
No part of this book may be copied, transmitted or stored in any form without the prior permission of the author, Fiona Angwin.

Acknowledgements

Once again, thanks are due to my ever patient and incredibly supportive husband Richard, especially for taking masses of photographs of Chester for me, and being dragged round every hidden corner of the city for research. Thanks also to our splendid god-daughter Becky Call, both for the use of her name and her encouragement to write the sequel.... as well as for always being so welcoming when I turn up on our (now your) doorstep unexpectedly. We're so proud of you.

In addition I'm very grateful to my friends Linda Mann, and Jan Ladhams for their help in preparing the manuscript for publication and to a host of other friends for their support, especially Martin for the formatting of the book, and Dan for creating a fantastic cover. It became a real Off Book Theatre team effort!

Mike Lockley, thank you for letting me use your excellent Chester Ghost Tours, and to the staff at Lee Louise, thanks for giving me permission to mention their shop. (To be fair, I have spent a fortune in there over the years).

For Richard Angwin, Dan (Peter) Jeffrey & Helen Bourne, Martin Williams, Ian Nenna, Steve Morse, Kirsty Brown, Richard Lewis and Chris Lucas, now you know why I was asking you all about your experiences in Chester...a city for which I am still very homesick. Lose yourselves in the pages and find yourselves in the story.

Bliss's Map of Chester

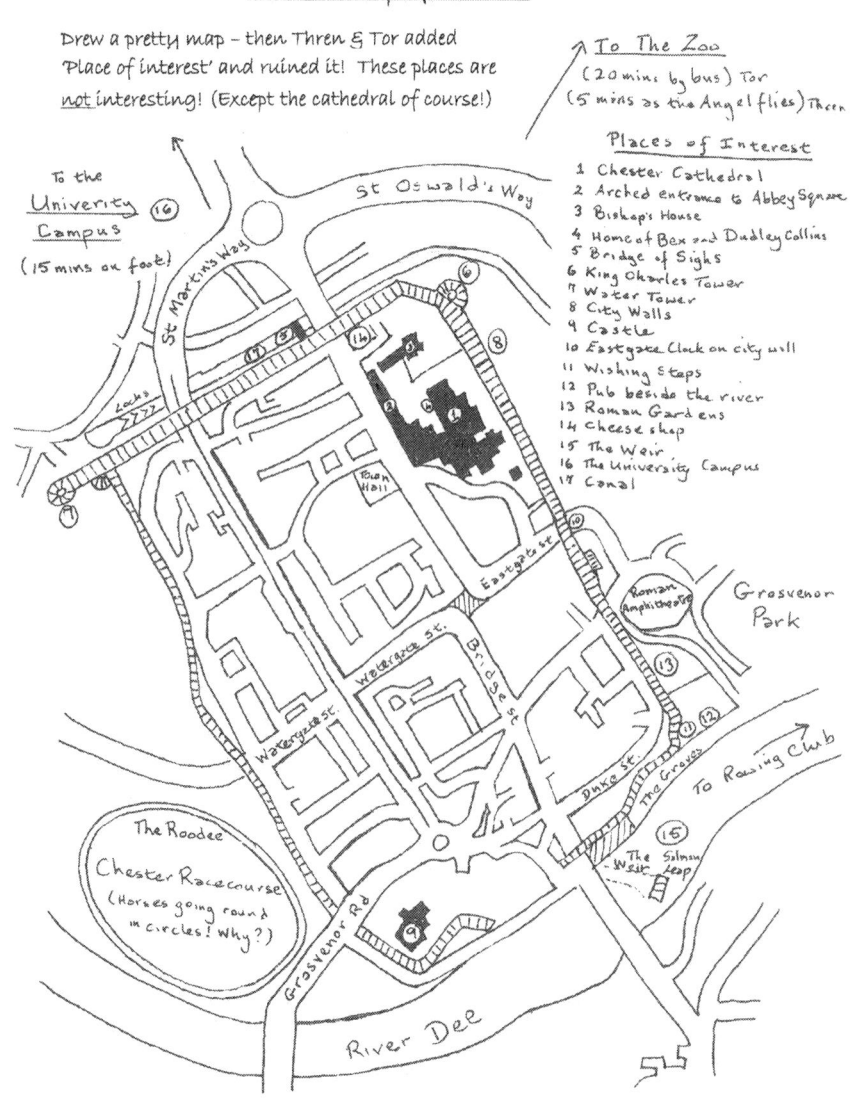

Drew a pretty map – then Thren & Tor added 'Place of interest' and ruined it! These places are <u>not</u> interesting! (Except the cathedral of course!)

↑ To The Zoo
(20 mins by bus) Tor
(5 mins as the Angel flies) Thren

Places of Interest
1. Chester Cathedral
2. Arched entrance to Abbey Square
3. Bishop's House
4. Home of Bex and Dudley Collins
5. Bridge of Sighs
6. King Charles Tower
7. Water Tower
8. City Walls
9. Castle
10. Eastgate Clock on city wall
11. Wishing Steps
12. Pub beside the river
13. Roman Gardens
14. Cheese shop
15. The Weir
16. The University Campus
17. Canal

To the University Campus (15 mins on foot)

St Martin's Way
St Oswald's Way
Locks
Bion Hall
Eastgate St
Watergate St
Bridge St
Roman Amphitheatre
Grosvenor Park
Duke St
The Groves
To Rowing Club
The Salmon Weir Leap
The Roodee Chester Racecourse (Horses going round in circles! Why?)
Grosvenor Rd
River Dee

Previously……… in "Soul-Lights"

When thirteen students at a party held a séance just for a laugh they had no idea of the terrifying consequences, but their actions unleashed evil across the city of Chester. By the end of the week one of them was dead, another as good as and a third had lost their soul. Their only hope was a probationary guardian angel, Thren, who'd been sent to look after the city as a punishment for his negative attitude, and wisecracking style, and his prim and proper mentor, Tor, a rather uptight and superior angel.

Thren's casual approach to his human charges led to a series of disasters as he learnt the ropes in his new role as guardian to the entire city, and he and Tor had to find a way to work together, at least some of the time, to defeat Dross, the demon that was attacking the students.

By the time the battle was over some of the students knew a whole lot more about what had really been going on than they would ever have expected, while others were still confused about the whole situation. However, they couldn't be told the truth without breaking the rules yet again, which would have led to further trouble…….

The Rules

(As written down by trainee angel Bliss during her guardianship training)

1. Good and evil are held in a balance and counterbalance situation.

2. If this balance is disturbed there is trouble. *(With a capital T, I suppose)*

3. If any angel allows a human to catch sight of them (other than fleetingly during an emergency) this breaks the rules. Talking to humans also breaks the rules *(I don't know why they even include that one on the list....we're hardly going to get chatting, are we?)*

4. If the rules get broken by any of the angels, then something from the Darkness has the right to come through, though anything as powerful as a demon needs an invitation from a human as well. The human who invites them is usually the first to be destroyed by the demon, who is only allowed to attack the person or people who let them into the human world. *(Honestly, who in their right mind would invite a demon into the world?)*

5. If lesser rules get broken, then Lesser Invisibles can come through into the world. *(Things like icky little imps I suppose....eeeew....I can't stand imps)*. This could be caused by giving humans more information than they're supposed to have....about soul-lights for instance, or by one human telling another about us. *(Of course, that would never happen, because no angel would be so unprofessional as to be seen in the first place)*.

6. All angels are supposed to stick to the rules. *(Well that's a bit obvious)*.

7. All demons cheat! *(Again......Obvious!!!)*

8. Prayer is Powerful *(Another obvious one!)*

9. <u>Remaining invisible</u>. It's all in the wing-beats (*apparently*). If you beat them at a certain frequency they set up such a disruption to the light pattern that you're almost invisible. People just see a very faint disturbance to the light, like a heat haze, around where the angel is standing. Most people won't even notice it, and will look right through an angel. If an angel suddenly stops beating their wings when they'd been using that frequency they'd still remain invisible for a few moments, until the light around them stops vibrating, and the haze disperses. If you change the frequency and the angle of the wing beats, your body can be seen, while your wings are just a faint haze behind you. (*Not sure what the point of that is, if we're meant o be invisible all the time!*)

10. <u>Soul-lights</u>. Little glowing globes of light inside people that angels can see and humans can't. These are peoples' souls (*apparently*), and come in lots of different colours because they reflect a person's personality. Very dark colours may mean the human has something troubling them and weighing them down, pale lights are a good sign....all of them can change over time, and are also affected by moods (*Moods?*) Red = Anger, Icy Blue = Fear etc (*Etc....what's that supposed to mean? Why don't they just tell us what every colour means? It would be so much easier*)

11. <u>Influencing people</u>. No angel can force a human to do anything they don't want to do. (*I should hope not!*) All an angel can do is whisper positive suggestions into a person's ear, appeal to their better nature, and encourage them to accept the angel's ideas, while letting the person think that they've come up with the plan themselves. This takes tact and patience. (*Easy!*)

12. Demons are fallen angels (*Yuck!*) and are desperate to collect soul-lights. The more souls they can take back into the Darkness with them, the more powerful they become there. (*All demons want power*).

Easy Peasey – I can do this!!!! I just need to take notes, write lists and be organised! (Note to self – create colour charts!)

Chapter One

Thren was lying on the cold, wet roof of the cathedral, tossing and turning in his sleep. His wings were rumpled, the feathers bent in all directions, and they had lost their former pristine whiteness. Tor perched on the battlements of the edifice watching over him with pity. She knew it wasn't the weather that was affecting his sleep like that....angels didn't really need to sleep anyway, just rest a little now and then ...but Thren wasn't getting any rest. Every attempt at sleep seemed to unsettle him even more. Tor, the more experienced of the two, recognised the signs. She should do, she'd been through it too. Every guardian went through what Thren was going through, eventually. Wiping the pitying look from her face, she nudged him with her foot. He might as well wake up, since dozing wasn't helping him anyway.

Thren sat up instantly, looking around with panic in his eyes.

"What's happened?" he asked blearily, "Did I miss anything?"

"No", said Tor, primly, "Everything is fine, as far as I can see". "You can't see", said Thren, anxiously, "That's the problem. You can only see that Bex is alright.....what about the others? What about the city?

How would you know if somebody needed me?"

"I wouldn't", agreed Tor, "That's your job, but the rest of the group must be fine, or Bex's soul-light would be showing me there was trouble, and it isn't".

Thren scrambled to his feet and moved over to the edge of the parapet, to look down over the city of Chester. He flicked his shoulder length golden hair out of his eyes with a nervous gesture of his hand, terrified of missing something. He could see people wandering through the streets, going about their business. Tor was right, there didn't appear to be any one in trouble, or in need of his help.

"You still shouldn't have let me sleep, lady, I might have been needed".

"You needed a rest", replied Tor.

"Well, I sure didn't get it", growled Thren.

"Same old nightmare?" asked Tor.

"Same old. Every time the same! I'm gonna give up on sleep, rest, all of it. It's doesn't do me any good anyhow". Thren spoke without taking his eyes off the people in the streets below him. He was glancing around almost obsessively, trying to look in all directions at once....trying not to miss anything.

Tor didn't ask Thren what the nightmare was about.....he always refused to tell her, but she knew it was always the same dream, prodding and pricking at him, stopping him getting any proper sleep. His eyes were still flicking from place to place, but they paused when he looked towards the University campus. Taking the time to check on the individuals he cared about. 'Cared about?' he thought, 'What a difference a couple of months makes'.

"Three months, actually", commented Tor, smugly. "You Came Down in February...."

"Er, did I say that out loud? Cos I sure didn't mean to.....though I gotta say, I'd rather know I spoke it aloud than find out that you know what I'm thinking. That I can do without".

"I don't need to hear your thoughts, in fact I'd much rather not, but I can generally guess what you're thinking....which I find rather depressing".

"Then quit hanging out with me, lady, I never invited you anyhow"

"I'm your mentor", she snapped, "I have to be here. Plus this is where Bex lives, and I'm responsible for her".

"And I'm responsible for putting her in danger. If it wasn't for me, they wouldn't have discovered her secret....they'd never have known she had angel blood in her".

"They haven't tried anything in the last three months. If the Invisibles were coming for her, they'd have shown their hand by now."

"Ya think? They just haven't found a way through yet", snapped Thren, "Either that, or they're lulling us into a false sense of security. I have to stop them, Tor. I can't let the demons hurt Bex....hurt any of them".

"Whatever happened to the 'I don't care about the Sheep' angel I knew and.....loathed?" queried Tor smugly. Thren just glared at her. "Nothing to say?" she continued, "You used to have a snappy answer for everything.....now you just snap!"

"Go and annoy somebody else, Wonderwings", groaned Thren, "Better still, go and do your own job. Keep an eye on Bex".

"I can do that from here!" she replied calmly.

"Well, I sure wish you wouldn't....please, Tor. Leave me in peace, just for a bit, ok?" Seeing the exhaustion in his eyes, Tor decided to stop goading him, for a while at least. She turned to leave. "I'll be with Bex, if you need me." "Like I ever do," he replied....but his voice lacked the edge it normally had when he was trading insults with her. Tor sighed, and glanced back at him, but he had already turned away from her, and was watching over the city.

She knew she ought to be pleased about that. When Thren had first Come Down to be the guardian angel for the City of Chester, he hadn't taken the job seriously. In fact, he'd been sent down as a punishment, for all the snide remarks he'd made about humans, (or sheep, as he called them) and comments about how He couldn't possibly love such pathetic creatures. Because of Thren's attitude, he hadn't listened during the guardianship training, and arrived on earth completely unprepared. He hadn't even understood about soul-lights, and what they could tell him about the state a person was in....how the colours could be so individual, giving him a clue about what its owner was like. He hadn't realised that his position as guardian wasn't just a punishment, but a test, too......to see which side he was really on. He'd passed that test....just about...but not before he'd broken a lot of rules. Rules he hadn't even realised existed.....rules that really mattered.....because they kept the dark things, the demons, out. Now he was suffering for it, and Tor felt for him.

"Go Away, Tor!" Thren growled, and she did, going down the stairs into the main body of the cathedral.....playing it by the book as usual....not just fluttering her wings and taking to the air. Oh no, Tor wasn't one to break the rules.

As soon as she was gone, Thren's body sagged. He sank to his knees, groaning, and opened the top of his long white robe with shaking hands, to stare at the scar on his chest. It was red, and throbbed where the broken shaft of wood was sticking out of it....and he could swear that the scar was getting bigger.

The wooden spike had been thrust into his chest a few months ago, during a battle with the demon, Dross, and nothing Thren tried enabled him to pull it out. Two things bothered him about that.....one was the pain it caused him "Angels do *not* do pain," he muttered to himself, again, as he tried to tug the shaft out of his chest once more. The other was fear....just before that battle he had had started to feel a pain in his chest, whenever any of the humans he was connected with were in trouble. Tor said it proved that he was getting better at being a guardian angel....starting to care about them. 'Which *totally* sucks', thought Thren, 'I mean, what's so great about that? If I was getting better at the job, you'd think there'd be some kinda reward. Pain's gotta be more of a punishment, whichever way you look at it'. Now, however, he was concerned. 'What if I can't tell any more....if one of them is in danger and I can't even feel it, with having this thing sticking into my chest all the time?'

    For a few minutes he crouched on the roof of the cathedral, willing himself to stay calm. After all, if he panicked he wouldn't be able to do his job properly....to protect everyone.... and he found he was being swamped by panic more and more often. Hauling himself to his feet he surveyed the city again. The rain had stopped and the sun was shining. There were no apparent problems, but he noticed that the good weather meant that there were more people on the streets than usual....especially down by the river. He took off into the air, adjusting his wing beats so that neither he nor his wings were visible to the human eye, and flew over the city and down to the edge of the River Dee. He'd always found that area peaceful and calming. 'Sure could do with some of that right now', he muttered to himself, as he landed on the roof of one of the pretty beach huts, built as colourful shelters in the grounds of one of the riverside pubs. He heard a scream, and tensed himself to launch into action, but when he looked round he found it was just a small child who had dropped his ice cream, and was kicking up a fuss about it.

    Thren glanced up and down the river. Two girls in kayaks were paddling along the stretch between the rowing club and the weir. One of them caught his eye, as she stopped for a moment, and took off her helmet to push her hair back under it more firmly. It was her hair that he noticed. It was long and purple and went rather well with an amazing tattoo that she had on her chest. Thren could just see part of it above her vest top. She returned to her paddling, and she and her friend moved out of his line of sight. Thren could feel the warmth of the sun on his skin and feathers and he began to relax.

'Guess I'm gonna have a quiet day after all', thought Thren, as he settled down on the roof of the beach hut. Of course, he was wrong.....as usual.

Chapter Two

Tor walked slowly through the cathedral; taking care to remain invisible to any humans she passed on her way out of the building. She strolled towards the university campus. It was a pleasant May afternoon, and the streets were filled with tourists and students. The students were a little more rushed than usual....exams were looming for most of them, and there were other deadlines too...essays, assignments and dissertations, all needing to be finished and handed in. Tor felt strangely relaxed. As Bex's personal guardian angel, she only had one human in her care, while Thren was still trying to look after everyone in the city. For the first couple of months after the battle with Dross, Tor had been tense too, waiting for the demon to make another attempt to break through, and carry Bex away. After all, now the creature knew that the girl had angel blood in her, he would be more determined than ever to kidnap Bex, and deliver her into The Darkness. However, as time passed Tor began to relax; none of the Invisibles could come through to this world unless one of the rules got broken, and Tor was very keen on sticking to the rules.

She thrust her hands into the pockets of her denim jacket, well, technically it was Bex's jacket, and meandered under the North Gate arch and down the hill. While she made an effort to remain invisible, anyone seeing her wouldn't have paid much attention anyway, apart from the wings. Aside from the denim jacket, she wore jeans and a black t-shirt, also borrowed from Bex, and had short curly golden hair, not that she was happy about it. Tor preferred the more traditional angelic look, but an incident with one of the Lesser Invisibles in the spring had ruined her robe, and resulted in her long tresses being chopped off. She'd hoped her hair would re-grow, but it hadn't happened yet.

When Tor reached the campus she made her way to the canteen....most of the students gravitated towards it between lectures, or when they were taking a study break. Bex was sitting there with Flint and Paul....they had become almost inseparable after the showdown with the demon who'd attacked them the previous term. The three of them, and Bex's adoptive father, Dudley, were the only humans directly involved in the culmination of the demon incursion... the only ones who knew what had really gone on, anyway. Not that that was on their minds at the moment. They were having the usual student argument about which of their courses had the heaviest workload.

Bex was trying to make the case for Applied Biology, the course she was on, but Flint just laughed.

"Everybody thinks that Drama is a dossers' course," he said scornfully, "But you wouldn't think that if you tried it. Physical exercises, vocal warm-ups, masses of lines to learn, character preparation.... trust me, there is far more to it than people think."

Paul didn't even try to make a case for his course, Art History, not because he didn't have plenty of work to do, but because he knew that none of the other students took his course seriously. He was content to simply sit there with his friends, and feel that he belonged. The tall, skinny young man tended to be so quiet that he was surprisingly easy to overlook, with his mousey coloured hair and his thick glasses hiding large blue eyes. He'd gone from being the geeky loner to part of the team....even if they very rarely talked about what had happened....the fact that they had beaten the demon....with help from a couple of angels and Bex's dad, of course.

Tor looked at Bex with pride...the girl had a soul-light of pure glowing silver, though only Tor could see it, as the angel responsible for Bex's welfare. Anyone else looking at her would just have seen a girl with shoulder-length brown hair, which never stayed tidy, a turned-up nose and a cheerful expression. Her hazel eyes, which were flecked with gold, were probably her best feature and although Bex was not exactly beautiful, she was attractive and likeable.

Flint and Paul seemed to like her, anyway, though Tor was hoping that all they felt was friendship. Tor still had reservations about Flint. She disapproved of the length of his wavy black hair, which was tied back into a pony-tail. When he had first met Bex he'd been so moody (or sulky, in Tor's opinion) that his good looks hadn't been obvious. Now he'd opened up a little, Tor was surprised that he didn't have a string of girlfriends, but he was still disinclined to trust anyone outside the tight little group of friends he'd made the term before. As far as Tor was concerned, that was rather a shame. The young man had very dark brown eyes set in a pale, lean face, reminding Tor of some of the romantic poets she could remember from her past. Tor had rather a low opinion of poets. It wasn't so much that she wanted Flint to find a girlfriend for his own sake, as to prevent him getting any closer to Bex. She was a little over protective of her charge.

Paul turned his head, and caught a hazy glimpse of Tor standing behind him, reflected in the lenses of his glasses. It still made him jump, the fact he could see the angels, at the edge of his vision, and sense their presence, when no-one else could. He shouldn't be able to do either....it was a quirk of his unusual eyesight....which he'd inherited from his grandmother. They both had an extra layer of cells on their retinas....his granny had always called it her "inner eye". Not for the first time Paul wished the old lady was still alive....he missed her, and he had so many questions he wanted to ask. He smiled as Sarah, another student, came over to join them. She was small, and a little plump, with frizzy fair hair, pulled into straggly bunches. As soon as she'd greeted the others at the table she turned to watch a young man who was limping towards the coffee bar. Normally Sarah was a cheerful girl, full of enthusiasm, and with a broad smile that accentuated her dimples, but now her expression was serious, and her light brown eyes were fixed on the student at the counter.

"Sarah", said Bex, quietly, "Stop looking at him, you'll make him nervous".

"I know", replied Sarah, "but I can't help it. Ever since his accident, I....well, I worry, that's all".

"He won't thank you for it," commented Flint, "And he's not your responsibility. You're not his...ouch! Bex!" He turned to glare at Bex, who had just kicked him on the shin to try and shut him up, before he upset Sarah by pointing out that she still wasn't Graham's girlfriend.

"Don't I know it", Sarah muttered, as Graham walked unsteadily towards them, spilling some of his coffee on the floor as he did so.

Tor watched as the young man sat down. His cropped fair hair was beginning to re-grow after the surgery he'd undergone the term before, but the injuries he'd sustained when the demon had attacked him were still healing, and it was likely that the limp was permanent. Of course, Graham didn't fully understand exactly what had tried to kill him, thinking of it as simply "something bad" that had taken over first a new student, David, and then Graham's friend Mark, causing them to flip out and attack people.

Graham smiled at Sarah, who practically beamed back at him, and Tor saw Paul look away sadly. 'So that's how it is', thought Tor. 'Oh well, at least Paul won't be asking Bex out then. He's obviously only interested in Sarah. One less thing for me to worry about'. As far as Tor was concerned, none of the young men that Bex knew would be good enough to go out with her. In fact, nobody would have measured up to Tor's standards. Not even Dudley, Bex's father, had such high expectations about boyfriends for Bex as her guardian angel.

Another young man flung himself down on a seat at the table. This was one of Flint's fellow students, on the drama course. Duncan, Tor thought his name was, though she hadn't paid him much attention up to now. He was a third year, and hadn't been involved in the events of the previous term. He was not as tall as Flint, or Paul, and had spiky, blond hair and multiple piercings in his ears. His stare was very intense, his green eyes darting from one student to another, as he erupted into their conversation.

"Flint" he announced, "I've got it....I know how to find my character for the production".

"Your character?" Flint answered, "Straight forward villain.....textbook stuff, isn't it?"

"Not the way I want to play it.....I want to make it real.....you see, when Redwood summons......" Duncan stopped mid-sentence and looked around at the others "Er....are you all coming to see the show?"

"I suppose so," said Paul.

"Since Flint is in it", added Bex. Graham and Sarah nodded, saying "Of course".

"You don't have to," Flint muttered, embarrassed. "I've only got a small role in it. It's really a showcase for the third years, like Duncan."

"And me", said another student, strolling over to join them.

"I'm Munroe", the man said, introducing himself to the others around the table, and sliding into a seat. His brown curly hair matched the colour of his eyes, and he had a broad, open smile. Bex decided she liked him at once. "I'm playing Redwood....he's the character who..."

"Wait," said Duncan interrupting his fellow third year. "If Flint's friends might come and see it, we shouldn't say anything else. No spoilers, eh Flint? Do you want to tag along with me? I'll tell you what I'm planning on the way to rehearsal". "I'm not needed this afternoon," said Flint, "Principals only".

"Shame", replied Duncan, grabbing his bag and heading for the door. "You'd love what I've got in mind. Tell you tomorrow." He glanced back over his shoulder, "Anybody seen Cath?" The other students shook their heads, and he hurried out of the canteen. "I suppose that means I'd better head off too", groaned Munroe.

"You don't sound very keen on going to rehearsal", said Sarah. "Don't you have much of a part in it?"

"Oh, I'm one of the leads", answered Munroe. "It's a great part. I'm just not that keen on the play, somehow. Still I guess I'd better go.

I don't want to be late. Good to meet you all, anyway". He stood up and headed for the door, giving Flint and his friends a parting wave. Tor decided that everything was under control, and there was no need for her to stay, so she left the canteen and headed back to the cathedral.

"What is the play?" Paul asked Flint, feeling more relaxed now that he couldn't see Tor any more.

"You never said", added Bex, "Which is weird". "You do normally go on about the shows you're in", chipped in Graham.

"Well", said Flint, "You might not like it. If fact, you really don't have to come, any of you. It's some old script one of our tutors found in a charity shop, a sort of modern take on the Faust story. The central character summons up the devil to try and do a deal with him."

Sarah looked at Flint, a worried frown creasing her face.

"I'm really not sure I like the sound of that", she said rather awkwardly.

"Neither do I, to be honest," Flint agreed, "Not after last term.....but it is just a play. It can't do any harm".

Chapter Three

Thren was still stretched out on his stomach on the roof of one of the beach huts beside the pub, enjoying the sunshine. The river was drifting past towards the weir, and beside it two young men were talking, trying to make their drinks last.

"I don't believe I could be that stupid", cried the younger one, a small, slightly built man with short dark hair, a pointed chin and big, soulful dark eyes. "How could I come away for a wedding and forget to bring my shoes? I can't wear trainers....not with a suit. Not to a wedding!"

"It's alright", said his companion, reassuringly "We'll go and buy you some shoes. Chester's full of shoe shops". He was a little older than the first speaker, and quite a lot taller. He gazed out over the river as he spoke, watching through his wire framed glasses as the rowers powered up and down. He patted the younger man on the shoulder, comfortingly, but the first man was in no mood to be consoled.

"If I buy a pair of shoes", he sighed, "I won't have any money left to buy them a wedding present. We can't go to a wedding and not take a present".

"I'm sure they'll understand," said the taller one. "You've said Paula & Mike are lovely people. They've invited us to share their day.....so stop stressing".

"But it's the first wedding I've ever been invited to, and the first one we're been to together. I wanted to do everything right!"

"I'm sure they'll just be happy we could get here". They smiled affectionately at each other. They couldn't change the situation, so they might as well relax and enjoy the day.

Thren let their voices wash over him. It was kinda nice to hear about little problems for once, instead of the big stuff he usually had to deal with. Nothing life or death, nothing that meant he had to help. Maybe he could close his eyes and try sleeping again after all, just for a moment. He was beginning to feel strangely peaceful, and for once the pain in his chest had subsided. He smiled as he listened to their conversation.

"I can't wait to see what Megan's wearing....Paula's daughter. I've only ever seen her in jeans", said the younger man. "I can't even imagine her in a dress.....she's usually a bit of a tomboy....she's an amazing girl though... and I wonder what kind of wedding cake they'll have....I mean, what they'll decorate it with? They're into rugby....so maybe...." the young man suddenly interrupted himself, his voice louder and more insistent "LOOK.....over there....downstream....is someone in trouble?"

Thren leapt to his feet, and scanned the river, trying to spot what the couple had already seen. Down by the weir he could see that someone's soul-light was flickering, and icy-blue in colour. He knew that meant that its owner was frightened, and at risk. He was in the air, flying towards the weir, almost as soon as the young man had spoken, thankful that he'd been alerted but annoyed with himself that, because of his exhaustion, it had taken a human to point out the danger.

When he reached that part of the river, he found the two kayakers he'd seen earlier. They'd been playing on the submerged steps of the weir, kayaking down, and then carrying their little craft back up again time after time, but now one of them, the girl with purple hair, was in trouble. Her kayak had overturned as she'd paddled down the steps, and her helmet had slipped off, so when she went under she'd cracked her head on the stonework of the weir, and she was stunned. Her friend was struggling to pull her out of the water, and onto a mud-bank, but she was hampered by still being in her own kayak, and having to reach across it and her friend's craft to keep the girl's head above water.

Thren dropped down beside them and helped to pull the semi-conscious girl out of the water. Neither of the girls could see him, but the one who was trying to rescue her friend suddenly found that the task was easier. The injured girl seemed lighter than she had been, and her kayak wasn't being tugged at so fiercely by the current.

Thren assisted the other kayaker to get the girl out of her canoe and onto the mud-bank, just as she opened her eyes blearily. She could see her friend, and she thought she caught a glimpse of someone....something.....else too. Tall, and pale and bright, with a.... feathery outline? She blinked, thinking she must have hit her head harder than she'd first thought. Her friend was getting a mobile out of its waterproof bag and calling an ambulance.

"I don't need one, I'm fine" said the injured girl, looking around. She swept her wet hair out of her eyes, and then rubbed some slime off the tattoo on her chest. The figure was gone, though she thought she heard someone whisper in her ear.

"Be more careful about fastening your helmet on next time.....nice tat though". The girl shook her head, slowly.

"Actually, maybe I do need a doctor, after all."

Thren left the girls on the riverbank and headed back towards the cathedral. 'Guess there's no such thing as a quiet day for me', he thought, as he trudged along, his wet robe squelching against his ankles. 'I can't even fly back like I used to, in case I drip on somebody, and make them curious. Some days I hate this job'.

When he reached the cathedral he paused before climbing up to the roof. Glancing around the green, he saw Dudley, Bex's father, returning to the little house tucked beside the ancient building. The old man worked as a canon in the cathedral, and filled his days with prayer, and with helping other people; he was one of Thren's favourite humans. Dudley's soul-light was almost pure white, and semi-transparent.....a sign that as he had aged any imperfections had gradually been put aside. It had taken Thren ages to understand the complex nature of soul-lights, and just how much their colours expressed their owners' personality. The angel saw Dudley step into the house, and smiled as the old man left the door open.

"You can come in if you like", Dudley called softly, and Thren sheepishly made his way into the house.

"How did you know I was there?" asked the angel. "I'm way more careful about not being seen than I used to be".

"There was a trail of wet footprints leading towards the cathedral, that's all", said Dudley. Thren settled himself on a stool in the kitchen and smiled tiredly at the old man.

"How are things going at the homeless shelter?"

"Very well" Dudley replied. "I've just come from there, in fact. Janet's doing a fine job managing the new premises....even Poole comes and lends a hand sometimes......and we can help so many more people now we're based in a bigger building".

"Poole?" Thren grinned, "You hanging out with Poole again?"

"Well, I don't know about 'hanging out', but he's quite a decent chap, really, when you get to know him" answered Dudley.

"I know it," said Thren, "I guess it's kinda cool that you two are friends now". The angel sighed, and Dudley looked at him more closely.

"Had a bad day?" he asked as he filled the kettle and got out two mugs.

"Kinda", admitted Thren, "It feels like every day is a bad day at the moment. I'm meant to watch over everyone in the city, all at the same time, and I just can't do it. What if I miss something....if one person gets killed while I'm taking care of somebody else?"

"Wasn't that always the case?" asked Dudley, making hot chocolate, and handing one of the mugs to Thren. The angel took it gratefully. Not that he needed food or drink, of course, but it was rather comforting.

"I guess," replied Thren, "It was kinda exciting at first, swooping in to rescue someone, feeling like a hero".

"So what changed?" said Dudley, passing Thren a plate of digestives.

"Me," replied Thren, munching on a biscuit. "It was ok when I didn't really care about anyone.....now I feel so darn responsible all the time.....and that's just the regular stuff, never mind if I make a mistake that let's something terrible through again."

"Is this a mistake?" asked Dudley softly, "Popping in to see me sometimes? Sitting here chatting?" Thren grinned.

"No, amazingly enough. Tor checked.....and it is a little unusual, but it's not breaking any rules. You already know about us, just like Bex and Flint do....and Paul, of course, so there's no point in pretending to you that we don't exist. You fought alongside us, when we defeated Dross, so it doesn't cause any trouble if any of you see us, so long as nobody else does."

"Not your sort of trouble, perhaps" smiled the old man, "But I think Bex is finding it a little difficult, feeling she's being watched all the time".

"Oh?" said Thren, puzzled, "OH!.....I kinda wondered why she wasn't dating anyone."

"Would you?" asked Dudley, "With Tor watching you like a hawk every moment of the day and night?"

"I guess not" agreed Thren. "In fact, I'm pretty sure not!"

Chapter Four

Cath was crouched in the corner of her room, shaking. She'd overslept again, and woken from a nightmare ridden sleep to discover that she'd missed all her lectures for that morning. It was happening more and more often, and she was getting very behind with her work....which wasn't like Cath, at all. Waves of terror swept over her. She'd hoped that these would diminish as time passed. It had been months, after all, but no....whatever was troubling her seemed to be getting worse, not better. She stared nervously round the room...there was nothing there...no reason to be frightened, yet she couldn't shake the feeling off. She took a deep breath then, sluggishly, she opened her laptop and spread her work out on the desk. She had to do something useful with her day, or it would be a complete waste. To Cath, it felt as if most of the last few months had been a total write off.

She had thought, when she'd woken up in hospital, that everything would return to normal quite quickly. She wasn't even sure of the reason she'd been admitted....something to do with David Ross, the new student on the English course....the new student who had some connection with a weird séance at Marty's party. The details were still fuzzy. In fact everything had been blurry to Cath after David had kissed her. Not in a pleasant, 'in love, floating on air, life's wonderful' way, but in a 'who am I, where am I, what's going on?' sort of a way. For several days after that strange, unpleasant kiss, Cath had wandered around confused and disconnected, not eating, not going to all her lectures. Not looking after herself at all, until eventually she'd collapsed, and woken up in the hospital.

She hated not knowing what had happened to her. It made her feel out of control, and if there was one thing Cath needed, it was to be in control....of herself, at any rate. Day after day she had tried to fill in the blanks....remember what had happened, and why she had let herself go in that strange fashion, but with no success. At first she feared that David had drugged her....and done more to her than just kiss her....she was terrified she might turn out to be pregnant, though she couldn't remember anything happening except that kiss.....but as time passed and no signs of pregnancy occurred, she felt that that was one fear she could tick off her list.

Cath used to love lists....what topics to study, what stationary to buy, what to get people for Christmas. Now her lists consisted of things like...Get some sleep.....Set the alarm.....Don't panic.... Set a second alarm......Don't panic ....Get some sleep......Don't think about the past....Don't think about that kiss...Don't... Don't...Don't.....

She looked at herself in the mirror. She'd started to wear her brown hair a little longer. It was still short, but no longer as severe looking as it had been. She was thinner too, much thinner. To be fair, she'd always been slim, but now she felt so stressed all the time that she was barely eating, and she looked almost skeletal. Her clothes were less businesslike than the ones she'd worn before, though she still tended to dress more smartly for lectures than anyone else on the English course. She'd made a conscious effort to change, partly because she was afraid that something about her old self had attracted David to do...whatever he did. She certainly didn't want anything like that to happen again....but the biggest change about her was in her eyes. Her confidence was gone, and she stared nervously at the world with fearful eyes, waiting for disaster to strike.

When all the students had got back together, after it....whatever IT was, had happened, they'd talked endlessly about it all, trying to put the pieces together. Cath had to admit, to herself at least, that she was the one pushing for answers....well, her and Sam. Marty couldn't remember much, apart from being rushed to hospital, though he felt guilty about suggesting the stupid séance in the first place, and they were all sure that David Ross had been connected to that somehow. He was the one who attacked Graham, throwing him off the city walls....but then Mark, one of their friends, had started acting oddly too and tried to kill some of the others students, even Sam, his best friend. Now Mark was dead, and they still didn't understand why.

However, when their endless speculation failed to produce any answers the others had decided to forget about it and move on. Cath, however, just couldn't do that, and she didn't think Sam could either. What really upset her though, was the feeling that some of her friends knew more than they were saying. Bex, Flint and Paul went very quiet whenever Cath brought the subject up, and always looked a little guilty.....and as for Sarah, she'd started talking about prayers being answered, and going to services at the cathedral sometimes, which Cath found rather frustrating. She wanted answers, not superstitious nonsense.

Her phone pinged loudly. She had a text from Duncan, asking her to meet him later, if she was free. She looked at her desk, piled up with work. She ought to concentrate on that, but she couldn't really focus on it anyway, so why not? All her friends had been surprised when she started spending time with Duncan....he wasn't her usual type at all....but that was the point....he wasn't like David Ross. Also, he'd had nothing to do with the events of last term, so there was nothing to explain, or worry about. He was just Duncan....an ordinary drama student, who wanted to spend a bit of time with her that evening....they weren't even dating really....they just enjoyed each other's company, which was as serious as Cath was prepared to get just yet.

She looked nervously at a bag of doughnuts that she'd just spotted on the desk, balanced on top of her work. She couldn't remember buying them, and she never ate doughnuts anyway.....even when she had felt like eating. So where had they come from? She always kept the door to her room locked, so who could have put them there? Cath shivered, and replied to Duncan's message, glad of an excuse to get away from the campus for an evening.

Over in his digs, Duncan smiled when he received Cath's text. He liked her nervous energy....it gave his own erratic emotions something to bounce off. It was one of the reasons why he enjoyed being with her. He sensed that, although she wasn't as on top of her work as she'd like to be, underneath, she was as driven as he was...they both wanted to be the best at what they'd chosen to do.

That evening he'd decided to try and do some more preparation for his role in the end of year production, and he was sure Cath would be happy to help him. She was always willing to read in with him, so he could rehearse his lines...and this was no different....well, maybe a little bit different. He opened the script and turned to the scene where Redwood summons the devil.

Chapter Five

Paul had wandered down to the bursar's office, to see if he had any post. The students who were in the halls of residence were expected to collect their own mail from the office. He flicked through the letters in the cubbyhole marked W. To his surprise he found a parcel addressed to him as Paul Williams Esq....which was odd, nobody used such an old fashioned title, these days....Esq.....short for esquire. The sign of a gentleman, his grandmother used to say. In fact, she'd always written to him as that, when she was alive, and the writing looked rather like hers too, now he looked at it more closely.....which was strange...actually it was beyond strange, and heading fast towards creepy.

He was shoving the rest of the post back into the cubbyhole, when he noticed that there were three envelopes for Sarah....whose surname was Wentworth. They were all coloured envelopes, and on the back of one of them was written "Not to be opened until the 7th", which was the next day. Collecting her post as well as his own, he headed up to her room, and knocked. "Come in" she called, and he put his head round the door. Sarah was lying on her bed, playing a Facebook game on her lap top, with a frustrated expression on her face.

"Not Candy Crush, AGAIN", joked Paul. "I think you're addicted to that game".

"I'm stuck on level 165, and I can't get passed it", she replied, without looking up from the game, "Nooooooo! Failed again......that's me out of lives for now". She shut down her laptop and looked up at Paul, saying, "You've got a lot of post."

"Most of it's for you," he replied, "So I thought I'd bring it over. Why didn't you say it's your birthday tomorrow?" Sarah shrugged, embarrassed.

"Got anything planned?" asked Paul.

"No," she replied, "I was hoping....." her voice trailed off, but they both knew what she meant. Sarah had had a crush on Graham for ages, and until the frightening events in the spring, he's really liked her too, but before they could get together Graham had been attacked, and seriously injured, and when he finally came out of hospital he'd been quieter, more subdued.....and seemed to be concentrating on his course work, and his physio sessions. He treated Sarah as a friend, but gave no sign of wanting to ask her out. Sarah had been hoping that

Graham would suddenly notice her again.....suggest doing something special for her birthday, but he hadn't.

"Let's go into town," said Paul, "I want to get you something, a birthday present".

"There's no need," replied Sarah.

"Are you turning down the chance to go shopping?" teased Paul, dumping the cards, and his parcel, on Sarah's bed. "At least let me try and cheer you up?"

"If you insist", grinned Sarah, grabbing her shoulder bag.

A few minutes later Thren, back up on the roof of the cathedral, saw Paul and Sarah strolling down Eastgate Street, and smiled. Sarah's fuzzy pink soul-light bobbed along cheerfully next to Paul's, which was an unusual mixture of sky blue and lemon yellow.

"Awwww. Cute!" Thren thought they'd make a good couple, if they ever got past Sarah's thing about Graham. For want of anything else to do, Thren took off from the roof, and landed a few feet behind them just as they ducked into a shop called Lee Louise. It sold funky, gothic clothing and Sarah paused to look at a skirt hanging on a rack just inside the doorway,

"This is pretty.... bit long for me though."

"Just wait here," said Paul, diving into the back of the shop. Thren followed him, intrigued. 'What the heck could he be looking for in a shop like this?' thought the angel, puzzled. 'In fact, how come he even knows what they stock.....this is so not Paul's kinda place!' Just then Thren felt himself being bumped into and jumped out of the way. A large girl with a ukulele case in one hand and a purple floaty top in the other was heading for the changing room.

"Keep an eye on my uke, will you?" she said with a grin, "I just want to try this on?"

"Me?" said Thren, shocked that she could see him.

"You don't mind, do you?" said the girl, dumping her case at his feet, "I won't be long...but you do have a trustworthy face.....and if someone walked off with my ukulele, I'd be gutted". She walked into a changing cubical, pulling the curtain shut behind her.

Thren was speechless. People weren't supposed to be able to see him.....if he was mixing with humans, he was supposed to keep his wing-beats going at a particular frequency, which would set up a disruption to the light pattern, making him almost invisible. He must have stopped concentrating, while he was speculating about Paul, and become visible....at least his body had.....thankfully his wings, though beating at the wrong frequency, were still going fast enough to deceive the human eye and remain unseen. The lack of concentration had to be a side effect of being so exhausted all the time, a dangerous side effect. He could have kicked himself for being seen without even realising it was happening.

Thren now had a dilemma......if he became invisible suddenly the girl in the changing room would think he'd just abandoned his duties, and left her ukulele lying about to be stolen, which seemed rude.....but if he stayed, he was giving her another opportunity to see him....which he wasn't meant to do. At least Paul hadn't noticed him....the young man was over beside a small glass fronted cabinet, getting the shop assistant to open it for him.

"What do you think?" the girl asked Thren, stepping out of the cubical to look at herself in the mirror. She had put on the purple cotton top, and was twirling round, trying to see herself from the back as well as the front.

"It looks....great," said Thren, and realised it did. He knew modern tastes insisted that everyone was supposed to be thin.... skinny even, but this big confident girl, with her lively smiling face, and brown hair tied back in a pony tail, looked terrific. The floaty top suited her, its long, trailing sleeves making her look like something out of another time period.

"Epic", he added with a grin, "It looks epic.....and so do you, lady. You just gotta buy that".

"I know", said the girl, grinning back at him before disappearing into the changing cubical again. She came out moments later wearing her original shirt and clutching the purple top, grabbed her ukulele case and headed for the counter to pay. "Thanks again", she called, as she left the shop. Thren made himself invisible as soon as she was out of sight, since there was nobody in that part of the shop at that moment. Paul had already completed his shopping, and he and Sarah were outside on the pavement.

Thren came out of the shop to stand beside them, and Paul turned his head, sensing that Thren was there.

"Sorry", whispered Thren in the young man ear, "I wasn't meaning to intrude, Paul". Of course, he was, actually, but he wasn't meaning to get caught doing it. That was embarrassing. "Err, I guess I'll leave you guys in peace". Thren turned away, heading towards the road....and promptly forgot about Paul and Sarah, as a car jumped the nearby traffic lights, and turned into the road with a squeal of breaks.

A woman on the crossing tried to leap out of the way, but misjudged the distance. The baby buggy she was pushing flew in one direction, while the car knocked the woman flying. Thren raced towards her, watching her soul-light turn icy blue with terror, and passersby who saw the incident came running to help. Thren flung himself under her body just as she was about to hit the pavement, breaking her fall, while Paul and Sarah ran up to help. Somebody had retrieved the baby buggy from the road, and wheeled it over to where the woman lay on the pavement, winded and battered from the impact of the car, but not unconscious, due to Thren's quick reactions. Sarah was already on her mobile, calling for an ambulance, while Paul rushed to the woman's side. He could see that she was rolling gently onto the pavement as Thren slid out from under her.

"You ok?" whispered Paul, to where he thought Thren must be lying.

"My baby!" screamed the woman, "Where's my baby?" Soon the woman was swamped with people telling her the child was alright, and trying to make her lie still until the ambulance arrived. Suddenly Paul heard a whisper in his ear

"I'm fine kid, just a bit squashed is all......I just wish I could have one quiet day. Is that too much to ask?"

Chapter Six

Dross was waiting in The Darkness. He had had to wait hundreds of years for his last chance to break though into the human world, and when he did reach it, he had failed in his efforts to steal the souls of the foolish students who had invited him in by holding their séance. He had managed to extract the souls of a few of the young people, briefly, but had been defeated by Thren and Tor, with the help of Dudley, and Bex, Flint and Paul, and the souls had been released again, and returned to their suffering owners......all except one. Even the soul of Mark, the young man he'd killed, had escaped him. How the other demons had ridiculed him when he was forced back into The Darkness....though they wouldn't have done so if he'd told them what he'd learnt. His one crumb of comfort, his secret discovery, his glowing, burning hope, was Bex. He had found out that the girl had traces of angel blood in her. She was descended from Eskarron, an angel who fell in love with a human, Phyllida, long ago, and had put aside his angel form to live on earth with her as a human......their children all had angel blood mixed in with their human heritage....and angel blood was powerful stuff, even diluted down though the generations.

Dross knew that if he could get hold of any human with angel blood and drag them into The Darkness to spill their blood there, he could let hell loose on the human world. They wouldn't have to wait for occasional chances to creep, one demon at a time, into the world when one of the rules of balance and counterbalance got broken....the whole army of the Invisibles could attack at once....drive back the angels, and take control of .....Everything. Which would be delicious, in Dross's opinion... well worth waiting for.

Of course, he knew now that Bex was not an unguarded target. It seemed that all of Eskarron's descendants were under special protection.... each had their own guardian angel. In Bex's case, Tor. Not that Dross rated her, particularly, and now he knew what he was up against, he had a plan, but before he could put it into action he had to get back into the human world.....a rule would have to be broken....and someone would need to invite him in. He was hoping it would be soon......

Bex and Flint were walking towards the cathedral, with Tor drifting along behind them. As they turned under the archway that led to the abbey green, Flint reached out and took Bex's hand. They kissed, briefly, in the privacy afforded by the great sandstone arch, then walked out towards the green, keeping a respectable distance between them. Although Tor was only a few steps behind them, and Thren was up on the roof of the cathedral, neither angel had spotted the intimate gesture.....which was exactly what the two young people were hoping for. Not that there was anything wrong with kissing, but Bex and Flint were a little shy about their relationship....they were only just moving from friendship to something more, and they certainly didn't want Thren, and especially Tor, knowing about it, and making disapproving comments.

Flint had started walking Bex home after her lectures earlier in the year, when they were all in danger, and the habit had stuck. Now he went back to hers most evenings, if he didn't have rehearsals. He often ate with Bex, and her father Dudley, and if he didn't want to go home at the end of the evening, he slept on their sofa. Sometimes Flint would catch the bus out of Chester to the village where his family lived, but he still felt unwelcome there, so he stayed on friends' floors, or anywhere he could scrounge a bed, as often as he could. He would have liked to rent somewhere in Chester, but he couldn't afford it.

"Are you coming in?" asked Bex, as they reached her front door.

"If you like", replied Flint, trying to look like he didn't care either way.

"I think it's time we told Dad about us, if you don't mind", Bex added. "It's one thing hiding it....pretending we're not going out, to Thren and Tor, but I hate having secrets from him".

"If you insist", groaned Flint, "But he won't like it."

"Don't be silly, you know how fond he is of you", Bex smiled encouragingly.

"As your friend, maybe......but as your boyfriend? That'll be a different matter, you'll see!"

Sarah unlocked the door to her room, and walked in, followed by Paul. They were both still a little shaken up after the accident they'd witnessed, and Paul longed to tell Sarah about Thren, and how much worse it could have been, if the angel hadn't flung himself under the falling woman, but he knew he shouldn't.

"I'd better go...leave you in peace", he said reluctantly, as he picked up the package he'd left on her bed.

"No", replied Sarah, "please don't, not yet.....I really don't feel like being alone. What's in that parcel anyway? It's not your birthday too, is it?"

"No. I'm not sure what it is....I'm not expecting anything".

"Then let's open it and see" she grinned. They sat side by side on her bed, and Paul ripped the brown paper open. Inside was a battered looking journal filled with scribbled handwritten notes.

"That's my grandmother's writing" remarked Paul, puzzled, "but she died a couple of years ago". A letter slipped out from the packaging of the book and fluttered to the floor. Sarah reached down to pick it up and handed it to Paul, who scanned it quickly.

"It's from my mum....the letter. She said she found this book all parcelled up and addressed to me, in a box of Gran's things, when she finally got round to sorting them out. Gran obviously wanted me to have it, so she's slipped this note into the wrapping, and sent it on."

"So what is the book? And why did your Gran want you to have it?" asked Sarah.

"I'm not sure," Paul answered. "I think it might be some kind of diary, or journal.... we were close, Gran and me....we had a lot in common....maybe that's why she wanted it sent to me."

"Like what?" Sarah looked at him expectantly.

Usually he'd have brushed off a question like that with something like "Oh, just family stuff", but this was Sarah, and he couldn't bring himself to lie to her. He wanted to tell her the truth....to be able to be completely himself with her, so he decided to explain. Surely he could do that without breaking any rules, or mentioning the angels? Bex and Flint both knew that he could see things other people couldn't, but he'd never mentioned it to any other friends. For years it had been a secret between his grandmother and himself. Nervously, Paul took a deep breath, and started to talk.

"We both see things....Gran and me.....well, I mean, she used to, before she died, and I still do."

"Things?" asked Sarah, "What kind of things?" "Things other people can't see. Things people say don't exist". Paul paused, and looked at Sarah. She didn't say anything, she just waited for him to carry on speaking.

"We both have an unusual eye condition....an extra layer of cells on our retinas.....Gran used to call it her 'inner eye'....she joked it was for seeing fairies with".

"Fairies?" asked Sarah, amazed "You've seen fairies?"

"Of course not", replied Paul, quickly. "That was just her little joke, but I do see other things.... sometimes.....not properly, like you can see me now, but sort of...... out of the corner of my eye, or reflected in the back of my glasses".

"Like what?" Sarah asked, firmly. Paul hesitated. "Paul, you can't not tell me, now you've started."

"Actually", replied Paul, realising that he really was in danger of saying too much, "Maybe my Gran explains it better. Here....in her journal ......look....." He started to read out an entry from the book, picking one at random.

"I saw them again today....the wings were very beautiful..... though rather disconcerting. It's most frustrating that nobody else can see them....though I sometimes get the feeling that little Paul senses them too...."

"Little Paul?" teased Sarah.

"This is from years ago" explained Paul embarrassed. "From the date written here, I think I was only two or three."

"But she mentioned wings.....so she must have thought she was seeing fairies!" declared Sarah, triumphantly.

"Fairies aren't the only creatures with wings" replied Paul, sharply, wishing he'd never started the conversation.

"Was she dotty?" asked Sarah. "Was it all in her imagination? But then, you said you saw things too....so what things? Come on Paul, you've got to tell me".

Paul stood up, awkwardly.

"What I've got to do is finish my essay. It's due in on Monday".

"Oh," said Sarah disappointed. "Please don't go....I wasn't meaning to make fun of your Gran, or of you. It's just a bit hard to understand, that's all."

"I really do have to go". Paul wished he'd kept his mouth shut. "I'm sorry, Sarah"

"Will I see you tomorrow?" she asked. Paul wasn't sure what to say. He wanted to see her, of course, but perhaps he should avoid her for a couple of days, until she forgot about what he'd just told her, otherwise she'd just keep pushing him for answers.

"I'm pretty busy this weekend. And I'm going round to Bex's tomorrow night......so...."

"But tomorrow's my birthday, remember? Surely you can spare me a few minutes?" Paul suddenly remembered the gift he'd bought her, and pulled it out of his pocket, thankful of a chance to change the subject.

"Here, Happy Birthday....in case I don't see you."
Sarah smiled and took the tiny gift. She grinned at Paul and started to open it.

"Well, if I'm not going to see you on my birthday....I'd rather open it now, when you're here with me". She held up a little carved opalite angel, dangling on a chain.

"Oh, Paul, it's lovely.....just perfect. Thank you!" She reached up and gave him a kiss on the cheek, then tried to fasten the chain around her neck, but fumbled with the catch. Paul was still blushing from her kiss as he helped her put on the pendant, and she turned to face him, suddenly feeling a little shy.

"How did you know? That I have a bit of a thing about angels? Ever since last term, when all that horrid stuff happened. I was really scared, but I had a feeling someone was watching over us, stopping things getting any worse. I know it sounds silly, but I did actually start to think that maybe an angel was looking after us". She looked up into Paul's horror struck face.

"You don't think I'm mad, do you? I haven't dared tell anyone else. I know what they'd say....that I was crazy......but I trust you. You'd never laugh at me, would you?" Paul was still staring at her, speechless.

"That's it, isn't it?" questioned Sarah, the truth dawning on her. "That's what you can see....you and your Gran. Things with wings, that aren't silly made-up fairies? You can see Angels!" Paul nodded, mutely, wondering if it counted as breaking the rules to tell Sarah about the angels, if she'd already guessed they existed. It was such a relief though, to be able to talk to her about it, that he couldn't resist. He explained about being able to see Thren and Tor....and what had really gone on the previous term....and how everything had culminated with a battle in the cathedral, when the demon they'd stupidly invited through had been driven back into The Darkness.

And in The Darkness, something shifted......only a little something, for only a little rule had been broken. Paul had simply confirmed what Sarah already suspected....but it was just enough to alter the balance slightly, and let Snig through.

Chapter Seven

The imp, Snig, was delighted to be back in the human world. Small, slimy and looking for trouble, he had had a marvellous time on his last visit, causing chaos and playing a nasty trick on Tor. This time, though, he was here on a different kind of business. His claws were clutching a sack filled with assorted objects, and he was bursting with pride at his assignment, for he had been chosen for salting.

He made his way through the streets, keeping to the shadows as dusk began to fall. He was searching for places to hide the objects... locations where they would eventually be found by people, and could be used to cause trouble. For centuries salting had been going on, whenever the opportunity arose. Imps would bury a relic here, or hide a book there, knowing it might be years before the object was discovered....but when it was, it would have the potential to open a doorway for something else to come through from The Darkness. Something much bigger and nastier than an imp like Snig. "This is gonna be fun!" he muttered to himself, as he slid into a second-hand book shop through an open window at the back of the premises. "I'm gonna be the best salter ever!"

Sitting on the sofa in Dudley's house, Bex and Flint waited for her father to say something. Flint was sure Dudley would hate the idea of them being more than friends. After all, Dudley was one of the few people who knew the truth about Flint's past. Surely the old man wouldn't think Flint was suitable boyfriend material for his beloved daughter? Flint had visions of being sent away from the house on the spot, and being told never to return.

He realised with a jolt that that would hurt him much more than he would have expected. The little house crouched beside the cathedral, where Bex and her father lived, felt far more like home than his real home ever had. He still felt his parents hated him.....and he couldn't even blame them. What he'd done had been unforgivable, and his whole family were still suffering. When he was there he could feel his parents looking at him all the time.....wondering why he was the son that had survived, when their favourite, their youngest boy, was dead. Blaming him......just as he blamed himself.

Dudley's acceptance of him, and Bex's friendship, had started to make him feel normal again....as if he had some kind of place in the world. But that place was here, in this house, and he was pretty sure that was all going to change.... right now.

"I did wonder why it was taking so long for you two to get together", said Dudley, after a long silence. "Why was that Flint? Because if you're not sure how you really feel about Bex...?"

"No," Flint interrupted quickly, "it's not that, really it's not. I've liked Bex for...well, for ages. It's just that I wasn't sure what she felt.....about me...once she knew what I'd done. And there was so much to get to grips with....about the angels, and Dross, and trying to make sense of it all. Even now, I'm not really sure if I imagined it. It all seems so unreal."

"It was real, Flint", said Dudley, reassuringly. "We were all there. It did happen"

"I know," said Flint, "But in some ways it would be easier if it wasn't. Because then I wouldn't know about....stuff. Like Tor watching over Bex...."

"ALL the time", Bex added. "Dad, have you any idea how embarrassing that is? I mean, I know Tor's always watched over me, even though I couldn't see her.....but it was so much easier when I didn't know about her either. Now, I know she might be around....but because I can't see her most of the time I don't know if she's there or not. It feels as if....as if...."

"She's spying on you?" finished Dudley.

"Yes, exactly", wailed Bex. "I mean, I know she's not. I realise she's only trying to protect me....but, I wish I had some privacy.....at least some of the time".

"Why don't you talk to her? Explain the problem, and set some ground rules?" suggested Dudley. "I'm sure she wouldn't mind".

"I'm pretty sure she would", answered Bex, "But I suppose it might be worth a try. Does that mean you don't mind? About Flint and me?"

"No father is ever ready for his daughter to grow up.....and no young man is ever supposed to be good enough for her, but you are growing up Bex. I trust you to make your own decisions, and I trust you, Flint, to treat my daughter with respect. You're a better person than you think you are, you know. You've always been welcome here....and you always will be".

Flint grinned sheepishly, and Bex gave him a reassuring nudge.

"I told you Dad would be alright with us going out", she said.

"Well, now that's settled", said Dudley, standing up, "Who's for a cup of coffee?"

Flint left the house a few minutes later, and headed for the cathedral refectory. He was due at another rehearsal for that summer's Mystery Plays. He'd seen a performance of the medieval cycle of plays years ago, and had been thrilled to get cast in the production that was coming up in July. He'd been less thrilled to discover that he was playing the role of Christ in the Crucifixion scene, even when, before February, he hadn't thought the biblical stories had any truth in them at all. Now, he felt even more embarrassed about the part he was performing. Secretly he felt it should be played by a better man than he was. The Mystery Plays were always a fantastic theatrical production though, with different community groups taking part, acting out various stories from the Bible, from the Creation to the Last Judgement. Audiences were always keen to see these spectacular performances, and came from across the country, as well as from around the city itself.

He was part of the group portraying The Trial and The Crucifixion, and he'd been delighted to find Munroe, from the third year of his course, was in the same group, playing the part of Peter. Flint really admired Munroe's acting ability, and was enjoying the chance to get to know him better, away from the hierarchy of the university, where everyone tended to stick to their own year groups. Munroe usually seemed really relaxed at the Mystery play rehearsals. Tonight however, he was looking rather stressed.

"What's up?" asked Flint, wandering over to join him. "No need to be worried about these scenes yet, the production isn't for a couple of months".

"It's not this show I'm worried about", Munroe replied. "It's the final year production. The director has just realised I'm in this one as well, and is giving me grief about spreading myself too thin. He thinks I should drop out of The Mysteries".

"That's crazy," said Flint, puzzled. "We've been rehearsing this for months. The final year show is on next week, and there aren't any rehearsal clashes. What's the point of dropping out of this now?"

"There isn't one", agreed Munroe. "I think he's just being difficult for the sake of it. He resents me being involved in an 'amateur' show when I should be concentrating on my finals. He's just mad at me because I've queried the script we're doing a couple of times. I knew he'd take it the wrong way, but I felt I had to say something....that play is just.... something feels wrong about it......"

"I know what you mean", agreed Flint, "And it's hardly fair to accuse The Mysteries of being amateur. We may not get paid but it's a fabulous production....and how often in our acting careers will we get the chance to take part in something on this scale". They grinned at each other for a moment, sharing the pleasure of being in a production to be proud of, then moved to take up their designated positions as the rehearsal began.

When Cath got to the front door of the student house where Duncan lived and rang the bell, the place seemed unnaturally quiet. She was beginning to wonder whether Duncan had forgotten about inviting her over, and was turning to leave when she heard his footsteps thundering down the stairs. A moment later he wrenched the door open, and stood grinning at her.

"You won't believe what I've got planned for tonight! Come on up". He led the way up to his attic bedroom, talking as he went.

"You know I was trying to think how to get into character for my role in this play? Well, I had an idea, but I'm going to need your help. Is that ok?" Cath was struggling to keep up with him.

"I expect so", she said, panting as they hurried up the stairs. "But you still haven't told me what the play is, or who you are in it".

"That's because I wanted it to be a surprise. I didn't want to spoil it for you, if you were going to come and see it".

"Of course I'll come", she replied.

"Even if I show you the script?" asked Duncan. "You see I want to try out a scene from the play, to help me think it through," he flung open the door to his room. Over his shoulder Cath could see that he'd cleared a space in the middle of the floor, and chalked a pentagram on it. A candle glowed at each of the five points of the star, and a bag of salt was placed in the circle. Cath stopped dead, her face white with fear. Duncan didn't notice, and carried on speaking enthusiastically.

"It's the scene where Redwood summons the Devil.....that's who I'm playing, you see.....the Devil. I need you to read in Redwood's lines for me, and ....Cath? Cath?" He heard her running down the stairs, and slamming the front door behind her. Cath was gone.

Chapter Eight

Peering down from the roof of the cathedral, Thren thought he saw something moving in the streets below.....something small, keeping to the shadows, sliding out of sight when people passed by. It didn't seem to have a soul-light, not that he could see, anyway. 'Kinda reminds me of something, but I can't recall what....just tired I guess. I don't usually have trouble remembering stuff. Reckon I might as well take a look'. Just as he was about to go and investigate, something more urgent distracted him. He recognised a brown soul light that was moving swiftly through the city. He knew it belonged to Cath, but it was tinged with icy blue light. 'Something sure has freaked her out. Guess I'd better go and see what's up'. He landed behind Cath, just as she ran under the clock on the arch over Eastgate Street. Making sure he'd adjusted his wing beats to remain invisible, he hurried along behind her. He could hear her breath catching in her throat, and she was veering from side to side as she ran. Thren knew the girl hardly touched alcohol, so she couldn't be drunk. He thought she must be having a panic attack 'I sure can relate to that, you poor kid'.

She was one of the students he felt guiltiest about. Dross had stolen her soul the previous term, leaving her to gradually decline and slip into a coma. Even when her soul-light had been recovered and returned to her body, she couldn't put the experience behind her. She had regular nightmares, Thren knew. Sometimes he sat on the floor beside her bed, as she tossed and turned and whimpered, and he tried to calm her down, holding her hand, and whispering softly to her, hoping to lull her into a more restful sleep. Not that Cath knew he was present of course, that was the point. Guardian angels are supposed to be unseen. 'Not much of a guardian to her, that's for sure. Let her down *real* bad'. Thren knew that one of the reasons Dross had been able to get to her was because he, Thren, just hadn't taken to the girl when he first saw her. She was organised, efficient, and just plain dull, in Thren's opinion, and because of that, he hadn't kept a close eye on her when the students were in danger. Every nightmare she'd had since was his fault.....every missed lecture, every panic attack. It was all down to him.

Cath, unable to keep running, sank onto a bench and tried to catch her breath. She was weeping, and wiping her eyes on the sleeve of her coat. The fact that she didn't have a hanky was another reminder to Thren of how much the strain of the few months had got to her. The old Cath wouldn't have dreamt of going out without one. The girl dug in her pocket and got out her phone. Her hands shook as she punched the keys. Thren heard voicemail kicking in.

"Duncan....Dunk....I'm sorry" Cath whispered, "Sorry I bailed on you....I just couldn't... I can't explain....something happened last term...there was this séance and.....and I don't know exactly what happened....but...something ....did, and I .....I think I'm going mad.....I just can't......and you mustn't....whatever you're planning to try.....just don't.....ok.....?" Cath's voice petered out. "What's the use" she said, as she stood up, shoving her phone into her coat pocket. "I can't do this anymore". She began walking again, purposefully striding up Eastgate Street, towards the sandstone pillar that marked the junction, and then down Watergate St. As she came within sight of the duel carriageway she began to run......towards it.

By the time Thren realised what she was up to, she had reached the edge of the road, and was looking at a car that was driving towards her at some speed. She stepped off the kerb, intending to throw herself in front of it. Thren caught a glimpse of the driver's horrified face speeding past as he grabbed Cath and pulled her back onto the pavement. The sudden movement caused them both to lose their balance, and they toppled over onto the hard slabs. Winded, they both lay still for a moment. The air seemed to shimmer in front of Cath's eyes, and she found herself face to face with what looked decidedly like a rather exasperated angel.

"Oh boy", groaned Thren. "This so wasn't meant to happen".

"Who.....are ....you?" asked Cath, as she scrabbled into a sitting position. "Are you what I ....think you are?" Thren ran through his options quickly, and decided he didn't have much choice. Not just because Cath had gotten a good long, no mistakes about it, look at him, but because he knew that what had happened before.....what he had let happen, had pushed her into this state. Pushed her to the point where being squashed by a car seemed better than trying to cope with a part of her life that didn't make sense.

Not knowing quite where to start he sat up and growled at her.

"Are you crazy? Just what did you think you were doing, Cath, stepping out into the road like that? Not only would you have been killed or injured, you'd have ruined some else's life too. What did that driver ever do to you that you have the right to make him feel guilty for the rest of his life......you gotta know that ain't fair, Cath....I thought better of you than that!"

"You....know me?" asked Cath, bemused. "You know my name?"

"Sure I do," answered Thren. "I know a whole lot about you. More than you know yourself....and that's the problem. The bits you don't know....the stuff that's making you freak out. That's what I gotta tell you, before you go and do something else stupid, and get yourself killed.....but first, do you mind if we get up off the sidewalk? I feel kinda stupid myself, sitting here".

He heaved himself to his feet, and then reached down to give Cath a hand up. "Let me walk you back to the campus, and I'll fill you in". Cath, speechless, just nodded her agreement, as Thren escorted her along the pavement towards the university, explaining everything to her as they went. By the time they reached her room in the hall of residence, the pieces were falling into place.

Snig was rubbing his claws together in delight. Each of the saltings he'd brought through had been hidden away. His work was done.....now it was time to have some fun. He heard voices and applause coming from an upstairs room in one of the old black and white timber pubs, and scrambled up the outside of the building to see what was going on. A group of people were listening to a woman reading out a poem.

"Nasty thing" muttered Snig "All that rhyming.....too much order. Chaos better". The woman finished, and sat down, to another round of applause. Snig was about to move on, bored, when he realised that the poetry reading was over and the group was about to scatter. There was nobody else around to annoy, so he decided to wait while people drained their glasses, said their goodbyes and wandered out of the building. Snig was clinging to the beams above the doorway, trying to decide who to have some fun with, when two of the men from the group caught his eye. At first glance they seemed an unlikely pair to be friends.

One was broadly built and older than the other, his hair just turning grey. He had a neatly trimmed beard and blue eyes that twinkled behind his black-framed glasses, and seemed to be the steadier of the two. He was quietly pleased about the way his poems had been received. The younger man, dressed entirely in black, was bouncing up and down as if he had springs on his feet. He was tall and lean, with shoulder length dark hair that flopped across his expressive face as he moved. Even Snig could see he was the more excitable of the two, as he walked backwards so that he could look at his friend as they talked. They both carried folders stuffed with papers.

"Weeeeheeeee", squealed Snig, scrambling down the side of the building, and beginning to follow the two men. Of course, they couldn't see him, but they could feel him tugging at their folders.

"I hadn't realised it was that windy", said the older man. "Wish I'd brought a sodding coat now". Snig gave a final tug and pulled the papers out of his hands, throwing them up into the air. The older man tried to catch them, but Snig had tossed them high above his head, and the night breeze was carrying the pages out of the man's reach. His friend tried to help him round up the poems, dropping his own folder in the process. Snig giggled and grabbed hold of that too. It was fancier than the first man's, and made of leather.....and if there was one thing Snig liked chewing on, it was leather. He began munching on a corner, expecting the men to spot the folder floating in mid-air as he bit it, but they were too busy trying to save the first collection of poems.

One sheet of paper had caught high up in the branches of a tree beside the road.

"I'll get it", cried the younger man, starting to scramble up into the tree.

"Come down", cried the older man. "You're too old to go climbing trees....and it's dark. If you slip you'll break your neck".

"No I won't" said the young man, grinning down at his friend from the upper branches. "I'm good at climbing trees. I always thought I'd make a good Robin Hood".

Snig, seeing the chance of causing more mischief, abandoned the leather folder and scurried up the tree, reaching the paper caught in the branches just as the young man put his hand out to grab it. Snig pulled the page just out of reach, so the man had to stretch further and further away from the tree trunk to try and catch hold of it.

"Can't catch!" called Snig to the young man, flapping the paper in his face.

"Don't be a bloody idiot", shouted the man at the bottom of the tree. "It's just a poem....it doesn't matter. Let it go!"

"But it's one of yours!" At that moment Snig found himself staring straight into the young man's blue eyes, which opened in surprise as Snig shoved him. The poem drifted to the ground as it slipped from Snig's claws, but the young man's decent was much more rapid, as he began to drop through the branches.

Snig froze for a moment, and then instinctively scrambled down to grab at the falling man.

"Got it!" cried the imp, triumphantly, dangling the man by his hair, before lowering him to the ground with a bump.

"Well, that wasn't embarrassing at all!" muttered the young man blearily, slumping over onto the pavement, as his friend knelt beside him, concerned.

"Are you ok, mate? That could have been nasty! What the hell were you thinking of....scrambling up there after a ruddy piece of paper? You could have been killed!"

"I'm fine, don't fuss", said the younger man, scrambling unsteadily to his feet. "Where's the poem? I saw it drop, just before....." He pounced on the paper, and triumphantly handed it to his friend.

"Here. See....it's one of your best......Worth the effort!"

"Nothing's worth watching you almost getting killed for, you twat!" said his friend, shaking him by the shoulders with a mixture of anger and affection. "Don't ever do anything like that again!"

"Are you ok mate? Honestly?"the older man asked more gently. "You do look pale".

"I do feel a bit strange....in fact, the whole thing was weird. It felt as if somebody pushed me out of the tree....I heard somebody too, I think.....or something". He shook his head, puzzled, causing his hair to flop into his eyes again. He swept it back with his fingers, and looked around as his friend collected the other loose poems.

"Speaking of strange", said his friend, picking up the leather folder "Did this look like that earlier?"

The two men inspected the chewed folder in silence.
"No, I'm pretty sure it didn't". They looked at each other, but neither could think of anything to say. Snig watched as they turned and walked away. The younger man, still rather shaken, stumbled, but the older one supported him until he regained his balance.

Snig perched in the branches, thinking. It wasn't something he did a lot of, and it made his head hurt.

"Friends.....must be friends". The whole idea of friendship puzzled him....it wasn't a concept he came across much in The Darkness....fiends yes, friends no....but the bond of friendship he'd seen between those two men was almost palpable. For a moment he wondered what it would be like to have a friend. It wasn't something he'd given much thought to before, but now the idea grabbed his imagination. He was also confused by his instinct to catch the young man when he fell. Of course imps weren't really supposed to go around killing people. It was the demons who had that right over certain humans....the ones who invited them in, at any rate. Imps weren't meant to draw attention to themselves in that way, but causing an accident wouldn't have got him into much trouble.....so why hadn't he just let the young man fall? The more he thought about it, the less sense it made it him.

Snig decided that the solution was to forget about the whole thing. He could go and find some more people to tease and have fun with, but somehow he wasn't in the mood. Perhaps he just needed a sleep. He was sure when he woke up he'd be back to his usual beastly, impish self. Sleep... that was it. Snig crept through the city looking for a nice quiet place to curl up and rest....somewhere where no one would find him.

Chapter Nine

"So you're telling me that...something.....took over a human body.....and....sucked my soul out of me? That's why my life fell apart?" asked Cath.

"I'm afraid so, kid" replied Thren. "I should have stopped it happening....but I didn't realise. Not until it was too late. I kinda took my eye off the ball. I couldn't protect all of you at once. I tried, but I failed".

"You mean you didn't try hard enough".

"Maybe, Cath, I just don't know......I've gone over and over it, trying to figure out how I could have stopped it all."

"Who else knows?" demanded Cath. "Which of my friends knows....and didn't tell me? I could have coped with it better if somebody had just explained what was going on."

"By the time it was all over, Bex, Flint and Paul knew what went on, but I swore them to secrecy. Talking about it....that's the kinda thing that could cause more trouble....and we couldn't handle that. We've been terrified about Dross getting back through....trying again".

"He'd come after us?" she asked, timidly.

"Not all of you", answered Thren, trying to sound reassuring, "I don't think so, anyhow. It's Bex he's after now."

"Why Bex?" Cath asked.

"I'm sorry," Thren shook his head, "But that's one thing I really ain't allowed to tell you".

"Somebody should have told us the truth about what happened!" she insisted.

"I'm real sorry, Cath", said Thren, unable to look her in the eye. "I knew you were having nightmares, but I didn't realise just how bad it was for you....not til tonight. Most of the others seem fine....they've put the whole thing behind them. Marty and Debbie are ok....so are Tim and Nesta......"

"What about Graham? And Sam? They're not alright, are they?" Thren stood up, pacing around her room nervously,

"Graham's getting better....I know he was badly injured, but he's making a good recovery."

"And Sam? He lost his best friend, he's still a wreck...we have to tell him".

"You can't, Cath.....you just can't, ok? I shouldn't have told you now, but I was scared you'd go and do something stupid......more stupid, I mean, and I just couldn't bear it". Cath stared at him for a moment, then cautiously asked Thren a question.

"Are you sure that....whatever it was...has gone? Because, well I think something's getting into my room sometimes....I found a bag of doughnuts on my desk this morning, and I didn't buy them.....it's creepy". Thren burst out laughing.

"Doughnuts? You think a demon would bring you doughnuts? They were from me.....you've hardly been eating, and I was kinda worried about you getting sick again, so I put them there. I hoped you'd find them and get the munchies".

Cath looked at him in amazement. "YOU? You brought me doughnuts? Didn't it occur to you that I'd find it rather odd? Food suddenly appearing in my room? Was it you who brought the biscuits last week? And that cake?" Thren blushed.

"I was just trying to look out for you, is all. I guess I goofed up again". Suddenly Cath grinned at him, and he realised that if she wasn't so stressed all the time she would be rather pretty.

"Have you even heard of healthy eating?" she asked, with a smile. He chuckled, realising that yet again he'd underestimated her....but perhaps now she knew the truth she'd start to relax. After all, her troubles were over now. Then he remembered something. He stared at her, and asked a question he dreading hearing answered.

"Cath, what did freak you out, tonight? Something pushed you over the edge.....is it something I need to know about?" Cath nodded, guiltily remembering Duncan, and why she had run away from his house, terrified.

She would have been even more terrified if she could have seen Dross, smiling in triumph, because Thren explaining everything to the girl had altered the balance even more. Now he had the right to come through to the human world again......all he needed was an invitation.

Bex took her father's keys and let herself into the cathedral. The interior felt even bigger in the dark, huge and full of echoes. She crept quietly up the steps to the roof, opened the door and called out softly.

"Tor? Thren? Are you here?" Suddenly Tor appeared in front of her, the angel looking oddly modern in Bex's old clothes, and with her short hair curling round her face.

"I'm here, Bex. What did you want?" Bex stalled, nervously,
"Er, it's a bit awkward.....is Thren here?"

Tor looked disappointed. She struggled with the fact that Bex, who she'd protected all her life, was much more relaxed and friendly with Thren, than with her. She tried to tell herself that it was just to do with the blood relationship Bex shared with Thren. They were from the same flight of angels, which was why the girl could always see Thren, if he was around, but only saw Tor, if Tor allowed her too.

"He's not here at the moment, as you can see. Can I help?" Tor knew her jealousy was making her sound uptight and formal.....like an old-fashioned librarian, but she couldn't help it. She turned her back on Bex saying, "Or you could come back tomorrow, if you prefer".

"Don't be like, Tor, please. I wanted to talk to both of you together, that's all".

"Oh," Tor sat down. "Well, it's up to you, but I'm happy to listen, if you think I can help".

Bex hesitated, sure that it would have been easier to have the conversation with Thren there to lighten things up a little, but she didn't want to upset Tor either.

"Yes", she said, "Ok, maybe it's better this way. You see, I've come to ask a favour...."

Tor smiled at her, benignly.

"Of course, Bex....anything you like. I'm always there for you. You know that."

"Actually, that's the problem", replied Bex, awkwardly. "You *are* always there....or you might be, and I wouldn't know, because I can't always see you.....which is starting to feel a bit.... well, very........... embarrassing".

"In what way?" asked Tor, genuinely puzzled. "Being there is my job.....I'm supposed to protect you"

"From danger, yes, sometimes....I know that" protested Bex, "But not from just normal stuff, Tor please. I need some privacy".

"For what?" Tor really couldn't see what Bex was getting at.

"Have you any idea how difficult it is to start going out with a boy, when you feel that someone is spying on you all the time?" asked Bex, exasperated.

"No", replied Tor. "I haven't. Angels don't have those sorts of relationships". Suddenly the meaning of Bex's words sank in. "You mean you have a boyfriend? Who is it? Do I know him?.....I suppose I must do....I know everyone you know". Tor stared at Bex. "Tell me it's not Flint". One look at Bex's face gave Tor her answer. "It *is* Flint, isn't it?"

45

Before Tor could ask any more questions Thren landed on the roof beside them. Bex had rarely been as glad to see anyone, but when she looked at him more closely, she realised he was not his normal, jokey self.

Ignoring her completely, he said to Tor.

"It's starting again....you gotta come with me. It might take both of us to stop it happening". Noticing Bex, her turned to her and added "Go home Bex, right now".

"Why?" asked Bex, confused.

"This is *so* not the time to stop for a catch-up kid. Just go home, lock the doors, and stay there. Things are about to turn real nasty".

Chapter Ten

Duncan was completely flummoxed by Cath's behaviour. While she always seemed a little nervous, and unsettled, he'd never known her to run off like that, and he didn't understand what had caused her strange reaction. He was disappointed in her too, he'd come to rely on her friendship, and her support, as he prepared for the different roles he'd played in his student productions over the last couple of months. He'd only kept this one secret, so that she could enjoy the show when she came to see it, and now she'd abandoned him, just when he needed her help to get to grips with one of his most challenging roles so far.

He'd intended to get Cath to read in Redwood's lines............... summoning the Devil....to help him get into the right mindset to play the Devil himself....the inverted pentagram chalked on the floor, the candles and salt were just set dressing, to create the atmosphere. They were described in the stage directions in the script, and would be used on stage during that scene in the performance, but Duncan didn't want to wait until the show to conjure up that mood. He wanted to set up the feel of the scene to find out how his character might think and behave, before the final rehearsals. He was convinced that he shouldn't play the character as a pantomime villain....that would be much too obvious. Duncan needed to find some real motivation, some layers to the character. He didn't want to take the obvious route and just portray cackling evil. Surely the devil was as complex as any human character? Maybe more so.

Well, he'd arranged the room, with a lighted candle at each point of the pentagram, so he might as well use it. He switched out the lights, so that only flickering candle-light illuminated the space. He'd just have to read in Redwood's lines himself, before he began his own monologue, in character.

Duncan opened the script and began to read out the speech that was used to summon the Devil. It was long and cumbersome, and Duncan noticed that Munroe, who was playing Redwood, had changed one or two lines, so that they differed from the script. Perhaps he'd done so by accident, misremembering them, but Duncan didn't approve of unauthorised script changes....he decided that he'd point out the mistakes to Munroe at the next rehearsal.

He read out the lines, loudly and clearly, as written, pausing in the middle of the speech to draw a sigil in the air with his finger. This was a simple symbol scratched into the text of the script they were using....it was meant to represent the name of the demon Redwood was supposed to be conjuring up.....in this case, the Devil. In rehearsal Munroe just seemed to wave his hand around vaguely at that point in the speech, so Duncan made a point of copying the sign in the air as precisely as he could.....though as it seemed to him to be more of a squiggle than a symbol that he could recognise, he wasn't sure if he was doing it right.

He knew he had one advantage over Munroe though. They were all working from photocopies of the script that their tutor had found in a charity shop, as the play wasn't in print, so they couldn't buy additional copies. However, Duncan's much thumbed copy had become rather feint and hard to read, so the tutor had lent him the original script for a few days. The symbol was carved onto the front cover, as well as marked in the middle of the speech he was reading, cutting into the slightly greying leather of the book's binding. Something about the feel of the leather was a little unpleasant, though Duncan couldn't think why he found it so.

He looked closely at the symbol on the cover, which was clearer than the photocopied version. It looked a little like a capitol D with squiggly lines running through it....D for Devil, he supposed. He made the sign in the air again, and then carried on proclaiming the speech.

"Mighty Master of Dark Realms", Duncan intoned, "Come before me now, summoned by my power, by fire and flame, by cold earth and warm air and smooth water.....and by the eternal power of your own name, used to bring you into my world" Duncan wished he'd made a recording of the music they were going to use in this scene, he felt it would really have added to the atmosphere." Come Dark One....I conjure you to appear before me. Come Dark Lord Come! Veni, Veni, Tenebrarum Domini. "

Still clutching the book, Duncan stepped into the space in the centre of the pentagram, and opened his mouth to start his own character's first line, but before a word came out he heard a sound behind him.....a soft whooshing sound, as smoke began to pour from the candles and swirl around the room. In the space beside him, in the middle of the chalk marks and candles, the smoke coalesced into two shapes.....that looked a little like hands.....huge smoky hands, clapping slowly.

"Very nice delivery", hissed a voice from somewhere in the room. "Very nice indeed. Might have made more of an effort with the props though.....those candles are white.....black are better for summoning a demon, or dark blue at a push......and where's the earth?.....there should be some soil, and a dish of water, and incense for air....Could Do Better...that's my assessment".

"Who's there?" asked Duncan, looking round nervously. "I can't see you".

"But I can see you", whispered the voice, "Every worthless, over-melodramatic inch of you.....not very appealing, are you? You forgot the salt, by the way."

"It's there", whispered Duncan, his voice strangled by fear. "In the bag, in the middle of the pentagram". At the back of his brain he was thinking "So this is what terror feels like, I should try to remember it, so I know how to portray someone who's terrified". The rest of his brain had already worked out that he was unlikely to survive to play any other parts at all.

"In the bag? In the bag? It's no use to you there! Didn't you do your homework? You're supposed to use it to make a circle around yourself......for protection, or around me, to keep me prisoner.....it's no use just sitting in a bag, is it? And where are the other props, eh? There's a full list of them in the stage directions".

"The director cut them," Duncan whimpered, barely audible, "Said we didn't need them......just the candles......for effect". The young man still couldn't make anything out in the swirling mist, the room was now so full of smoke, or fog, or......whatever it was. The stuff was trailing round him now, covering his face and wrapping itself around his throat.

"You did bring the most important prop though.....the item with the real power to summon me out of The Darkness. You brought the script."

"What's so special about that?" asked Duncan, timidly.

"Well, it's not the words" replied the voice in the smoke, "They're nothing special, I've persuaded better playwrights than that one to pen what I wanted.....the words aren't what brought me here. Especially without any intension behind them....you weren't expecting me were you?....You didn't actually think I'd appear? No, I thought not.....it's the cover. Do you know what it's made of?"

"Leather?"

"In a manner of speaking.....it's made from the skin of a prisoner of mine, from a very long time ago. He was a killer, you know, a mass murderer, though not even he really deserved what I did to him, but that's what you get for trying to do a deal with me.....I carved my name into his skin days before he died…..makes a rather impressive binding, don't you think?"

"Human?" gasped Duncan, dropping the book in disgust. "It's made from human skin?"

"Every inch of it….that's what brought me here in answer to your invitation…..the power of my name, carved into the skin of one of my victims…..that, and the fact that I wanted to come!"

"You're the Devil?" Duncan was trembling with fear by this time.

"Very flattering, but no!" the smoke was twisting itself round him, more and more tightly, making it hard for him to breathe. "My name is Dross", said the voice in the darkness, just before the boy passed out.

Chapter Eleven

Dross hovered over Duncan's unconscious form. The demon needed a body to inhabit, and he had the right to try and seize this one, and devour the boy's soul-light, since the young man had been foolish enough to invite him into the world. The dark blue soul-light was flickering gently, exciting Dross's gnawing hunger. How he longed to devour it, how he ached to kill the boy and take over his perfect shell, uninjured and fresh. If all Dross had come to do was cause trouble, kill any humans he had the power to assault and steal their soul-lights to strengthen his own status and influence in The Darkness, he'd have finished the young man off there and then. But Dross had learnt from his last incursion into the human world, and he had bigger plans afoot.

His real target was Bex, and he had to force himself to stop and think whether killing this boy would help or hinder his plans. He couldn't believe his good fortune in being invited back into the world by someone who knew her. Dross had seen Cath bolting from the house earlier as he hovered between here and The Darkness, waiting for his chance. And he knew Cath....he knew her deliciously well, for he was the demon who had stolen her soul earlier that year. Her tasty brown soul-light....he could still remember how it had felt when he had kissed it out of her and swallowed it. Of course, he hadn't looked the same at the time. He had been "wearing" a good-looking human body, going by the name of David Ross. He knew that Cath knew Bex, was part of that circle of friends, and if she knew this young man, the chances were that Bex knew him too.

Dross glanced around the room, and caught sight of a poster for the play. It was due on in a few days, which was simply perfect. The script itself had been a salting.....something randomly sent through from The Darkness years ago, with the power to cause trouble, if it ever fell into foolish hands. And it had. Dross was delighted at how it had turned out. The Powers of Darkness were definitely on his side. After sitting on dusty bookshelves and in old libraries for years, the book had fallen into the hands of a director, in the very town Dross needed to return to, and been used by someone who knew the person he was determined to capture.

Killing the boy would put the group he was trying to reach on guard, and alert Thren and Tor to his presence, and it was too early to do that. Plus, the student obviously had an important role in the play that was about to be staged....a play that, with a few little alterations, could be turned to Dross's advantage. Better to keep the boy alive than risk having the production cancelled.

Dross was still in his disembodied form, but he concentrated on forming the substance of his being back into the shape of hands, and picked up the book. A shiver of delight ran through him as he touched the human skin that bound it, remembering the pleasure he'd felt while torturing the man whose flesh it was. Placing the book on a table, Dross focused on picking up a pen, and making a few minor changes to the text. Then he turned the boy's inert body over, so that the young man was face up, and sent delicate tendrils of himself into Duncan's mind, blowing out a memory here, planting an idea there. Unconscious and unable to defend himself, the young man seemed deliciously easy to influence. If Dross had had a face at that moment, it would have been smiling.

Reluctantly the demon withdrew from Duncan's brain, resisting the almost overwhelming temptation to steal the soul-light, and finish the boy off. If he did that now, the body would be rotting by the time the play was due to be staged. He would have to go and find himself a body, but not this one. Not yet, anyway.....

Thren and Tor burst into Duncan's room. The young man was still on the floor, unconscious but alive, the candles were guttering, and although the misty essence of the demon had vanished, there was a strange bitter smell in the room. The bag of salt had been knocked over, and some of it was scattered across the floor.
Tor felt disappointed. She had been ready to battle any demon who might have come though at the young man's invitation, but there was no-one to fight. Thren was just relieved that Duncan was alive, his soul-light glowing weakly, but still present. Both angels made sure that they were invisible as the boy groaned and hauled himself to his feet. He looked dazed...unsure of what had just happened. He switched on the light and blew out the candles, though a couple of them had burned out of their own accord, and then walked over to a table, where an open book lay.

Duncan's hand hesitated before he picked it up, and began to glance through the pages. There seemed to be alterations to the script, but perhaps they had always been there.....and the cover.... there was something about the cover. No, he couldn't recall what it was. He fetched himself a glass of water and returned to the book, closing it.

With his finger tip he traced the sign carved into the surface of the book's binding, a puzzled look on his face, before stumbling over to his bed, and collapsing onto it, falling into an exhausted sleep.
Both Thren and Tor longed to question the young man, and discover exactly what had happened, and who had come through, but that would mean him seeing and hearing them....another breach of the rules, another chance for something bad to happen. Tor moved over to the table, and picked up the book, then flung it to the floor, looking at Thren in horror.

"It's...it's....it's...."

Surprised by Tor's reaction, Thren bent down to pick up the book himself. The moment his fingers touched it, he felt a searing pain in his chest.....this time it was so acute that it look his breath away. Doubling up in agony, Thren fainted.

Thren woke up, feeling his body being battered as he was jolted down step after step, dragged along by his arms.

"Hey, what'ca doing....let go". The movement stopped, and Thren opened his eyes to see Tor glaring down at him.

"You fainted", she muttered sternly, "I can't believe you fainted. I admit that the cover of the book was......" She paused, trying to find words strong enough to describe her revulsion, "......but to faint? Is that any way for a guardian angel to behave?"

"It was gross," said Thren weakly, "it was *way beyond* gross".

"Well, now you've come round you can jolly well walk! I only started to drag you out of the house so there was no risk of you being seen when that boy woke up. You were completely visible while you were unconscious".

They made their way slowly back to the cathedral and up to the roof. They needed to try and understand exactly what had happened, and how....and to assess what danger everyone was in. When they climbed up the stairs and emerged onto the flat roof, they found Bex waiting for them.

"Hey", murmured Thren, weakly, "I thought I told you to go home....lock yourself in......"

"Yes, young lady," added Tor, sternly, "You should be in bed".

"But I was worried about you", Bex replied, "Both of you. And it looks like I was right to be. What happened, Thren? You look terrible....and you're bleeding!"

"Nonsense", snapped Tor, "Angels don't bleed".

"Ya think?" Thren tried to make light of it, before collapsing onto the roof, blood staining his robe, where the broken shaft of wood stuck out of his chest.

Chapter Twelve

Cath couldn't sleep. Everything that Thren had told her was going round and round in her head. The whole idea of good and evil actually existing in terms of angels and demons, and not just moral concepts seemed bizarre to her, and yet knowing what had happened to her made sense of everything. The fact that Thren had intervened to prevent her getting herself killed did make her feel a bit better, even if she was still angry that he hadn't protected her from having her soul stolen in the first place.

Part of her wanted to rest, to sleep, to make up for the endless nightmare nights, but she was still too wired. Information overload.... that was the phrase people used, but it didn't begin to describe how she felt at that moment. She decided that she needed some fresh air, even though it was late. It might be dark outside, but the weather was warm. And she felt that if she stayed in her room for much longer she'd be bouncing off the walls. She headed downstairs and wandered across the campus. Groups of students were making their way back from the pubs or setting off for nightclubs in giggly, girly groups. Cath felt completely detached from it all, thankful that the nameless terror she'd been struggling with for months was not a sign that she was cracking up, but not yet ready to put it all behind her and feel "normal" again.

She noticed a lone figure weaving towards the halls of residence. He was unsteady on his feet and as he passed a security light she realised it was Sam. His short ginger hair looked ruffled, and his green eyes were unfocused. Cath remembered how he'd always been smiling and joking about with Mark, but now Mark was dead, and it was rare to see Sam smile these days. She hesitated, then walked towards him.

"Hiya Sam", she said, trying to sound casual. "Been out for a drink?" It wasn't the most original line, she knew, but she didn't want to sound too critical.

"Just a few", replied Sam, his speech slightly slurred. "No need to get in a stew....few...stew....get it?"

"Yes," said Cath, "I get it. Who were you with?" she asked, thinking she might have a word with them in the morning about encouraging Sam to get that drunk, and then leaving him to make his way back alone.

"Nobody" said Sam, swaying a little, "All on my own. Bad company, that's me. No-one wants to go boozing with poor old Sam any more. Say I make them gloomy.....like Eeyore ......That's me, good old Eeyore."

"I'm not really a Winnie the Pooh sort of person", smiled Cath, "But you are a little.....solemn.... these days. You haven't been yourself for a while".

"No, 'strue enough .....don't know who I am any more....not really. Don't care mucsssh either. Night, Cath". He turned to walk away from her, but lost his balance, and Cath reached out a hand to steady him.

"Here, take my arm", she offered, "I'll see you back to your room."

Dross was drifting over the city, looking for a body to inhabit. Having spared Duncan, for his own purposes, he didn't have the right to take someone else's life or body. Not someone who hadn't welcomed him in.....so he needed to find a person who was recently deceased. If he had a choice he'd go for someone of student age, to give him the easiest access to the group he was interested in, Bex and her friends. Not that he could go after any of them yet....the rules didn't allow it....he'd had his chance at each of them, and lost. He needed more power, so that he could overthrow those rules, and help The Darkness to break through into the human world. Then he could take whoever he chose.

First, however, he needed a body. For a while he hung around road junctions, hoping to spot a traffic accident, and take advantage of it, but it was a quiet night, with good weather conditions. Abandoning that idea, he headed for the hospital, his smoke-like essence sliding in through an open door, and drifted down to the morgue area. There were a couple of bodies on gurneys, but one was a frail elderly woman, of no use to him, another was a middle-aged man who had died in surgery, and the open chest wound would be difficult to disguise. Then he noticed that one of the morgue drawers had been left slightly ajar. Enough for him to ease it open and look inside. Perfect. A female of about the same age as Bex and her friends, perhaps a little younger. Dross couldn't see any obvious marks on her body, and was not certain how or why she was dead. He hesitated, knowing that that could be a problem in the long run. He heard footsteps coming along the corridor towards the morgue, and knew he'd had to make his decision quickly. Pouring himself into the girl's body, he began to animate it. First he used her hands to pull the sliding trolley out of the locker, then he stood up....a little shakily at first, and draped the sheet around her body. He knew humans had a thing about naked bodies, and he didn't want to attract attention. Then Dross crawled under the gurney with the dead middle-aged man on it. The sheets over the body came almost down to the floor, creating a safe hiding place. Crouched there, Dross saw that the morgue attendant had entered the room, and seen the empty body locker, with the door still open and the trolley sticking out.

"What the......" the attendant checked the name on the locker door, glanced around the room to make sure that the girl hadn't just been moved to one of the slabs, then hurried away to call security. Dross could have kicked himself for not shutting the locker door. Now the alarm would be raised immediately.

He shuffled out from under the table, pleased his new body didn't seem to have any broken bones, then checked the name on the locker she'd come from. Lizzy Brett. It would do. Dross searched the room until he found a large plastic bag with the girl's name on it, which contained her clothes and personal belongings, then hurried away from the morgue and went in search of somewhere to change. There was a cleaning cupboard in the corridor, and he's just closed the door of it behind him when he heard feet rushing in the direction of the morgue. Hurriedly Dross slipped into Lizzy's clothing.

Fastening the bra gave him some problems, so did putting on the girl's high heeled shoes and clinging party dress. He abandoned the tights altogether, after wrestling with them for a few minutes, picked up her bag, and let himself out of the cupboard. He tottered down the corridor on the heels, wishing repeatedly that he'd found a male body to inhabit....or at least one that wore flat shoes.....and left the hospital behind him, walking towards the city.

By the time he reached the heart of Chester, it was late. Only drinkers and party goers were out and about. According to Lizzy's address, she lived on the opposite side of the city to the hospital, and all he wanted to do was get back to her home, get out of her ridiculous clothes, and think. He had to decide what to do and when to do it. He had a campaign to organise.

Cath lowered an unsteady Sam onto a chair, and glanced around his room in the hall of residence. She'd not been in there for months.

Although she was fond of Sam and spent quite a bit of time with him, generally they hung out in other places. Cath found most student rooms a little too claustrophobic, though Duncan's attic room was better than most. Looking at the photos pinned to the wall, she was overwhelmed with sadness. Most of them were of Sam and his best friend, Mark. Even though Mark had been dead for months, Sam had left the pictures up. Cath knew that he was as trapped in the events of the spring as she had been, but since her conversation with Thren, she was beginning to make sense of it all. Perhaps that's what Sam needed too, to understand what had happened so that he could begin to move on.

"Sam,", she said nervously. "I need to tell you something, but you've got to promise not to laugh at me......and you mustn't tell anyone else, alright?" Sam stared at her blurrily.

"Sooo it's a secret....ok, I can keep secrets.......I can keep m'mouth shut, if you need me too, Cathy. I'mmmmmm good at tha'". She knew he was. From being the life and soul of the party when he'd first started at university and teamed up with Mark, he'd become quiet and withdrawn. He tended to spend some time with the other students in the day, but at night he often chose to be alone......and increasingly often, he drank. Although he was studying Biology and Cath was on the English course, she knew he was struggling to keep up with his work. He handled things differently to her, but she was sure they both had the same problem....and now she understood what had happened, she wanted Sam to know too.

Dudley knelt beside Thren on the roof of the cathedral, and looked at the blood stain on the angel's robe. He gently opened the neck of the garment to reveal the spike of wood sticking out of the angel's chest, the blood starting to clot around it, and made a tutting sound.

"Thren", said the old man softly, "Thren, how long has it been like this?"
Thren tried to lift his head to answer, but somehow it seemed as if he was weighed down by lead. Any movement was exhausting.

"Since February", he replied weakly, "It's been there since the battle.....it hurts, but it hasn't been bleeding..........that only started tonight".

"Why didn't you say something, you idiot?" Tor snapped, anger hiding her concern.

"Not your problem, lady" he whispered. "Anyhow, I deserved it....what happened last term...it was my fault. I figured it was kinda fair I should be punished".

"Don't you dare blame Him for this!" cried Tor indignantly. "You know He wouldn't do this to you".

"But I messed up, let everything go wrong......I deserve what's coming to me". Bex sat behind Thren, trying to comfort him by holding his hand. Tor didn't go in for comfort. "Never mind what you deserve....that's not how He works....and you should know it. Why on earth would He make it harder for you to do the very job he's sent you here to do?"

"I must say", Dudley added, "Tor is making sense. Surely your 'punishment', if you deserve one, is knowing what happened, and how you failed? Living with our mistakes is painful enough. It's not like Him to do this to you".

"Well, somebody sure has," growled Thren, "And I just can't get the damn thing out. Believe me, I've tried, but if any of you wanta give it a go, feel free".

Snig was perched on top of the Eastgate Clock, looking idly down at people wandering through the darkened streets. From up there he could see people strolling along, laughing and joking. One couple stopped to kiss each other in the shadow of the arch that supported the clock, another pair were bickering as they hurried down the road. Snig considered playing some tricks on them, but somehow he didn't feel like it.

The imp noticed some people in high visibility jackets talking to some of the individuals who were wandering home rather the worse for alcohol. The jackets had the words Street Pastor written on them, and Snig was trying to work out what they were doing. Two of them were comforting a girl who was upset after a row with her boyfriend, while some others were calming down a group of young men who were on the point of getting into a fight. Snig was trying to understand what the Street Pastors got out of it, but he couldn't figure out what their angle was. They just seemed to be there to help.

His eye was caught by a tall, blond girl in a tight-fitting party dress. She was attempting to stride along purposefully, but seemed to be struggling. She was wearing high heels which were difficult to balance on. Snig really couldn't grasp why females chose to wear such things. They looked more like instruments of torture than shoes; in fact, perhaps he should suggest them, as a form of punishment in The Darkness....but then Snig wasn't important enough to suggest anything to anyone. As he watched he saw the girl stumble and fall, the heel on one of her shoes snapping. She looked up sharply, her face distorted by rage, and locked glances with the imp. She could see him. Humans weren't supposed to be able to see him!

Then he realised that the girl wasn't really a human at all, just a dead shell, being worn by a demon. An angry, fierce, cruel demon, who looked ready to lash out as the street pastors hurried towards him. Snig couldn't hear what they said, but he saw them giving the "girl" a pair of flip-flops to walk the rest of the way home in. The demon snatched the flip-flops out of their hands, and pulled them on in place of the high heeled shoes, which "she" threw angrily in the direction of a bin. Then the creature got up and stormed off, annoyed at the delay. The twisted smile Snig could see on its lips told the imp that the demon fully appreciated the irony of being helped on his way by Christians, of all people. Snig, however, wasn't relishing the situation as much as he once would have done. He was more intrigued by the kindness of the Street Pastors, going out in the middle of the night to help their fellow humans.

Snig found himself smiling, and stopped. What was happening to him? He wasn't supposed to be impressed by humans, he was meant to cause trouble, to make them miserable, or angry, or distressed. Imps feed off negative emotions, not positive ones. Perhaps he was coming down with something, not that he'd ever heard of imps getting sick. He scuttled off along the city walls, looking for somewhere else to settle for the night....somewhere with no distracting humans about. He came across an open area labelled "The Roman Gardens", made up of ruins and pillars scattered across the grass. There was an old Roman under floor heating system displayed in the grounds, a Hypocaust. That's what the signs said anyway, though Snig couldn't really read them properly. The imp crawled into the reassuringly dark space underneath it. As he closed his eyes to rest, he found himself thinking of the humans he'd watched that night, of their friendships, and their kindnesses. He tried to recall the last time anyone had been kind to him, but it was too long ago for him to be able to remember it. The thought made him feel strangely sad.

Chapter Thirteen

As the sun came up over the city Tor, Dudley, and Bex sat with Thren on the roof of the cathedral. They'd all tried to remove the piece of wood from Thren's chest, without success. If anything, their efforts just made the bleeding worse. Even Dudley's prayers hadn't had any effect.

"Perhaps it's not about strength", said Bex, after another futile effort. "Perhaps it's about who's supposed to remove the stake". The others looked at her, puzzled. "Like King Arthur, in 'The Sword and The Stone'? You know what I mean....you got this stuck in you during the battle. Perhaps it's to do with that. Flint and Paul were there too. Maybe one of them can pull it out". As she finished speaking Bex pulled her mobile phone out of her pocket and started texting.

"They're sure gonna love you", muttered Thren, "Getting messages this early in the morning."

"They'll come, though," replied Bex, "I've told them you need them".

"Like that's gonna get a student outta bed at this hour on a Saturday morning.....and even if they do, it'll take 'em a while to get here. You two might as well go and get some breakfast. You've been up all night."

Reluctantly, Bex stood up, and then helped her father to his feet.

"I must be getting old", said Dudley apologetically, "I never used to have to think about something as basic as how to stand up!"

"Sitting on a cold, hard roof all night'll do that to a guy!" Thren grinned weakly, "Thanks for trying, though, both of you. I sure do appreciate it".

"Now", said Tor firmly, once Bex and her father had left, "What are we going to do about this demon?"

"Like I said to Dudley", Thren answered, "There's no reason to think this demon knows anything about Bex, so it's not your problem. Dross ain't gonna share that information with anyone. He'd keep it to himself until he could use it for his own gain. This demon that's come through....it'll be some random, grabbing an opportunity. I need to concentrate on protecting that boy, Duncan.....and maybe Cath... but it least it isn't a whole big group this time. That's gotta make things easier, right?"

"Thren," said Tor, gently, "You're in no state to protect anybody. Can't you see that?"

"I gotta try, Tor. You know I gotta. Can't you remember what it was like, when you had lots of people to look out for? I bet you wouldn't have sat back and ignored them, just cos you were sick. In fact, I'd better get back to the job...."

"At least wait for Flint and Paul to get here. Maybe Bex is right, and one of them can help you".

It was Paul who arrived first, since Flint was staying on the sofa at Marty's house, on the other side of town. The beeping of Bex's text message had woken him, and Paul had dragged on his clothes and hurried away from the campus towards the cathedral. Barely awake, he didn't notice Sarah waving to him on her way to breakfast. He didn't notice, either, when she changed direction and started to follow him. After what she's learned from Paul the day before, Sarah wanted to see the angels for herself. This was her birthday, after all....and meeting angels had to count as a pretty interesting way to celebrate. When she saw Paul let himself into the cathedral, she knew where he must be going.

Paul opened the door onto the roof hurriedly, too concerned about Thren to close it behind him. He could sense the angels' presence, but not see them directly.

"Hello", he called softly, "It's me, Paul".

"We know who you are", explained Tor, patiently. "We can see you, remember. It's you who can't see us....most of the time, anyway". Sarah, looking round the edge of the door, saw a sort of heat haze, which solidified into the shape of two angels, one of them sprawled on the roof. She gasped.

Tor, hearing the sound, turned, and caught a glimpse of the girl, tucked into the shadows.

"Paul", said the angel, sternly, "What have you done?"

"Nothing!" Paul replied, nervously, "I've done nothing".

"Then what is she doing here?"

"Ah," said Paul, "Er, yes, about that. I didn't actually tell her.....she just sort of....guessed..... yesterday. And I didn't know she was following me....but...well....since she'd already figured it out, does it really matter if she....sees you?"

Tor shook her head in disbelief.

"Of course it matters, you foolish boy. We've got enough trouble already".

"I'm really sorry", said Sarah, stepping out onto the roof. "I didn't mean to cause any trouble....and it wasn't Paul's fault, honestly it wasn't".

"You said we had enough trouble already," commented Paul. "What's going on?"

Dross was still getting to grips with his new body. For a start, it was female, and he couldn't get the hang of female anatomy. It made getting dressed so much more complicated. Secondly, he'd begun to figure out how Lizzy Brett....his current host....well, hostess.... had been killed. She'd been in a fire and died of smoke inhalation. He'd been in too much of a rush, the night before, to notice the smell of smoke on her clothes when he'd pulled them on, but now, in the little bedsit she rented, the scent was intense. Even pulling on fresh clothing from her wardrobe didn't get the taste of smoke out of his mouth. And her hands were burnt and blistered. She must have tried to escape from the fire, or put it out, as she was dying.

He was thankful to discover Lizzy owned jeans and trainers, as well as party frocks and high heels. Dross wanted the freedom to move quickly, if he had to. Pulling on a pair of gloves to hide his burnt hands, he slipped out of the bed-sit and headed into town.

Paul and Sarah had already left the cathedral when Flint arrived, having dashed across the city from Marty's place when he'd received Bex's text.

"Are you ok, Thren?" he asked, out of breath from racing up the stairs to the cathedral roof.

"Bex said....where is she, anyway?"

"Oh, trust you to ask that question first", said Tor disapprovingly. "You're supposed to be here to help Thren".

"And I will, if I can," said Flint, then he noticed the ferocity of Tor's glare. "She's told you, hasn't she? About us going out?"

"You're dating?" said Thren, surprised. "You and Bex? About time! What took ya so long? I was beginning to think you'd never get it together". He looked at his fellow angel, puzzled, "You knew? You knew, and you didn't tell me? This is Big News! How long has this been going on?"

"I don't know", snapped Tor, "But it stops now. You know how special Bex is, Flint. Do you honestly think you're worthy of her?"

"After what I did, you mean? No, of course I'm not....that's why I waited so long before asking her out....but she....she can see past that....and her dad, he's ok with it too."

"Well I'm not!" said Tor briskly, "I want you to stop seeing her...right away. In fact, it would be better if you weren't even friends......"

"Hey, Wonderwings", said Thren, stumbling to his feet. "Will ya cut the guy some slack? He's on our side, ya know......and it ain't up to you who Bex goes out with, your job is to protect her, not run her life for her.....'sides.....prioritise?" He pointed at the shaft of wood protruding from his chest, where the dried blood was staining his robe. Tor fell silent, leaving Thren to explain his situation to Flint.

"So you see, Flint, I need you to try and get this outta me, if you can", he finished. As Flint stepped up to the angel, and took hold of the piece of wood, Thren whispered "Don't worry about Tor, I'll calm her down....and don't, for heaven's sake, break up with Bex about it. She's a good kid. She knows all about your past, and if she loves you anyway, that's good enough for me". Flint looked away from Thren's face, and the angel noticed that the young man's soul-light, which was usually a paler shade of grey these days, darkened. Thren was just wondering what was wrong when Flint attempted to tug the stake out of his chest. The waves of pain that followed washed over Thren, driving all other thoughts from his mind, briefly, but it was no use. No matter how hard Flint tried, the wood wouldn't budge. Thren sunk back down onto the roof, trying to catch his breath.

"I'm sorry, Thren", said Flint, crouching down beside him. "I really am. I can't seem to shift it at all".

"That's ok kid, not your fault". "What are you going to do?" asked Flint. "Try to keep going, I guess. I've managed this long with the thing sticking into me....I figure I can carry on for a while yet....at least until we've beaten the demon that's just come through, anyhow".

Thren hauled himself to his feet and looked down from the roof. None of the soul-lights he could see were showing signs of being in trouble, so it looked as if the demon hadn't started anything yet. Thren didn't notice the body of Lizzy Brett hurrying through town, minus a soul. He was finding it harder and harder to focus. In fact, he was beginning to wonder if angels could die, and if so, how long he had to try and sort things out before he became too weak. Not just for dealing with the demon, but for settling some other issues involving some of the humans he'd been trying to help. Time to get back to work, before it was too late.

Chapter Fourteen

While Thren set off into the city, Tor and Flint went to Bex's, to join the others for breakfast. There was a frosty silence between them as they walked down the steps from the roof. Tor had made herself invisible again, but Flint could feel her disapproval even without being able to see her.

"I know you don't like me", murmured Flint, "But I'm going to take care of Bex, honestly I am".

"Like you took care of your younger brother?" sniped Tor. As soon as she spoke the words she regretted them, but before she could apologise Flint had speeded up, running down the steps and out towards the cathedral green. He decided to skip breakfast. What right did he have to relax with his friends anyway, after what he'd done? He turned to head for the archway out to the street, but then he heard Bex, calling him.

"Aren't you coming in for breakfast?" she asked, smiling. He shook his head.

"Things to do", he muttered. A few months ago Bex might have accepted his explanation, but now she knew him too well.

"What's up? Has someone upset you?" Flint shrugged. "It was Tor, wasn't it? What did she say? She had no right to have a go at you".

"She's your guardian angel, Bex, she can say what she likes".

"Maybe, but she's not my mother, and she's not supposed to interfere, not like that anyway".

"I knew it would be a mistake, telling them", groaned Flint.

"I only asked her to give us some privacy", protested Bex. "Hang on... Them? Thren knows? How did he take it? Don't tell me he had a go at you as well?"

"No, he was ok about it. Good in fact, but think about it Bex.... how can we be together with Tor breathing down your neck all the time? It can't work". They looked at each other bleakly.

"It can if I give you some space", Tor was nearby, but speaking so softly they could hardly hear her. "I'm sorry Flint. I didn't have the right to say what I did. I know you've made mistakes in the past, but you've been honest about them", Flint looked at the ground, embarrassed. "You regret what you did, I know that", Tor continued, "And it's not for me to judge you anyway. Thren's right, you're on our side....and I'll try to be on yours. I'll even back off a little.... but not until we contained whatever demon came through last night.....so you may have to put up with my presence for a little while longer".

"No problem" muttered Flint, awkwardly.

"Thanks Tor," said Bex, grinning. "I know you're just doing 'the mum thing'....but I'm not a kid anymore." It was rather nice to hear her guardian angel being a little less bossy. "Now come inside, both of you".

Thren had looked in on Duncan, who was still sleeping, and, more importantly, still in possession of his dark blue soul-light, and now he was heading across the city to check up on some of what he thought of as "his" humans. Being a guardian angel had turned out to be far more complicated than he had thought at first. Some humans just needed to be pulled out of danger ....and then he might never run into them again. Others needed more long-term help. These were some of the ones he was worried about if he......well, if he stopped being able to do his job.

He made his way to Grosvenor Park, the largest public park in the city, where one corner was enclosed, to allow an archaeological dig to take place undisturbed. The rest of the park took him by surprise that morning. It was full of tents, and people were wandering around dressed as Roman soldiers, druids and Celts. Some of them were even speaking in Latin. Thren stopped dead, trying to make sense of what he was seeing, wondering if he's slipped through time. Then he saw one of the soldiers talking into a mobile phone, and he realised that these were re-enactors. People who were acting out what that period of time would have been like....and Chester was the perfect place to do it in. He smiled. Humans were weird, but in a good way. A cold wind was gusting across the park, making it seemed much cooler than yesterday. 'The guys in the togas sure must be feeling that', he thought. He allowed himself a few minutes to wander through the encampment, tasting a little mead here, and a mouthful of rabbit stew there, before pulling himself together and getting back to work. Making his way to the section where the dig was, he fluttered invisibly down into the enclosed area. The first person he saw was Amy, who had just turned eleven, sitting cross legged under a tree reading a rather battered letter.

Her green soul-light, usually flecked with gold, was a little dulled for a moment and her dark blond hair was neatly plaited.

Nearby her foster parents, Jay and Harriet, were excavating in a trench.

"Please" Amy was asking them. "Please! I really want to see him".

"I'm not sure it's a good idea", replied Harriet, brushing her long brown hair out of her eyes. "You said he drank, and he used to push you around.....you and Luke".

"He did", agreed the child, "but he couldn't help it......and he's much better now.....listen...." and she started to read out a paragraph from the letter she was clutching. "As I said in my last letter, Amy, I've been getting help....both with my drinking and my temper ....and I'm much better than I was. Still a long way to go though. I know it didn't work out, you and Luke living with me after your mother died, but I haven't forgotten you, and I'd really like to see you both again, for your own sake, and your mother's. Social services have said I can see you, so long as it's a sur...ser..."

"Supervised?" Jay chipped in. Amy nodded briskly, and continued "A supervised visit....and so long as everyone agrees to it". She looked at her foster parents "Please agree to it.....please......"

"Why do you even want to see him again, after he treated you both so badly?" asked Jay climbing out of the trench and going to sit beside Amy.

"Because he's Harry....and he wasn't always like that. He was nice in the beginning.....when mum first moved in with him. I liked him.....he was like a dad". She looked shyly at Jay, hoping he wouldn't be jealous of how she felt about Harry. She didn't want to be disloyal. Jay and Harriet were the best foster parents she's had so far, but she hadn't been with the couple for long, and felt uncertain about where she stood with them. Her big brother Luke had been bounced around a few foster homes too.....but fewer people wanted teenagers, and he was currently in a children's home, which he hated. Amy missed her brother so much, but she didn't like to complain about it, in case Jay and Harriet got sick of her, and sent her away.

Thren knew that the couple saw foster caring as a short term role, while they waited to have a child of their own, but he was trying to influence them into offering Luke a place with them too, and making the arrangement more permanent. Even though he was an angel, he didn't have to power to force anyone to do anything. All he could do was whisper in their ear, appeal to their better nature, and encourage them to accept his suggestions, while thinking that they'd come up with the idea themselves. Influencing people like that required tact and patience, and Thren was short of both. It was one of the hardest parts of his job, but he had the satisfaction of knowing that he succeeded sometimes. So far Jay and Harriet hadn't even met Luke. Amy was allowed to visit him at the children's home once a week, but her foster parents just dropped her at the door and picked her up later.

Now he was trying to convince them to let Amy meet up with Harry. Social services had suggested the meeting take place at the children's home on Sunday afternoon....the time when Amy went there to see Luke. That way Harry could see both children together, and the staff of the children's home could supervise the visit.

"Go on, lady" Thren whispered in Harriet's ear, "What do you got to lose? You gotta take the kid to the home anyway.....where's the harm in letting her see the guy, if that's what she wants?" Thren stared at Harriet, willing her to agree. He really liked this couple. They were both dedicated archaeologists, committed to their work, and fascinated by history, and the traces it left behind, but they were fun too, and ready to give up their time to look after foster children. Harriet was in her early thirties, tall and slim, with long brown hair, and a soft, hazel brown soul-light. Jay was a little older, and stockier. His black hair was lanky, making him look a little like a hippy, and his soul-light was royal blue. The couple didn't have much money, as archaeologists are never well paid, but they did the best they could for the children they fostered. Thren knew that they were each beginning to feel anxious that they hadn't had a baby of their own yet. He'd checked them out thoroughly when he discovered that Amy was being placed with them. He wished he could tell them that even if they didn't have their own child eventually, it might not be the end of their world...it might leave them free to parent the other children....the ones who didn't have anybody else....but they'd have to figure that out for themselves.

"Come on, Jay" whispered Thren, "What harm can it do. You can see how much Amy wants to see him".

"Alright", said Jay to Amy, "If you're really sure you want to see this man, and it won't upset you too much, you can see him".

"Result!" thought Thren, delighted to see a huge smile on Amy's face. The child's soul-light brightened too.

"Are you sure this is a good idea Jay?" Harriet whispered, "I'm worried she'll be unsettled by seeing him. I think I'd rather be there at the meeting, if it's going to happen. Then at least we can support her, if things get difficult." 'Even better', thought Thren, 'that way they get to meet Luke too. Am I good or am I good?'

Snig peered out from under the Hypocaust, his shelter in the Roman Gardens, trying to decide what to do next. He saw a very tall, thin man with extremely short brown hair and a neat beard, walking through the gardens, reading the various descriptive signs.

"Time to have some fun", Snig decided. He crept up behind his target to take a closer look, and noticed that the man was alternating reading the plaques describing different objects in the gardens, with pulling a small book out of his pocket and glancing at it, while muttering to himself.

"We've got a fellow who is better on the cello than any other ship can brag" sang the man, under his breath. The man snapped the book shut in frustration, "Whose idea was it to have us acting, singing and playing instruments at the same time! And why did I get landed with the cello???" Snig backed off, wondering if the man was dangerous. Not knowing that actors often recited their lines aloud when they were learning a script, the imp wasn't sure what to make of someone who was talking to himself. Humans were definitely a little strange. Then he saw the corner of a price tag sticking out from under the back of the man's hat. It was obviously brand new. Perhaps the man had bought it that morning, because of the cold wind. Whatever the reason, Snig couldn't resist. He leapt up and snatched the hat, and started waving it about in front of his victim. The man turned, puzzled. Surely the wind wasn't strong enough to wrench the hat from his head? And why was it moving about in the air like that?

The weather was cold, but the wind was dropping. It wasn't that fierce now. He reached for his hat, and it seemed to leap away from him, which was most peculiar. Snig was invisible, of course, but the hat was behaving very erratically. Every time the man made a grab for it, it jumped away from him, dancing in mid-air. The man started to run after the hat, but after a few minutes, he began to cough, stopped running and bent double, trying to catch his breath. Snig stopped cavorting with the woollen hat and crept closer. Most people would have become angry with the frustration of the situation, and started shouting and swearing. Snig would have enjoyed that. He loved negative emotions. This man seemed gentle and quiet, except for the sounds he made as he struggled to get his breath back. Snig began to feel a little guilty, for making the man ill.....and suddenly dropped the hat at his victim's feet.

"Have it back", croaked the imp, "You're no fun anyway". The man just stared at it as his breathing began to settle, then he reached down and picked it up, looking thoughtful. He ripped off the price tag, put the hat back on his head and carried on exploring the Roman Gardens.

Thren was flying back towards the cathedral when he looked down and caught a glimpse of what he thought might be an imp, taunting a human in the gardens. He saw the creature return something to the man then scurry off out of sight. 'That's real strange behaviour for one of those' thought Thren, 'Guess I'd better get after it though. It sure shouldn't be here'. He tried to turn in mid air, but the pain in his chest was too great, and he dropped to the ground, crashing to his knees. He managed to remain invisible, but one of his feathers drifted down to land at the man's feet. The man bent down and picked it up, holding it to the light.

"Beautiful", he said, wonderingly, before looking around to see where it had come from. There weren't any birds nearby large enough to shed such a feather. The man tucked it into his coat pocket and carried on walking.

Thren picked himself up off the ground muttering.

"Great....so now I'm moulting? My life just gets better and better". He looked round for the imp, but there was no trace of it. The angel didn't have the strength to start searching for the creature, all he could do was hobble back towards the cathedral.

Snig, meanwhile, had curled up back in the shadows under the Hypocaust. He was shaking with shock. He must be ill. What was wrong with him? Feeling guilty? Imps didn't do that! Giving the man back his hat? This was terrible! Something frightful must be happening to him.

"Scared", he whispered to himself. "Snig's sick. Snig's dying".

Chapter Fifteen

Paul and Sarah were still munching on pieces of toast in Dudley's kitchen when Bex walked back in, followed by Flint and Tor....who was allowing herself to be visible, since everyone in the room had seen her anyway. Sarah choked on her toast at the sight of the angel, and Paul had to thump her on the back several times, until she'd coughed it up.

"Sorry", said Sarah, embarrassed. "I wasn't expecting....I'm mean....inside....I thought...."

"We're not glued to the roof of the cathedral, you know", snapped Tor, huffily. She paused, remembering the awkward moment when she had actually been glued there. Bex caught her eye, and grinned. The angel carried on speaking, crisply, "We wouldn't be able to do our job if we were."

"Er....I'm sorry", muttered Sarah.

"More toast, anyone?" asked Dudley, to fill the awkward silence. Soon Tor and the others were tucking into hot buttered toast smeared with strawberry jam. When Thren arrived, Dudley offered him some as well, but Thren just shook his head. Somehow food seemed less appealing since he'd crashed to the ground earlier. He was quiet too, which worried everyone except Sarah. She didn't know what he was normally like.

"There was an imp, in the Roman Gardens," Thren said eventually. "Only small fry, and acting kinda oddly....but I couldn't catch it. Seems like we've got more than one problem to deal with". Tor took a deep breath, and glared at Paul.

"That would be because Somebody was foolish enough to tell Sarah what was going on".

"Paul didn't tell me," protested Sarah. "I just guessed....that wouldn't count, would it?"

"It might explain an imp", Tor replied. "But that wouldn't be enough to let a demon through. So who else has said something, and to whom?"

At that moment the doorbell rang, and Bex hurried at answer it. Cath was at the door, and as soon as Bex opened it, the usually quiet girl stormed into the house, dragging Sam behind her. She erupted into the kitchen before the angels had had a chance to make themselves invisible.

"How could you?" she ranted at her friends, "How could you keep it from me? Everything that happened last term....I thought I was losing my mind, and you let me! What kind of friends would do that to a person?"

Tor rose to her full height; well actually she cheated and floated just above the ground, to look more impressive.

"The kind of friends who know that if they go around telling everybody what really happened, there'd be even more trouble. More demons would come through, more people would get killed. Is that what you wanted?"

"What I wanted.....what I needed, was to understand what had happened" the girl replied, suddenly feeling rather overawed at arguing with an angel.

"And now you do!" snarled Tor. "And another demon has come through. I hope you're satisfied!"

"Don't blame her," said Thren, trying to calm things down. "It was me that told her....I had ta, to stop her doing anything foolish. So if ya gonna take it out on someone, blame me".

"Don't worry, Thren, I always do!" Tor glared at him.

Sam had been looking around the kitchen in amazement. He was still hung-over from the night before. He'd refused to believe anything Cath had told him, about the angels, and the demon who'd caused so much trouble, stealing her soul, and taking his best friend's life. Cath couldn't bear to have one of the few people she felt safe with to think she'd gone crazy. She was so determined that he should understand what had happened that as soon as she saw him on campus that morning, she'd practically hauled him up to Bex's home.

Now he was speechless. He could see Thren, and Tor. They were real. Either that or he was hallucinating. He'd partially understood what had happened to Mark, but that didn't stop him from feeling guilty that he hadn't managed to do anything to save his friend's life. Now he was beginning to see that what had happened was part of a bigger, and much more complicated, picture. One he could barely grasp, and had been in no position to control. The shock, and the relief of the discovery, was overwhelming. Sam felt his legs buckling under him and he slid to the floor, shaking. Cath knelt down next to him, and put her arm around his shoulders. Her anger faded, and she suddenly felt small, and foolish. She looked round at her friends, ashamed at having shouted at them. It wasn't like her to lose control like that. Not like the old her, anyway.

"It's ok, kid" said Thren, gently. "They'll forgive you." The others nodded. "And put your wings down, Tor, they don't need you towering over them. They're just trying to get their heads round everything". Tor floated down until her feet rested on the kitchen floor once more.

"Well, now you know", said Tor, then added, more gently, "I'm sorry nobody could tell you what happened, but they really weren't supposed to. It's completely against the rules for people to see us, or know what we do in any detail. ....and when the rules get broken..... that's when things go wrong".

"So I've made things worse? Coming here, seeing you, telling Sam?" Cath asked guiltily, looking up at the angel.

"It's not your fault," said Tor, "Thren should have told you about the dangers". Tor looked at Thren, disappointed that he'd been reckless, yet again. Thren opened his mouth to protest, but Cath looked guilty enough already. He didn't want to make her feel any worse. Most of his energy was going into keeping himself upright, and trying to block out the pain in his chest, but with what was left, he could recognise the irony of annoying Tor to protect Cath. He'd always thought of her as the dull one amongst the students, but seeing her all riled up made him reassess his opinion. And in a way, he was glad that Sam knew too. Over the recent weeks the boy's copper coloured soul-light had darkened, as he brooded over his friend's death, blaming himself for not doing more. Now Thren could sense a lightening of the boy's spirits, and hoped that one day the jokey, smiling boy would emerge from the gloom he'd been struggling with. Thren was beginning to feel he might not be around to see the transformation, but he was pleased anyhow, even though it meant the rules had been broken.

"Dudley", said Thren, smiling at the old man. "Would you mind making these two some toast? Cath hasn't been eating properly, and I reckon Sam could do with something in his stomach, too".

"Of course", Bex's father replied. "Are you sure you don't want any yourself?" Thren shook his head and tried to focus. His job was to deal with the consequences of all these broken rules. He wasn't sure how much the balance of the world and The Darkness had been altered, but he was sure trouble was coming their way, and he had to be ready to fight it. "Guess I'd better get back to work", he said, moving towards the door with difficulty.

"Will you been joining us tonight?" asked Dudley. "Seven o'clock".

"What for?" asked Sam, speaking for the first time. "Some kind of prayer meeting?"

"Nothing so serious," replied Thren, grinning weakly. "Seven o'clock on a Saturday night??? Think about it!" Sam continued to look confused.

"I'll be here tonight, Dudley" answered Thren, as he left. "If I can, anyhow. Just my luck if all hell breaks loose right in the middle of the show".

Debbie turned this way and that in front of the mirror, trying to assess the effect her new dress would have on Marty. She smiled, pleased with what she saw, and slipped the fascinator into her beautiful blond hair. Perfect. Her outfit was complete! She couldn't believe it the day before when Marty said he was taking her to the races. Most of the time Debbie was content to simply hang out with Marty, doing nothing in particular, but it was lovely to have a special afternoon to look forward to. She enjoyed having a reason to dress up and look her best....and her best was pretty fabulous, if she did say so herself. She'd always loved fashion, and if there had been an award for "best dressed student" in the first term she'd been at university, Debbie would have won it hands down.

Admittedly, it helped that her father had happily supplemented her finances when she first went away to study, and even now, the odd extra cheque would arrive for her, just in case she needed it. It was also handy that her mother knew a couple of people who were magazine editors....and that was Debbie's plan, once she graduated, to be a fashion journalist.

The term before, when Marty was sick in the hospital, Debbie had resolved to be less frivolous and fashion conscious, and concentrate on the more important things in life, like her relationship with Marty, and her English course work, and on the whole she'd stuck to her decision, but today... well, today she was determined to revel in the chance to glam up and slap on some makeup for the trip to the Chester Races. After a final glance in the mirror, she set off, in brand new high heeled shoes, clutching a matching handbag....and thinking to herself that Marty was the best boyfriend in the world!

Chapter Sixteen

Marty had asked Debbie to meet him at one of the gates into the race course. She looked through it into the crowded arena, and could see all the marquees filling the spaces around the track. Men in smart suits were calling to each other, and strutting around with bottles of champagne, while groups of ladies, resplendent in their best frocks, clustered together, like flocks of brightly coloured birds, chatting and waving greetings to other race goers. Debbie could sense the excitement building up around the track. Soon it would be time for the first race to begin. She hoped Marty would turn up quickly, so that they would have time to buy a drink before the event started and make their way to a good position beside the track, to watch the horses galloping past.

Marty appeared a few minutes later, casually dressed in jeans and a t-shirt, his fair hair clipped close to his head. He wasn't anything special to look at, in fact Debbie had considered him rather plain when they first met, but now she only noticed his friendly smile.

"Sorry," he muttered, as he kissed Debbie's cheek, "I was watching the end of the Grand Prix Qualifying Session on TV before I came out, and lost track of the time." He stepped back to admire her outfit, "You look...amazing....but aren't you a bit overdressed?"

"Not for the races, no", replied Debbie, "You're the one who looks too scruffy to be allowed in, if anything. Shouldn't you have put a jacket on, or something? I thought there was a dress code".

"Not for watching the races from up here," laughed Marty. "You didn't think we were going in, did you? The view of the race track is just as good from up on the walls....better, even....and it's free."
He took a second look at Debbie, and realised that was exactly what she had thought. "Sorry, I didn't mean....I haven't bought tickets, or anything."

"We could buy them now?" suggested Debbie. "How much are they?"

"More than I've got left at the moment", said Marty, embarrassed. "Unless you've got any cash?" Debbie glared at her now not so perfect boyfriend.

"I spent mine on the dress!" she snapped.

"It's a very...nice dress" said Marty, sliding an arm around her waist. She stepped away from him.

"Nice....this dress is just NICE?" From inside the race course they could hear the first race starting, and moved along the city walls, until they found a spot that overlooked the race track. They both looked down at the jockeys steering their mounts around the course, a chilly distance separating them. Marty reached out to take Debbie's hand, and then thought better of it. He considered telling her about his debts, which had started to spiral out of control.

Debbie had invited him to stay with her and her parents over Easter, and in an effort to fit in, and make a good impression, he'd offered to take them all out for a meal. Unfortunately, Debbie's parents, who never seemed to worry about money, chose a rather expensive restaurant, and Marty had used up a whole term's worth of money in one night. Since then he'd taken out several pay day loans, but since, as a student, he didn't have a pay day, he was getting further and further behind with his repayments, and his debts were rising at a terrifying speed. He'd already decided he'd need to look for work the moment he finished his exams, but he was beginning to worry that he would need more than just one job to clear his debts. At this rate he'd need two, or even three.

Living at home while he was studying had been keeping his living expenses down, but once he started going out with Debbie, his efforts to impress her seemed to land him deeper and deeper in the red. He'd tried to get some work as a waiter at the beginning of term, but in a city full of students there was fierce competition for any work that didn't clash with classes. The hand he'd reached out to take Debbie's dropped to his side as they watched the horses thundering round the track in silence. He wished he'd placed a bet on one of them....but the odds on him winning enough money to get out of debt were remote. He reached into his pocket, pulled out a packet of cigarettes, and a box of matches, and lit up. Debbie hated him smoking, but since she was mad at him anyway, he didn't think it would make things any worse.

Thren was making his way through the crowded streets of the city centre, unaware that Tor was following him. She was so concerned about the state he was in, that she thought she should be nearby, in case he needed any help, even if that did mean leaving Bex unprotected.

Thren was trying to scan the people around him, to see if anyone needed assistance, if their soul-lights were indicating that they were in trouble, but there were so many people packed onto the pavements that it was difficult for him to move, let alone be aware of anyone more than a few steps away. The Roman event included a procession through the streets, with all the participants in costume. Thren recognised the director of the Chester Mystery Plays dressed as an Emperor and riding on a horse. Roman soldiers were striding along the roads, along with a smaller group of people dressed as Celts. Thren was so intrigued by what was happening that he didn't look where he was going, and bumped into a young man who, like him, was watching the event.

The man was big built, with close cropped dark hair, bronze skin, bright eyes and a wide infectious smile, full of energy and the joy of life. Thren found himself smiling back, then remembered that he was invisible. The angel was about to move on when he heard the stranger humming a melody, very softly, as his fingers moved in time to the music that nobody else could hear. The tune seemed simple enough to begin with, but the man kept making tiny alterations until it leapt and soared....Thren looked around, amazed that no-one else was noticing the beauty of the music, then realised that he was hearing it more in his head than with his ears....The young man must be a composer, and, briefly Thren felt jealous of humans ability to be creative........but soon even that thought was washed away by the glory of what he was hearing... it reminded him of Home, and everything he missed about it, and as Thren let the music flow though him, the pain in his chest eased slightly, and for a few moments he felt whole again. A young woman brushed against Thren's shoulder as she wove her way through the crowd, but the angel didn't even notice her, or the strange look she gave him.

'This guy sure has talent', thought Thren, 'I could listen to him all day'. Just then the young man broke off and started laughing. Another group of Roman soldiers were marching past, and one of them started to shout out orders.

"Sin Dex Sin". The composer waved to the soldier, obviously recognising him.
"Bet you don't even know what that means, do you mate?" the young man shouted to his friend, who just shrugged and carried on marching, still calling out in Latin.

"Sin Dex Sin".

"Left, Right, Left ....the sound of marching armies the world over", whispered Tor softly, in Thren's ear. "Romans, they still make me uncomfortable, even after all this time. The things they did......"

"Don't stress it, Wonderwings, it's all in the past....and these guys are just pretending....they're not even real Romans".

"Just as well", said Tor, "The real Romans were barbaric.... though I did enjoy speaking in Latin....Hinc spes effulget...".

"Lady, do *Not* start talking to me in Latin" replied Thren. "I got no idea what you just said".

"Nothing new there then," said Tor, resignedly. "It's the Latin for 'hence hope shines forth', a rather comforting thought, under the circumstances".

"Hence hope shines forth," muttered Thren, dejectedly, "not much chance of that right now". The composer turned away, humming his music again....then paused and said softly to himself.

"Hence hope shines forth! That might work." The man wandered off, softly experimenting with setting those words to his melody.

"Are you sure that you're managing to stay invisible?" Tor asked Thren, determined to get back to business. "A girl who bumped into you gave you a very odd look".

"I didn't see a girl", shrugged Thren, "Guess I was too taken up with listening to that guy's music....did you hear it Tor? Wasn't it amazing?"

Tor shook her head, sadly.

"You know I can't hear human thoughts the way you sometimes can, Thren. I can't even see their soul-lights, except for Bex's". Which was why she hadn't noticed that the girl who bumped into Thren didn't have a soul-light at all.....which would have been a really useful thing to know. Another mistake to add to Thren's already very long list!

Debbie and Marty were still leaning against the city walls, watching the races. Even Debbie had to admit that the view of the race track was good from that viewpoint, but that still didn't get Marty off the hook. Debbie had been expecting to experience the glamour of feeling part of the crowd within the grounds, and she felt foolish being all dressed up, but on the outside looking in. She moved further along the wall, putting a little more distance between herself and Marty.

A girl wove her way through the crowd and came to stand beside her, looking out over the race track.

"You don't mind if I shove in, do you?" asked the girl. Debbie shook her head politely.

"No, feel free". She took a tiny step away from the newcomer, trying to avoid the bitter, smoky smell she seemed to carry with her.

"I love the outfit", the girl commented, grinning. "Guessing someone let you down, then?" Debbie hesitated, torn between her loyalty to Marty, and annoyance at her disappointing afternoon. "I'm Lizzy, by the way," said the girl, offering her gloved hand for Debbie to shake.

'Lizzy' smiled as they exchanged names. She already knew exactly who Debbie was, of course. One of Dross's targets on the last occasion that he'd come through from The Darkness. He'd come close to capturing Debbie's tempting pink and orange soul-light before....but not close enough. According to the rules, Dross didn't have the right to go after her again.....or any of the other students in that group. He'd had his chance with them, and failed. Debbie and her friends had had no part in inviting the demon through this time, so Dross had no claim on them, but then, Dross was a demon, with a score to settle, and he was toying with the idea of breaking a few rules. After all, if his plan worked, in a few days he'd have broken the power that held the rules in place completely. The balance that kept The Darkness in check would be overthrown, and he could do as he pleased. So long as he kept things subtle, and nobody realised who they were dealing with, perhaps he could get away with taking his revenge. 'Lizzy' pointed to Marty, who was standing a little distance away.

"That your boyfriend?" she asked, wheezing, as if she didn't know, as if she wasn't drooling to swallow Marty's tasty amber soul-light again, and draw strength from it. Dross had missed out on Debbie's soul-light last time, and Marty's had been wrested back from him, but now he was determined to correct that mistake.

'Lizzy' glanced down from where she leant against the wall, weighing up the possibilities. The drop to the ground wasn't far enough to do any major damage, so there was no point in pushing either of them over the city wall...besides, it was broad daylight, and they were surrounded by people. She needed to try something less obvious. Debbie's pretty little clutch bag was unclipped, and Lizzy could see the girl's phone, sitting on top of a make-up bag. Lizzy waited a few moments, until the horses galloping round the track caught Debbie's attention, and then slipped the phone out of Debbie's bag and into her own pocket. Dross once again regretted his choice of a female corpse. Women's clothing was too tight fitting, the pockets were too small, and the demon was sure the phone was sticking out. Debbie would notice it, surely? At that moment Marty edged back towards his girlfriend, and reached for her hand. As she slipped away 'Lizzy' noticed that Debbie put her hand in his. She was starting to enjoy the afternoon, even if it wasn't what she'd expected, and Marty seemed to have been forgiven.

"Enjoy your fun," thought Dross, as Lizzy's body moved away from the couple. "It'll be over soon enough".

Chapter Seventeen

Despite Thren and Tor being on the lookout for trouble, the rest of the afternoon passed uneventfully. They had checked on Duncan several times, but there was no sign of any danger threatening him. The student seemed perfectly normal, though he was a little pale and tired. Thren's concerns over having another demon to deal with were causing him more and more stress. The angel was feverish, and the pain in his chest was becoming unbearable. He wasn't even sure if the pain was purely due purely to the wooden stake or to a sense of impending trouble for the people under his protection.

Thren decided to allow himself a few minutes in the one place that always helped him to feel at peace....the heart of the cathedral. Moving invisibly through the tourists who were wandering around it, he made his way up the nave and through the arch in the carved wooden rood screen, to the choir stalls. In Thren's opinion they were one of the glories of the cathedral. They were ancient, and festooned with intricately carved spiky wooden canopies. The backs of the stalls, and the benches themselves, were decorated with strange grotesque wooden faces of sedate angels and mischievous imps. Not that Thren liked real imps, but these carvings always made him smile. Every inch of the elaborate wooden structure had been created hundreds of years before, by people producing their best work, for His glory. For a few minutes Thren allowed himself to rest, absorbing the soothing atmosphere built up by generations of worshipers, and the pain in his chest subsided.

Then he glanced up at the golden ceiling, where the beautifully painted angels stared down at the world serenely, and sighed. 'Gee, they look relaxed', he thought, 'Why don't I ever get to feel that way?' He felt an intense longing for Home. He missed the place so much that it hurt....but not as much as the wooden stake in his chest was starting to hurt again....a reminder of everything he still had to do here. Putting aside his homesickness, he stood up, patted a wooden lion on the end of one of the choir stalls on the head, and went to check on Duncan again.

At half past six Thren and Tor were back on the roof of the cathedral, hoping to see any disturbance from above, but the city seemed remarkably calm.

"You might as well go and join the others at Dudley's", suggested Tor. "I can keep an eye on things from up here".

"But then you have to miss out.... that's kinda rough....I know you enjoy it too".

"Nonsense," said Tor sharply, "I only go along to be sociable". This was not true, and Tor was shocked at herself for telling even such a tiny lie, but she didn't want Thren to feel guilty about leaving her on guard over the city, which was really his responsibility. "You go," commanded Tor firmly, steering Thren towards the stairs down into the cathedral. "You need the distraction, and they'll only worry if neither of us are there". Thren nodded weakly, and began to walk down the stairs, but stumbled, almost losing his balance. "Here," said Tor, hurrying after him, "Lean on me". She draped Thren's arm around her shoulders and supported him down the stairs and round the green to Dudley's little house.

As his fellow angel took his weight, Thren remembered the night he first met Bex....not long after his Come Down. He's had a foolish accident, and the girl, who could see him even when she wasn't supposed to, had witnessed it, and helped him back to the cathedral. 'Things sure have changed since then', mused Thren. 'Who'd have thought it? Me? Getting so involved with these humans, making friends with them, and with Tor. I guess she ain't so bad really, even if she does act all bossy most of the time'. He turned to glace at his fellow angel, who was concentrating on holding him upright.

"Tor", he said softly, "I'm real sorry about how snappy I've been with you lately. I'm just a bit stressed out is all, and I guess I've been taking it out on you".

"Nothing new there then", replied Tor curtly, then she turned and smiled at him. "That's alright Thren, I do know what you're going through. I can cope, if you need someone to lash out at sometimes". Thren was stunned. Tor was being nice to him? He realised with a jolt that he must really be sick.

When they reached the door it was open, so that anyone who was joining them could let themselves in. Dudley was in an armchair in the sitting room, Bex, Flint, Paul and, on this occasion, Sarah, were squeezed onto the sofa, which wasn't really big enough to accommodate four people. Usually, it was just Dudley, Bex, Flint and Paul, and the angels.

The television was on, but the programme hadn't started yet. Tor settled Thren into the other armchair, giving the others warning glances not to comment about the state he was in. Flint reached into his rucksack and pulled out a big bag of popcorn, nipping out into the kitchen to fetch a bowl to put it in. Tor frowned, noticing how familiar he seemed with the house. She was still convinced that he spent too much time with Bex, but was determined not to comment. Just before seven o'clock there was a shy tap on the door and Cath and Sam walked in, hesitating in the doorway.

"We came to find out what's going on", announced Cath, defiantly, "You didn't say earlier. Is it something important?" Sam had the hangdog look of someone being dragged along in his friend's wake.....again.

"That depends," said Dudley smiling ruefully, "On whether you're a fan of 'Dr Who', or not. I've loved it ever since started.....I watched the very first episode, and I've been hooked ever since. And now it's back.....and better than ever. It's my biggest vice. I never miss it....and sometimes people join me".

"I'm just here to be sociable, I provide the popcorn", Flint added quickly. He didn't want Sam labelling him as a geek, and spreading it all around the campus, though Sam no longer spent as much time winding people up as he used to. Cath glanced round the room, and stared at Thren, amazed. "You watch Dr Who?"

"Sure", Thren replied "It's cool, and it's the only time I take off all week". Tor smirked; glad no one dared to ask her if she enjoyed the television programme, or just came along for the company.

The programme started, and they all settled down to watch, even Cath and Sam secretly enjoying it, though they didn't usually follow it.

"Not a bad episode.....and the new doctor's growing on me, but I still miss the Brigadier", said Dudley, sadly, as the credits began to roll. "He was always my favourite companion. Such a shame he was never in the new series".

"Rory was my kind of hero" argued Paul, through a mouthful of popcorn. "I'm just glad that it wasn't an episode with the Weeping Angels in" added Tor. "They really do creep me out".

Everyone turned to look at her.

"Creep you out?" queried Bex. "You really have been spending too much time with Thren, haven't you?" Tor reddened, self conscious about the choice of phrase, and the fact that her comment showed that she really did watch the series. Dudley took pity on her and changed the subject.

"I'll put the kettle on", he said, "Anyone for a cup of tea?" The old man walked into the kitchen, then called out "Tor, I think you'd better come out here, if you wouldn't mind".

Tor raced out to the kitchen, followed by the students, and more slowly, by Thren. The room was in chaos, packets and tins of food pulled out of the cupboards, and containers of flour and sugar emptied onto the floor.

"Perhaps it was a mistake to leave the front door open this evening", remarked Dudley calmly. "Rather a big mistake". In the scattered granules on the kitchen floor, someone had written the word "Next" in clumsy lettering.

Dross walked out from under the stone arch, turned onto Northgate Street and headed towards the university campus. He peeled the sugar speckled gloves off Lizzy's burnt and blistered fingers and tossed them into a litter bin. He was through with this particular body….the smell of smoke disgusted him, her burnt hands were not functioning well enough for his purposes, and her slim frame lacked the strength he needed to put some of his plans into action. Her lungs, damaged in the fire, tended to wheeze and rattle, and he had to concentrate to make her voice sound normal. Plus, she was beginning to decompose internally, and Dross knew from past experience just how difficult that could make things. He needed a new body, and he had decided exactly where to start looking.

Thren was staring down at the word scrawled in the spilt sugar.
"I kinda think it could be an imp. This place looks like an imp has trashed it….and if that word was written with a finger, it was a fairly small one".

"An imp?" asked Sarah incredulously. "They exist too?"

"Oh yes," said Tor in her best "teacher" voice. "The Lesser Invisibles can be quite a nuisance, though there are limits to how much real harm they can do…..but I'm afraid I have to ask….Flint, this wasn't done by you, was it? As some kind of a joke?" Flint looked at Bex's guardian angel in horror.

"Me?" he replied, shocked. "You think I did this?"

"Well, you did come out here to fetch a bowl for the popcorn", the angel continued. "That took about thirty seconds", countered Flint.

"I couldn't have done all this in that time, and I wouldn't have. This isn't a joke. It's sick".

"I'm sorry Flint" said Tor, guiltily, "But I had to ask. You were the last one to come out here. …and, if I'm honest, I'd much rather it

85

was some foolish prank, and not a deliberate challenge from a demon, or an imp".

"I sure wish we knew for certain which it was", added Thren. "A random imp could have just spotted the open door and seen a chance to cause a bit of mischief, but then, why write the word Next? That's some kinda threat. And a demon wouldn't bother with something as lightweight as trashing a room. They'd rather do something terrible to a person. I just can't get my head around this at all". Which was exactly what Dross had intended...to keep them all confused and off balance while he made his next move.

How he'd struggled when he realised that all his most hated adversaries, the very ones who had defeated him, were gathered in the next room, innocently watching the television together....and with the front door wide open! The demon felt almost weak with the desire to go in rip them all limb from limb, and gulp down the soul-lights of the humans, to give himself the power he needed....but the body he inhabited didn't have the strength. So he had settled for setting them a puzzle, something to keep them guessing, while he put his plan into action.

Snig had just crawled out of his hiding place, determined to pull himself together and start causing chaos again. No more thoughts of friendship, kindness, or gentleness. No more guilt. Just make trouble, that's what he was there to do.....and he was going to do it....big style!

When Dross reached the campus he stared around in delight. He Was Back. He might have been defeated last time, but now was his chance for revenge. With a bigger, better plan he was convinced that he could upset the balance between the powers of light, and The Darkness, for good.....And have another chance to collect the soul-lights of the students who invited him through last time, as well. Starting with.......Graham. He watched as the young man limped across the quad, a Chinese takeaway carton in his hand, heading for his room in the halls of residence, where he'd be all alone....an easy target. Dross smiled.

Chapter Eighteen

Graham made his way to his room. He'd been assigned one on the ground floor when he came out of hospital. He still found going up and down stairs a bit of a struggle, though he could manage them when he had to. He dug out a fork, and started to tuck into his takeaway, after slipping a DVD into his computer. 'Good old box sets' he thought, 'Always something to watch, something to keep you company'. He looked round his room. He'd kept it very plain since he moved into it. No posters or photos on the walls, just the basic furniture, his clothes and textbooks, and folders spread out on the desk. A few pieces of physio equipment took up the remaining space. For the first few weeks back at university just getting through each day had been a struggle. He still didn't really understand what had happened to him, or why.

His course work was a struggle too. He'd been behind on it, even before his accident, and then he'd been off for ages. He half expected his friend Cath to chivvy him along, and help him to catch up, but she seemed preoccupied and different somehow. Now he was making such an effort to catch up on his work, and study for the exams, that he was spending less time with his friends on the English course, like Debbie, Cath and Sarah.

Seeing less of Sarah was one of the hardest things. He'd liked her, before everything went wrong, and had been clumsily trying to ask her out, though he had always bottled it at the last minute. When he first returned to university, battling his injuries had left him too exhausted to cope with the social side of life, but there was more to it than that. Being injured had knocked his confidence, and he couldn't see how Sarah could still be interested in him as a potential boyfriend, when he felt like such a failure. He glanced over to where a brightly coloured envelope with her name written on it leaned against his pillow. He'd known that today was her birthday, and had the card all ready to give to her, and then chickened out at the last minute. Why would she even care whether he gave her a birthday card or not? Why would anyone be bothered with a loser like him?

He'd just thrown the empty takeaway carton in the bin, when there was a knock at the door. He opened it to find a young woman he didn't recognise smiling at him. He smiled back awkwardly.

"Can I come in?" asked the girl. "My name's Lizzy, and I'm doing a survey about what students think of university life".

"I'm probably the wrong person to ask", Graham replied. "Look at me, all alone in my room on a Saturday night. Come to that, isn't this a bit of a bad time to do a survey? Most people will be out at the moment."

"Of course," said the girl, "I should have thought of that". Dross could have kicked himself. He should have come up with a better explanation, but all he wanted was to get into Graham's room for a few minutes, and overpower him, which he didn't expect to be too difficult, given the injuries the boy was recovering from. Injuries Dross himself had inflicted. The demon eyed the young man's yellow soul-light hungrily. "But since you are in, can I ask you my questions? It won't take long". Graham hesitated, uncertain about letting her into his room. The last time he'd invited an 'almost stranger' in things had gone very badly wrong. Now he kept himself to himself, and only mixed with the students he already knew, when he mixed at all, that is.

On the other hand, this was a girl, quite young and presumably harmless. It seemed almost rude to refuse her request. "Alright then, as long as it doesn't take too long", he muttered, ungraciously. He didn't know why he wanted to sound busy, it was obvious that he had no plans for the evening, but it did mean he could try and limit how long she spent with him. Something about her made him feel uncomfortable, whether it was the smoky smell that clung to her, or the burnt hands....that should have been holding a clipboard....and weren't. As soon as she stepped into his room, he regretted allowing her in.

"Well," he asked, "Let's get this over with. What are your questions?"

"Questions?" asked the girl, sounding rather wheezy.

"Yes," replied Graham, "The questions for your survey". Dross hadn't actually prepared any questions, his only plan was to kill Graham and take over his body. He hadn't expected the young man to be so on edge. He considered flirting with Graham, Lizzy had been quite good looking, when alive, but he got the impression that that wasn't going to work.

"Straight for the kill then," thought Dross, picking up one of Graham's weights that were stacked on the desk. Dross raised it up, ready to bring it down on Graham's head, but Graham saw the move coming, and dodged towards the door. He wrenched it open, to find his friend Tim just outside, with Nesta just behind him in her wheelchair.

"Run" said Graham, tersely, "There's some nutter in my room, she's trying to attack me".

After a shocked pause, they heard the weight slam into the doorframe, and the three friends hurried down the corridor. They weren't exactly running, neither Graham nor Nesta were able too, but they were moving pretty fast. Tim looked back and saw a girl fleeing room his friend's room, going in the other direction along the corridor.

"She's gone", called Tim, "I think we can stop now. Graham, what on earth is going on?" Graham looked completely confused,

"I have no idea", he muttered.

Thren and Tor were still trying to get to grips with what the message in the kitchen meant as Bex and Flint tidied up the mess.

"Perhaps it was just some vandal?" suggested Bex. "It might not be anything to do with.....well, anything." Thren shook his head sadly.

"I kinda doubt it. I did see an imp earlier, and it sure seems like more of an imp thing". Suddenly Thren howled in pain, bending double as the sensation shot through his body. "Something's happened", he croaked weakly, "Someone's in danger, I gotta go see what's going on". Tor shook her head. It was clear that Thren was no longer capable of going anywhere. The sudden jolt of pain had weakened him even more, and now he was slumped on the floor.

"I'll go," she said firmly. "I can check up on the other students, and that boy Duncan, even if I can't see their soul-lights".

Just then Bex's mobile rang, and she pulled it out of her pocket. She was silent briefly, as she listened to Nesta talking very quickly.

"He's not hurt though? Good. Come round here then", said Bex, when she got a chance to speak. "Almost everyone is round here anyway. You'd better not go back to your rooms for a bit." She put the phone down and knelt beside Thren. "Thren", she said gently. "Some girl just tried to attack Graham, a couple of minutes ago. I think it was when you keeled over. He's alright though. He's coming here, along with Tim and Nesta".

"What's going on, Tor?" asked Thren . "If it's the demon, why is it going after Graham? It doesn't have the right to. Graham didn't have anything to do with inviting it through this time".

"It's a demon alright, and it's breaking the rules". Tor was horrified,   "What makes it think it can get away with that?"

"I got no idea", said Thren, weakly, "But I think it's time we broke a few ourselves. Bex, can you get hold of Debbie and Marty, and see if they can join us? It's time everyone knew what's really going on."

"You can't do that", said Tor, "It'll cause even more trouble".

"Look at me, Tor", said Thren weakly. "It's my job to defend everyone. Does it look to you like I can do that anymore? 'Cos I'm kinda thinking not. So the best I can do is put them on their guard". Tor nodded, reluctantly.

"I do see your point, but we're taking a very big risk. We could be making everything much, much worse". The ghost of a smile touched Thren's lips at Tor's use of the word 'we'. Not long ago she would have washed her hands of such a risky decision.

"I can't reach Debbie, or Marty," said Bex, who'd been trying their numbers. "They must have their phones off. At least they're likely to be together, that should make them a bit safer, shouldn't it?"

"Of course, dear" said Tor, trying to sound reassuring, "Much safer. Now Thren, you'll have to stay here, you don't look as if you have the strength to leave the house. You can explain to those who don't know, exactly what we're up against. I'll go and see if I can locate Debbie and Marty, and check on Duncan. I honestly don't know why the creature hasn't attacked him first! He's the one who invited it in". The senior angel turned to Bex, and spoke very softly "Look after Thren for me, please. I don't think he can take much more". Then she was gone. By the time Flint and Bex had helped Thren back into the sitting-room, Graham, Tim and Nesta were at the door.

Chapter Nineteen

Dross was furious with himself. He should have planned things better, prepared what he was going to say to Graham, chosen the best approach to take. Instead he had just assumed that Graham would take him at face value, and be as easy a target as the boy had been the first time. Humans were obviously better at learning from their experiences than he had realised. Time to try a more subtle method. He got out Debbie's phone and, ignoring a missed call from Bex, he scrolled through the list of names and numbers, then smiled.

He typed a text message, noticing with annoyance that the blistered skin on his fingertips was peeling off and sticking to the keys as he did so. He needed a new corpse, and quickly. The bigger plan would have to wait until the morning, but for tonight, he was determined to find himself a new shell to inhabit.

Dross found that Lizzy's body was increasingly wheezy as he hurried through the city looking for a victim. There was a large group of people gathered beneath the clock on Eastgate Street. They were being addressed by some kind of Master of Ceremonies, wearing a top hat and frock coat. He had short black hair and a neatly trimmed beard, and seemed to be a jovial sort of a man, cheerfully looking after everyone as he led the group off up the street. They stopped in front of one of the closed shops, and he began to tell the crowd a ghost story related to the building. The man relished his work, and told the story well, but watching from a distance Dross quickly decided that he wouldn't be easy to pick off, not with everybody focused on him. He was obviously the leader of what must be a "ghost tour" of the city, and it would mean Dross waiting until the tour was over before he could attack. That would require patience, and Dross wasn't feeling patient at all. He wanted a new body, and he wanted it now.

At Dudley's house Graham, Nesta and Tim were staring at Thren in disbelief. Too exhausted to keep beating his wings at the right frequency to remain invisible, Thren just had to accept that they would see him, and there was nothing he could do about it. The little sitting-room was now full to bursting, with some of the students sitting on the floor at Thren's feet. Dudley brought the exhausted angel a hot chocolate, in an attempt to lift his spirits, but Thren couldn't even bring himself to sip it. The energy required to lift the mug was more than he could muster.

It was down to Dudley, Bex, Flint and Paul to explain what had really happened in February, when this same group of students, along with Debbie, Marty, Mark and a girl called Joanna, had held that jokey séance at Marty's house, and invited a demon into their world. Not all of them had realised the very real consequences at the time, and Tim and Nesta had tried to forget about it, while being grateful that the dangers of the situation had brought them together. Nesta had thought she's caught a glimpse of an angel at the time, but had eventually chosen to dismiss it, and Tim and Graham had never quite understood the supernatural aspects of what had gone on.

"So why tell us now?" asked Nesta, her hand in Tim's. "Why wait so long?"

Thren gazed fondly at her, seeing her bright yellow soul-light dimming with concern. The angel had always admired Nesta's determination to study Biology, even though it wasn't easy to do the field work in her wheelchair. She'd had a bit of a wobble about her course the term before, but with Tim's encouragement she'd persevered, and now she was doing really well. In appearance she reminded him of an elf, with her long dark hair, green eyes and slightly pointed ears. Usually she was smiling and positive, but now she looked worried, and she was right to be.

"Because it's dangerous to tell you," Thren groaned weakly. "It breaks all the rules, and when the rules get broken, more trouble can cross over from The Darkness....like we need any more!"

"Then why tell us at all?" asked Graham, insistently.

"Because I'm afraid for you," said Thren, honestly. "I don't get what's going on. The demon that got invited in this time.....it oughtta go after the student who invited it....instead it goes after one of you. It doesn't make sense. You've got no connection....."

"Unless it's the same demon?" suggested Dudley. "Could that happen?"

"I guess it could at that," groaned Thren, his heart sinking. "In which case we've got a whole heap of trouble". He looked warningly at Bex. The fewer people who knew why the demon would want her in particular, the better. That was one secret he really wasn't planning on telling.

"The problem is", said Thren looking guiltily around the group of students, "It's kinda my fault he got through from The Darkness last time, as well as yours, and now he's back, it's my job to protect you all...." his voice trailed off.

"And you're too ill to help us", finished Sarah, softly.

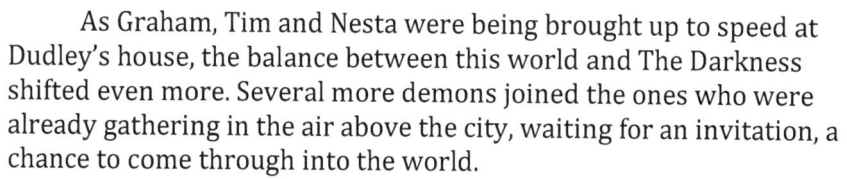

As Graham, Tim and Nesta were being brought up to speed at Dudley's house, the balance between this world and The Darkness shifted even more. Several more demons joined the ones who were already gathering in the air above the city, waiting for an invitation, a chance to come through into the world.

Snig was skittering through the shadows of the city streets. He too had noticed the ghost tour and stopped for a closer look. This should be the kind of situation where he could really cause some trouble.

"Tricks!" he muttered to himself, grinning. "Time for some tricks!" He noticed a girl, hanging back from the main group, following them from a distance, and realised it was the creature he'd seen the night before, the one wearing a now slightly smelly human shell. Maybe he wouldn't play any tricks just yet after all...maybe it would be more entertaining just to watch.

Stunned by what they had been told, the students sat quietly chatting to each other. Bex fetched a blanket to wrap around Thren, who was becoming sleepy. Tim perched on the arm of a chair, holding onto Nesta's hand. He was trying to make sense of what had happened earlier in the year, a worried frown creasing his normally cheerful, freckled face. He ran his other hand through his curly brown hair as if he could sweep away everything that he'd just been told, and Thren noticed the young man's usually steady light green soul-light was flickering in confusion.

Sam, too, was still working through the ramifications of the situation.

"So this....Thing....can take over any human body, just like it did with Mark, and control it....and attack any of us?"

Thren struggled to concentrate, to explain things properly to Sam and the others.

"No Sam, he's so not supposed to be able to attack just anyone....only the poor sucker who invited him through this time....but he seems to be breaking the rules left, right and centre, so....." "So we don't know who we can trust?" Sam completed the sentence for him.

"That's about the size of it, kid", agreed Thren. "And I ain't got a clue what's going on, or how to make it stop."

Graham moved over to where Sarah was sitting, and awkwardly handed her the birthday card. He had insisted on nipping back to his room to fetch it, and lock up, once the girl who attacked him had run away.

"Happy Birthday, Sarah", he said shyly. An enormous smile spread over Sarah's face, as she opened the envelope and saw there was a picture of a rabbit on the card. Graham must have recalled what she'd told him months ago, about how much she missed her pet while she was away at university.

"Thanks Graham," she replied, "I'm really pleased you remembered....with everything else that's been going on."

"I wasn't going to forget, was I?" he answered, shyly. "Not my favourite girl's birthday."

"Am I your favourite girl?" she asked. He looked away, embarrassed. "You know", Sarah continued, "Last term, I thought you were going to ask me out....."

"I was," admitted Graham, "But it kept going wrong, and then.......well, you know." He paused for a moment, and then blurted out, "Would you have said yes?"

"I still would", Sarah said firmly, deciding that she was having such a strange birthday that she might as well go for it, and ask Graham out herself, if he still liked her.

"So what do you think?" she asked. Graham leaned over and gave her a kiss, and Paul, watching from across the room, turned away sadly.

Sam, was starting to feel more like his own self, now that his guilt about Mark's death was beginning to fade a little, suddenly reached over and started rooting around in Flint's open rucksack.

"I'm hungry, have you got any more snacks in your bag, Flint?" Sam pulled out a slightly battered looking envelope with a card inside it. "Is this for Sarah?" he asked, and handed it over to her. Flint lunged for the card, waking Thren up in the process, but Sarah had already opened it.

"Oh", she said, disappointed. "This isn't for me. It's to Flint, not from him". She started to read it out, "Happy 21st birthday, from Julie.....who's Julie?"

"My sister", said Flint tersely.

"Hang on," commented Sam, "21st birthday? But you're only in the first year....how come you're older than the rest of us? Don't tell me you had to do re-sits or something?"

Flint hung his head. This was exactly what he had hoped wouldn't happen, the moment when everyone would learn the truth, even the parts of the truth he had kept hidden from Bex.

"You don't have to say anything, kid", Thren said softly. "Not until you're ready".

"I'm not sure I ever will be", Flint turned to leave. "I think I need some space", he said, heading for the door.

"Not tonight", said Bex firmly, blocking his exit. "We all need to stay together at the moment. I don't want you going out there and getting yourself killed, whatever's wrong". She took his hand and pulled him back towards the rest of the group.

"Come on, it's 'be kind to Thren night'", she joked, "You know if you go out there, he'll have to follow you, to protect you....and I really don't think he can. Not tonight." Flint looked at Thren, and realised just how sick the angel was looking.

"Ok" said Flint, settling down, "But please, don't ask me any more questions". Thren reached out and put a comforting hand on the young man's shoulder, and Flint began to relax, a little.

Dross, however, was far from relaxed, as he observed the group of people on the ghost tour, and decided who to kill.

Chapter Twenty

The ghost tour was moving through the streets of the city, with Dross following behind, assessing who would be easy to pick off. There were two small groups of work colleagues, out for a bit of a giggle. They'd already had a drink or two and were tending to cling to each other. Dross dismissed them within a few minutes.....a family with a nervous little girl? No, the child would notice if he tried anything with the parents.....and children can scream very loudly. His eye was caught by a group of three adults, who seemed to be friends of the man leading the tour.

Listening in to their conversation, Dross gathered that they were a married couple and their friend. The older man was in his early fifties, big and bearded, with fair hair turning silver-blond and smiling blue-grey eyes. He had obviously been dragged along by the other two, but was tolerant enough to go with the flow and enjoy himself. His wife was small, and plump, with mid-length wavy brown hair. Her right foot twisted outwards slightly, and whenever she stumbled on the cobbled streets both her husband and her friend would reach out protectively to support her. Dross wasn't sure either of them suited his purpose. They would hardly blend in with the students he was targeting.

Their friend, however, was a possibility. He was in his early thirties, clean-shaven, with light brown hair, an open face, and a gentle expression. He seemed to be enjoying the company of his friends and taking pleasure in seeing the ghost tour going so well, especially since he knew the man in the top hat. Whenever audience participation was called for, this young man and his friends were happy to get involved, giving support and encouragement to the man in charge of the event. Even Snig was drawn to this enthusiastic young fellow who was so protective of his friend, and the imp found himself puzzled once again by human behaviour.

By now the group was near a covered archway, listening to another tale, and a spooky figure approached up the alley, carrying its head under its arm. The audience turned and saw it, some of them squealing with fright, while others were impressed with the theatrical effect. Snig couldn't resist. He'd been hanging back, waiting to see what the demon would do, trying not to draw its attention, but now he leapt forward and grabbed the head, leaping and bounding invisibly through the air, making the severed head appear to turn somersaults. The group froze, some genuinely scared, others trying to figure out how the amazing trick was being performed. The child started to cry, and the man in the top hat, who was almost as puzzled as everyone else, was desperately trying to stay in character and calm everybody down.

He hurried the group away, trying to signal to the headless body to get away itself, and leave the head to do its own thing. He could replace the head, if need be, costly as the prop was, but he didn't want anything to happen to a member of his team, and he couldn't understand what was going on.

As the group was chivvied away down the street, Dross stepped out of the shadows and grabbed Snig by the throat. The imp dropped the head and hung in mid-air choking.

"Get away from here, or I'll rip you apart!" growled Dross, menacingly, and Snig was in no doubt the demon meant it. Dross threw him forcefully down the alleyway and turned to follow the tour group, so confident that the imp would do as it was told that he didn't even glance backwards to check. Even in the relatively weak body of Lizzy Brett the demon's throw was enough to smash Snig against a wall, knocking the air from the imp's lungs, and crushing one of his clawed hands. The imp was furious.

"Thinks he can push me about....tell me off? Not fair! I'll play tricks if I want to". And Snig picked himself up and began to hurry after the ghost tour.

Dross followed the group through back alleys and quiet roads that most of the tour party hadn't even known existed, despite being only a few minutes away from the main streets of the city. He heard tale after tale.....but he wasn't there to listen to stories, even if the rest of the group were fascinated. The demon needed to find a way to separate the young man he wanted from the remainder of the tour party, and his chance came towards the end of the evening. They had walked along beside the river, briefly, and were heading up a flight of stone steps, while being told the tale of a ghostly monk. The steps were narrow and poorly lit, and Dross had already ripped a white parasol cover from one of the tables beside the waterfront. With this draped over Lizzy's body, to make himself look ghostlike, Dross raced up the steps, screaming and shoving, scattering the audience in all directions. He grabbed the young man he'd chosen by the arm, and tried to drag him away from the group and into the darkness of a nearby ruined building.

Snig however, suddenly found himself intervening. Something about the victim's enthusiasm and protectiveness appealed to him, and he was angry at the demon for the earlier attack. The imp grabbed a fallen tree branch and started battering Dross about the head with it. Hampered by the parasol cover Dross couldn't fight off the imp while holding onto his prey. The demon dropped the young man's arm, and the imp gave the human a kick, to send him stumbling back towards the rest of the group who were scattered across the flight of steps. The streetlight at the top of the stairs enabled the humans to see what was happening in the ruins, where a branch appeared to be beating up a pale figure.

The audience looked to the tour leader for an explanation, but even he was at a loss.

"Ladies and gentlemen," he said, "I suggest we RUN!" and they did, back towards the better lit streets. The father of the little family picked up his child and ran with her as she screamed in fright, and the husband and wife helped their friend up, and began to race along the alleyway. The woman got wheezy very quickly as they rushed through the streets, and soon they had to slow down to let her catch her breath.

"Is everyone ok?" she asked weakly. The man in the top hat was a few paces ahead of them. He turned to them and said "I think so, but I've no idea what just happened. Trust me, that was not a normal ghost tour".

"Look on the bright side" said the big, blond, bearded man, as he handed his wife her inhaler, "At least nobody stopped and asked for their money back!" Their young friend was shaken, but unhurt after his strange experience.

"I should hope they didn't," he grinned, "If they came for an interesting time, they certainly got one".

"Not exactly the evening I planned for them, though, and they didn't even get to the end of the tour", said the tour guide, sadly. The woman, beginning to recover, gave both her husband and her friend a hug, thankful that nothing too terrible had happened.

There was no sign of the rest of the audience.

"I'll just have to email everyone later" said the man in the top hat, resignedly, "And check they're alright. For now I'd better go and find the rest of my team, and let them know we've finished early." The tour leader turned back to his friends, "Are you coming for a drink?"

"Definitely!" said the older man, "After that experience, I think we could all do with one....and I'm buying!"

Back amongst the ruins Dross had finally managed to free himself from the enveloping parasol cover. He reached out and grabbed Snig, determined to punish the imp for his interference.

"What did you think you were doing? Did you imagine you could defy Dross and get away with it?" shrieked the demon, as he shook the imp by the scruff of the neck. "I wanted that human, I needed that body, and then you interfered! Why?" Dross raised Snig up, and then smashed his face against the remains of a stone wall. "What possessed you?" screamed Dross, battering Snig against the wall again, this time snapping the bones in the imp's spindly little arm. "Well?" Dross continued, grabbing one of Snig claws, and attempting to pull it off. Snig screamed, then muttered defiantly.

"Cos you're a bully, and young man...." the imp groped for a word to describe the man's unfamiliar behaviour "...kindly."

"Kindly?" howled Dross. "What sort of a word is that for a creature like you to use?" He snapped the imp's toe between his fingers, and the little creature wailed. "What do you care about humans, and kindness anyway? You're an imp....you're here to cause trouble for them, not rescue them".

"Don't want to", protested the imp. "Humans are nice....nicer than you......nicer than me too. Don't want to hurt them".

"NICE!" roared Dross. "What kind of imp cares about nice?" The demon lifted the little creature up by its broken arm, and deliberately snapped the bones in the other arm by swinging the imp into the stones again. "That'll teach you to behave yourself", said Dross with satisfaction.

"Noooo", cried Snig, rebelliously. "Teaches me demons bad and cruel....humans nicer...they has friendships. Nobody friends with you".

"Friends? I haven't come here to make friends. I've come for power, and I'm going to get it". With a final kick, which made damaging contact with Snig's brittle ribcage, Dross turned and left. Lizzy's corpse was beginning to wheeze, and weaken, and Dross knew he had to go in search of another body immediately. He didn't want his whole glorious plan to fail, just because he couldn't find a suitable temporary host.

Chapter Twenty-One

Thren was beginning to get worried about Tor. She'd been gone for ages, much longer than it should have taken her to check up on Marty and Debbie, and on Duncan. Despite how much he tended to complain about her, he realised he had come to rely on his fellow angel, especially lately, as he had become weaker and weaker.

"I'm sure she's alright, Thren" said Bex, quietly. She was sitting on the floor beside him, as the other students prepared to head back to their various homes. Thren tried to pull himself up onto his feet, aware that he should try to protect them all. He was their guardian angel, after all. He collapsed back into his chair.

"It's ok, Thren", said Paul. "We can walk back together. Nothing's going to attack a big group of us". Paul remembered the horror of the final battle with Dross. He wasn't completely sure about the truth of his statement, but it was obvious that Thren was beyond being able to protect them, and he didn't want the angel to feel any guiltier. Even though being able to half see the angels when they were supposed to be invisible was un-nerving, he'd grown fond of them, and was keen to reassure Thren.

"I'll see Sarah back to her door".

"No need", said Graham, smiling shyly. "I can do that". Paul nodded, trying not to let his disappointment show. Since yesterday, he'd begun to hope that Sarah liked him as much as he liked her, but now it was obvious that she was still soft on Graham. Paul was conscious of being the geeky outsider, again.

Flint hesitated when the others left. He knew if he didn't leave the conversation might turn to the very place he didn't want it to go, but in the end he decided to stay and get it over with. Within a few minutes only Thren, Dudley, Bex and Flint were left in the sitting room. Flint looked around nervously, but forgot his own worries as he could see Thren looking increasingly concerned.

"Do you want me to go and look for Tor?" Flint offered, but Thren shook his head. "No point in putting yourself in danger kid, not when we don't even know if she's in trouble. She sure wouldn't thank me for that".

"She might," said Flint gloomily. "I'm the one person she would be glad to see the back of, and you know it".

"She is trying to be ....a little less difficult with you," said Bex, encouragingly.

"She'll change her mind about that when she knows......" he hesitated. "Well, I suppose I'd better get it over with..." Flint was about to continue when Dudley interrupted him gently. "Not tonight, Flint", said the old man. "Whatever it is, you should only tell us when you want to....not because you feel you've been backed into a corner. We're prepared to wait, aren't we Bex?"

"Of course", she replied. "We trust you Flint....whatever it is, it can't be that bad." Looking at the young man's worried expression, and the way his pale grey soul-light was darkening with stress, Thren wasn't so sure. Still, he hadn't exactly been the world's best guardian angel, so he figured it wasn't for him to judge. Besides, he liked Flint, and wanted to believe the best of him. Thren glanced affectionately at Dudley and Bex. They were such good people, and he was so grateful for what he'd learned from them. Dudley was a godly man who always looked for the best in people, but accepted their failings with kindness and encouragement. Bex was loving and cheerful, and to Thren it felt as if she was often looking after him, rather than the other way around. Not that she was his responsibility, she was in Tor's care, but he still thought of her as one of 'his humans'.

Bex and Thren had got off on the wrong foot when Thren first Came Down, but now they were genuinely fond of each other. Thren was thankful to have been a part of this funny little family. Even though they weren't connected by blood (Bex was Dudley's adopted daughter) the bonds between father and daughter were very strong. They'd accepted Thren, not just as an angel, but a friend, and welcomed the sometimes awkward Flint in too. As the angel felt his strength slipping away, he knew he'd been fortunate, despite the sorrows that were crowding in on him. There was so much he still wanted to do, unfinished business, situations that needed sorting out, but he doubted now that he's get the chance to do it. His eyes closed and he drifted into sleep....perhaps when he woke up, he'd be Home....the very thought of it warmed him, but he dreaded seeing the disappointment in His eyes, when He realised how much Thren had let Him down, by becoming too weak to protect everyone.

"This is bad, isn't it?" Bex whispered to her father. The old man nodded, sadly.

"I didn't think angels could die", Flint muttered.

"Isn't there anything we can do?" asked Bex.

"Other than praying, I have no idea", Dudley answered. "But at least we can stay with him, he shouldn't be alone".

The other students strolled back towards the university. They felt reasonably safe in such a large group, and managed to chat to each other in a fairly relaxed way. Graham and Sarah hung back to snatch a brief kiss, but then hurried to catch up with the others. Paul noticed, of course, though none of the rest of the group seemed to. He resolved to keep an eye on both of them, and make sure that they both got back to their respective rooms safely. Even though all of these students had now seen Thren, and were beginning to understand the situation, Paul was the only one who'd seen Dross, in his natural, hideous form, the only one who realised exactly what they were up against.

The fact that Thren had admitted he couldn't defend them terrified Paul, and he racked his brain, trying to think of what he could do himself, to help everyone. Last time, when he realised there was a crisis looming, he'd done as much research as he could in the library, but it was late on a Saturday night, and the library was shut. On the other hand, he did have his grandmother's journal. Maybe there was something in there that could help. Forgetting his intension of seeing everyone else safely back to their rooms when they reached the campus, Paul began to hurry ahead, to start his research as quickly as possible. He practically bumped into a young woman standing in the shadows, and hurried past without paying her much attention. Dross, still encased in Lizzy's body, watched as the students walked across the quad, scattering off to their rooms....so much choice, the demon didn't know where to start. ...... Oh, well, decision time.....

Paul had reached his room and unlocked the door, when something that had been niggling at his memory for a couple of minutes hit him. The smell, the funny smell of the girl he'd nearly bumped into outside....there was a smoky scent, but underneath that there was another aroma. It reminded him of a body that had been worn too long.....by a demon. Paul froze, horrified. It was out there, watching them....and he hadn't realised.....hadn't warned everybody. Part of him, a very large part of him, wanted to lock the door and hide under the bed. He'd had two terrifying encounters with Dross, and really, really didn't want a third. But another part of him, the better, braver part, knew he had to go and warn the others.

Snig slowly hauled himself upright. He was battered and bruised, and some of his bones were broken, but that was not the most terrifying thing. What frightened him most was the change in himself. He had stood up to a demon. He had chosen to take the side of a human against a creature from The Darkness. Where did that leave him? Would he ever be able to go home to The Darkness again? Did he even want to?

His broken toe hurt when he stood up, both of his arms were broken too, some of his claws dangled limply from his wrists and his rib bones were sticking out through his skin. "What do I do now? Snig sore. Snig sick. Snig scared". He wanted help, but didn't know where to go to find it. He dimly remembered that some humans prayed when they needed help, but he couldn't do that. None of the powers in The Darkness would be bothered with listening to or helping a confused and injured imp. If he was of no more use to them, they'd simply discard him. As for praying to the other side, out there in the light, it simply didn't occur to him. He was just a nasty little imp, nobody would care about him.... but if prayer was out of the question... perhaps wishing would work. He limped out of the ruins and down the stone steps, then hobbled along beside the river for a short distance, and walked painfully up onto the city walls. He'd noticed a flight of steps, part of the walls themselves, called 'The Wishing Steps'. Perhaps he could get some help there.

Dross crept along the corridor of the halls of residence, hovering outside one door and then another. In theory any new body would do to replace the one he was wearing. It didn't have to belong to one of the students who'd invited him through the last time. In fact, it would be easier to stay hidden if he picked someone else. That way he could stay under the radar and keep the angels guessing until he was ready to reveal his plan in all its splendour......but something about destroying the students he already knew appealed to him. There was a certain symmetry to it, and he knew it would distress Tor, and especially his old friend Thren, far more than if he killed some random stranger. Besides, once he'd put his plan into action in a few days time, he was planning to round up each of the humans he'd failed to kill last time, and annihilate them. Then, finally, he'd get to savour their tasty soul-lights.. ....the greatest delicacy known to demonkind.

Chapter Twenty-Two

Paul had made himself stop panicking and think logically about warning the others. He realised that if he just ran randomly about the campus, visiting each of his friends' rooms, he might get to one of them too late. Instead he sat down and texted a warning to everyone whose number he had, which included Debbie and Marty, though he had to be rather vague with them, as he wasn't sure how much they knew. Which just left Sam and Graham to warn in person. He armed himself as best he could, placing a cross around his neck, and rooting though his desk for a small bottle of holy water. He knew from past experience that both could be effective. Then, taking a deep breath, he opened his door, and looked up and down the corridor.

Because it was late at night, the lighting in the public areas of the building had automatically dimmed. Somewhere, he could hear the sound of a text landing in somebody's mobile phone. Odd, he couldn't usually hear phones in his fellow students' rooms, not when the doors were shut. It must belong to somebody walking along the corridors. Sam's room was nearest, so Paul headed there first. Sam opened the door much too quickly, in Paul's opinion, a whisky bottle clutched in his hand.

"You need to be more careful", Paul cautioned him, "It's out there, right now. You'd better lock your door, and keep it locked until the morning". He looked at the bottle in Sam's hand, then looked away. After all, it wasn't up to him how Sam chose to deal with the pressure of the situation.

"If you must know", Sam said, answering the question Paul never even asked, "I'm pouring it down the sink". Paul shrugged, embarrassed.

"Do you want to come in?" Sam asked "For a coffee, I mean? I could use some company. I'm still trying to make sense of it all."

"Thanks", replied Paul, "But I need to warn Graham that's it's here too". He paused, the offer of company was tempting, a lot more tempting than walking along the dimly lit corridors to Graham's room, especially when Graham had just started going out with Sarah.

Paul had to admit he felt jealous but that was no excuse for not going to warn his friend. Besides, if something bad happened to Graham and Paul could have prevented it, Sarah would never forgive him. He refused Sam's offer, and walked down the stairs.

Dross had come prepared this time. Clutching a fire extinguisher that he'd pulled off the wall, he tapped at the door of Graham's room. From his position in the shadows earlier, the demon had noticed Graham and Sarah's lingering goodnight kiss when they parted, so pitching Lizzy's voice down a little, to copy Sarah's he whispered "Graham, it's me, Sarah. Can I come in? I need to talk to you". Within moments Graham had unlocked and opened the door. He glanced down the corridor to his right, but there was no sign of Sarah. Before he could look in the other direction, Dross brought the heavy extinguisher down on the back of Graham's head, knocking him out. Knowing from the text that Paul had sent to Debbie's phone that the students knew he was on the campus, he realised he had to act quickly.

Dross was aware that Lizzy's decaying body wouldn't be able to carry Graham any distance, so he'd already located one of the trolleys that the service staff used when they cleaned the building. Throwing the mops and buckets into a cupboard, Dross hoisted Graham's body onto the trolley and pushed him away along the corridor and out of the building. The demon needed to find somewhere private.

When Paul reached Graham's room, he found to his horror that the door was open, and Graham had vanished. An abandoned fire extinguisher lay in the doorway, and a few drops of blood from the wound on Graham's head spotted the floor. Paul sank to his knees, terrified. Dross had succeeded, he'd taken one of them, and Paul had been too late to stop it happening.

Snig had reached the bottom of The Wishing Steps. They stretched up in front of him, built to connect the south and east walls, which were on different levels. Six sets of steps, with three steps in each set. He'd heard a rumour that if up you ran up the steps, and down them and then back up again, without taking a breath while you did it, your wish would come true. Of course, you were meant to have walked the walls of the city first, so that you were tired to start with, but after his fight with Dross, Snig felt he was quite tired enough already.

The imp took a deep breath and started to run up The Wishing Steps. They looked easy enough to climb, but they weren't, not for Snig anyway. Between each of the sets of three stone steps there was

a level area, which it took Snig four paces to cross. This meant he couldn't get into his stride as he ran up the steps, because he had to change pace on the flat sections. He couldn't even get to the top once without gasping for breath, never mind doing it three times.
It was hopeless. It seemed even wishing wasn't going to be of any use to him. Aimlessly, he hobbled on around the city walls, wondering what would happen to him now. It felt as if he didn't belong here, or in The Darkness, and nobody even cared. The street lights cast a dim glow, even high up on the city walls, and looming up ahead of him, within the circle of those walls, Snig could see the massive shape of the floodlit cathedral, the sandstone from which it had been built giving it a mellow, rosy glow.

Thren had assumed, or at least hoped, that Tor was with Duncan, making sure that the drama student wasn't in any immediate danger, but by the time the other students returned to the campus, she was no longer in the attic room. Duncan had felt unaccountably tired and gone to bed early.....ridiculously early for a Saturday night, and was having troubled dreams. There had been a few peaceful moments, when Tor had come to check up on him, and sat beside him as he dozed, humming quietly to sooth him. Tor had smiled ruefully, thankful that Thren wasn't with her to tease her about singing lullabies to a human....but then she remembered the reason that Thren wasn't there, and the smile faded on her face. She glanced around the room, grateful that there was no sign of the horrible, skin covered book, the book that seemed to have made Thren's condition so much more acute when he touched it.
    Earlier she'd made sure that Debbie and Marty were safe, though it had taken ages to track them down to the cinema where they were enjoying a movie. ...it was a Rom-Com......Debbie's choice, to make up for her disappointment over the races. Tor had thought that the film looked rather fun, but tore herself away to look in on Duncan. Once that task was finished, and the angel was sure that he was safe too, for the moment at least, she decided that it was time for her to act. Thren was no longer able to protect the city, and Tor knew that they needed reinforcements. It meant leaving Bex undefended, while she was gone, but it was a risk that Tor felt she had to take, before things got any worse. Of course, Tor wasn't aware that things were getting worse already.

After she'd gone Duncan's dreams became increasingly disturbed. There were snatches of memories, and things he couldn't quite remember, all mixed up together. Every so often he dreamt of the book, which seemed more menacing in his dreams than it did in reality. Suddenly he jolted awake, and scrambled out of bed. He had to make sure it was safe....that no one had stolen it.

He reached under the bed, and pulled out an old shoe box. Inside it, carefully wrapped in tissue paper, was the book. Duncan breathed a sigh of relief. He couldn't even explain why it had suddenly become so important to him. It was just an old script, borrowed from his lecturer, but it seemed to reach out to him, demanding him to protect it. He ran his fingers over the old leather, simultaneously attracted and repelled by its oily feel. As he put the book back in its hiding place he noticed his fingers were stained with a thin coating of powder, the colour of dried blood. Without even knowing why, the young man shivered.

Dross had wheeled the cleaning trolley, with Graham draped across it, out into the quad. The darkness hid the movement, not that anyone was watching. The demon rapidly steered the trolley into another accommodation block, opened the door to a cleaning cupboard, and shoved it inside.

Dross entered the cupboard, closing the door behind him. He examined the back of Graham's head first. It wasn't too dented where the fire extinguisher had hit it. It would do well enough for a day or two. The demon placed his hands around the unconscious young man's throat, and carefully choked the life out of him. Graham's final breath sighed itself out of his body, without him even waking up, and his flickering yellow soul-light began to spin in the air above his corpse. Dross reached out and grabbed the glowing ball of light, stuffing it greedily into his mouth. He swallowed, and smiled as he felt the power flowing through his body. "Delicious", he murmured, licking his lips. He'd come close to capturing the boy's soul-light last time. Now he had succeeded....just as he would succeed with the rest of his plan.

Bex's phone ringing insistently woke her up. She stretched uncomfortably, realising she's fallen asleep on the floor at Thren's feet. The angel was twisting and turning in his sleep, her father was stirring in his armchair, and Flint was laying uncomfortably half on and half off the sofa. Bex grabbed the phone, aware that it was still dark. Paul's voice sounded terrible as he tried to put what he feared into words. That Graham was missing, and Paul was afraid that Dross had got him. Bex started to try and calm Paul down, but before she succeeded, Thren suddenly jerked forward, eyes wide open, and full of horror. He screamed and clutched his chest, before collapsing completely.

"We have to try and find Graham," Paul was saying "We have to rescue him before it's too late". Looking at Thren, barely breathing, blood pouring from the wound in his chest, Bex burst into tears, and whispered down the phone.

"I think it's already too late, Paul. Graham must be dead...and I'm afraid Thren will be soon, too".

Chapter Twenty-Three

Tor arrived back on the roof of the cathedral, with another angel in tow. She glanced around, hoping to see Thren, but was hardly surprised that he wasn't there. He'd been so weak when she left, she expected he was still at the little house on the green, being looked after by Bex and Dudley.

"Come along", Tor said crisply to her new companion. "Follow me. We'd better find Thren".

"Shouldn't he be at his post?" asked the new angel, consulting the notes attached to her clipboard. "It says here that a guardian angel should always be at their post.....unless dealing with an actual emergency." She glanced up, nervously, "You don't think that there's been an actual emergency do you? Do they happen very often?"

"You'd be surprised", replied Tor, drily, as she led the newcomer off the roof and down the stairs into the cathedral. Tor found herself hurrying as she made her way to Dudley's house. She'd only been gone for a few hours, but things were moving so quickly that anything could have happened in that time. She could see Bex's usually bright silver soul-light though the walls, darkened with grief, and hesitated for a moment before she knocked softly on the front door, trying to prepare herself for what was to come. "Wait out here for now", she whispered to the other angel, "And stay out of sight".

By the time Bex answered the door, Tor had composed herself, and wore her best reassuring smile. She was completely unprepared for Bex bursting into tears and flinging herself at her guardian angel, hugging her tightly, as if she was afraid to let go. Tor let the girl cry for a few moments, then gently detached herself and walked into the sitting room. She was horrified when she saw Thren's body lying on the floor, his chest covered in fresh blood from the wooden stake sticking out of it.

"How long has he been like this?" Tor demanded, kneeling beside him.

"Since Graham died, last night". Flint whispered his answers, as if afraid to disturb Thren by speaking, but Tor doubted if anything would disturb the angel now, he seemed so far gone. "At least, we think Graham's dead. He disappeared, and then Thren collapsed".

"Can angels die?" asked Bex, looking Tor in the eye, insisting on being told the truth.

"Well........" said Tor, hesitating.

"Tell Me!" shouted Bex, then lowered her voice. "Sorry, but I need to know. We all do".

"I don't know" Tor replied wearily. "I haven't heard of it happening, but I suppose it could. We all go through this stage you know. Every guardian angel. You start out thinking you can be a hero, and save lives, and make things better, then gradually you begin to notice your failures. The ones you didn't save, the people you couldn't help.....and it all starts to get on top of you. Eventually, every guardian angel has....well, I suppose you'd call it a nervous breakdown. They....we.....realise that we can't protect a whole city, and the pressure gets to us. Usually we get moved on to somewhere smaller, a town, or a group, or an individual in need of extra protection.....like you, Bex".

"You mean you were like this?" asked Flint, finding it hard to picture.

"Not quite this bad", answered Tor. "I did.....crack up....but it wasn't so extreme. I never expected Thren to end up like this. When he first Came Down he didn't take his responsibilities at all seriously..... I would have thought that he would have been the last to fall apart. He never used to care about anyone".

"And now he cares too much", said Dudley, softly, from his seat in a shadowy corner of the room.

"Yes", agreed Tor. "Much too much".

"So what can we do?" asked Dudley, which was the first practical thing anyone had said since Tor arrived. She smiled at the old man.

"Find a way to help him, if we can".

Dross had had to wait a few hours, of course, before he could shed the body of Lizzy Brett, and transfer himself into Graham's corpse. He didn't want to rush the process, and find that putting the boy's own soul-light back into the dead body revived it, or made the transfer into his corpse difficult. By first light it was done. Perfect timing, thought Dross, as he slipped out of the cupboard and headed for his appointment. He had used Debbie's phone the night before to send a message to Marty, inviting him to come round to Tim's early that Sunday morning to watch the Grand Prix.

Dross knew from his earlier time with the students that both Marty and Tim were heavily into Formula 1, and never missed a race. Mostly they watched them at Marty's parents' house, where they had

Sky, and could watch every race in full. This Sunday, however, Dross knew from glancing at the TV schedule on Debbie's smartphone, the race was also being broadcast in full on the BBC.

It seemed to Dross to be the perfect trap, "Debbie's" text explained that she'd decided to join them to watch the race, and see what all the fuss was about, so why didn't Marty met her at Tim's and they could all watch it together, since Tim's was so much nearer her. Dross didn't bother to text the arrangement to Tim, as he didn't expect Marty to get that far.

Sure enough, as Marty approached the campus, where both Debbie and Tim had rooms in the halls of residence, he saw Graham waiting for him. His friend looked a little pale, but then, he'd hardly been himself for ages, not since his accident, so Marty didn't think anything of it. Dross was delighted his plan had worked. He'd really set the trap for Marty as a fall back, in case he hadn't already got hold of a replacement body, but since the young man was on the spot, as well as being on his personal hit list, the demon thought it would be a shame to waste the opportunity. Besides, the energy that Marty's soul-light would give him would strengthen the demon to carry out his bigger purpose.

"You're up early", said Marty approaching his friend.

"Yep", replied Graham, "You too. Where are you off to at this time of day?"

"Tim's, to see if McLaren are back on form yet".

"McLaren?" Graham looked puzzled.

"Jenson Button's team?" Marty clarified, "Their car just hasn't got the pace at the moment. He's barely scraping into the points in each race, no matter how well he drives, but they're adding some new parts to the car this weekend. I'm hoping it will make a difference".

Dross glanced around to check that the coast was clear. He didn't want to waste another minute talking about motor racing, when he could be devouring the sparkling amber soul-light of this cheerful young man. He needed to kill him now, while there was nobody about. He put a hand on Marty's shoulder, gripping the boy tightly, and was about to bring the other hand up to grab the student by the throat when he heard a voice calling out.

"Marty? What are you doing here? I thought I was coming over to yours? I know I'm a bit late, but we had a bit of a funny time of it last night, and I guess I overslept".

Tim was coming up behind Graham and Marty, and in the sharp morning light he had an excellent view of the back of Graham's head, bloodied from where he'd been hit with the fire extinguisher. Putting two and two together with remarkable clarity for dawn on a Sunday morning, Tim rushed towards them, grabbed Marty's arm and pulled him away.

"Come on then, Marty", he started talking very quickly. "We'd better hurry up or we'll miss the start. Might as well come and watch it at mine, now you're here." He herded his friend away, calling back over his shoulder.

"Sorry .....Graham....got to dash...see you later", and he ushered a bewildered Marty into the building.

"What's this all about?" asked Marty as they entered Tim's room.

"I'm not sure you're going to believe me", said Tim, sadly, "But for starters, I don't think that was really Graham".

"What do you mean, it wasn't Graham? He looked like Graham....he sounded like Graham....he was Graham! Did you have too much to drink last night or something? You're not making any sense".

"I know it's not Graham" Tim replied heavily. "Graham disappeared last night. Someone tried to attack him earlier, but he got away. Then, later, when we all got back, Paul went to check on him. Graham's door was open and there was blood...we think he'd been hit with a fire extinguisher. We searched all night and couldn't find him. Then I saw him out there, with you....and I had to get you away from him".

"So if he's been injured", said Marty, confused. "We should be helping him, not avoiding him. You're not making any sense."

"Then let me explain", said Tim, "But first we'd better go and wake Debbie, she needs to hear this too, and I don't think I can cope with explaining it twice."

"What about the Grand Prix?" asked Marty, glancing at his watch, "It'll be starting any minute".

"Trust me", said Tim, "Some things are more important".

"You're kidding!" said Marty, shocked.

"I wish I was", answered Tim, grimly.

Snig dragged his broken bones around the city walls, heading for the cathedral. He was grateful that he was invisible to humans. He didn't have the energy to stop and hide whenever people came past.

Even though it was early in the morning, there were still joggers and tourists about, but he was beyond wanting to play tricks on them. His only thought now, the only thing that might be able to help him, was to get to the cathedral and claim sanctuary. He didn't know why the idea had popped into his head, but it had, and now he was determined to reach his goal.

He found it odd being out and about so soon after dawn. Imps are not naturally morning creatures. The air felt clean, and the light made him feel strangely optimistic, despite his injuries.

"Snig's stupid" he muttered to himself, "Nothing to be glad about. Snig's in big trouble". He reached one of the doors into the building and crept inside. He thought he ought to find one of the black clad humans, who were scurrying about the building, and tell them what he wanted....but he wasn't sure who to speak to, so he just crept into the choir stalls and hid in the shadows beneath the seats. Once there, he fell into an exhausted sleep.

Chapter Twenty-Four

Sarah had spent the early hours of the morning weeping. Paul had roused the others on the campus after he had phoned Bex, and between them Tim, Nesta, Sam, Cath and Sarah had searched for Graham, but there was no sign of him. They all feared that what Bex had said was true. That Graham was already beyond help.

For Sarah especially, it had all been too much. She'd gone from having the best birthday ever..... meeting the angels.....spending time with her friends, especially Paul, who she counted as her best friend....and finally....finally....starting a relationship with Graham, whom she'd liked since the first moment she met him, only to have everything go horribly wrong before they even got as far as their first date. Graham was missing, possibly dead, and there was nothing she could do about it. She was distressed and angry and exhausted, which might have been why she wasn't thinking straight when she heard someone tapping on her door, and softly calling her name.

"Sarah", the voice whispered, "It's me, Graham".

She rushed to the door and pulled it open. Graham stood there, looking a little pale and shaky, but alive, and Sarah practically dragged him into her room, relief washing over her like a tidal wave. Dross had decided to capitalise on the relationship he'd noticed the night before, when he'd observed the students walking back to the campus. He didn't know that the group were already aware that something had happened to Graham, but having been frustrated over his hopes of killing Marty, the demon decided to pick off one more student before getting back to developing his master plan.

Sarah had flung her arms around Graham, holding him tight, but it suddenly dawned on her that something wasn't quite right. Graham was hugging her back, but not in a gentle, nervous, Graham-like way. This was more like being held in an iron vice, and she began to struggle to free herself. Graham's skin felt cold, and his lips were forcing themselves against hers. She remembered what she'd learnt had happened to Cath, about how the demon, wearing a human body, had kissed the soul out of her friend. Well, Sarah was determined not to let that happen to her. She opened her lips slightly, and bit Graham's bottom lip hard. As he pulled back in surprise she shouted for help at the top of her lungs, and at the same time sent up a prayer, hoping someone, anyone, human or otherwise, would hear her and come running.

Paul made himself yet another cup of coffee and perched on the side of his bed. Once they'd given up looking for Graham, he'd spent the remainder of the night reading his grandmother's journal, and the more he'd read, the more he wished she was still alive, so that he could ask her about some of the remarkable things she'd seen.
It appeared that, like him, she's had more than just passing glimpses of angels. She too had gotten to know one, and learnt a little about how they operated in the world, but unlike Paul, she'd never had anyone to share her experiences with. Still, her journal made fascinating reading, and Paul wished he could go and find Sarah, and show her a couple of passages he thought she'd find interesting.

    Not that he would be going to find Sarah anytime soon. She'd been furious with him last night, when the students finally gave up searching for Graham, and had to admit that something terrible had probably happened to him. She blamed Paul for not going to warn Graham quickly enough, accusing him of being jealous that she had started going out with Graham, rather than him. There was just enough truth in her comment to leave Paul defenceless.....and when he had offered to stay with her overnight, so that she wouldn't be alone with her grief, she had kicked him out and told him very firmly not to come back. He had hated leaving her on her own, but she had been very insistent, even sending Cath and Nesta away.....and if Sarah wanted to be alone, what right did he have to go and seek her out. He was the last person she wanted to see right then....or possibly ever.

    Tor sat on the floor beside the unconscious Thren. She was trying very hard not to cry. It wasn't something that angels did, and she felt she had to be strong, for everyone's sake. She was relieved however, when Dudley announced that he was going over to the cathedral to pray, and Bex and Flint slipped into the kitchen to make some more coffee. Finally she had a moment to herself, and she felt the tears beginning to flow down her face. She tried to wipe them away with the sleeve of her denim jacket, but more kept coming.
"This is ridiculous", she muttered to herself, "Pull yourself together, Tor, you're not helping anyone by sitting here weeping".
"Is that Thren?" said a voice from behind her. "I know you said to wait outside, but you've been ages. I got bored.....I want to get started". The new angel nudged Thren's body with her foot. "Does he always look like that? He's a bit of a mess, isn't he? No wonder the High Council want to replace him....he seems completely useless".

"Don't you dare say that", said Tor, leaping to her feet. "Don't you dare! You have no idea what he's been through....what any of us have been through".

"Sorry", said the new angel, huffily, "I was only making an observation. I just expected a guardian angel to be more.....well....." She hesitated, at a loss for words, "Professional..... that's all!"

"It's being 'Professional'.....taking the job so seriously.....that's got him into this state. Don't you dare criticise him for that. This is what happens to us when we do our work properly, so show some compassion, for pity's sake!"

"You mean I'm going to end up like this?" asked Bliss, horrified, "How disgusting!"

"Well," said Tor, calming down a little, "His is a particularly bad case. You might get off more lightly. It depends how committed you are to your job".

"I intend to be totally committed....in a 'not ending up like that' sort of way", said the new angel primly.

Bex walked into the room carrying a mug of coffee.

"Who are you talking to Tor? Has Thren woken up?" She stopped and stared at the unknown angel. "Who's this?"

"You can see me? Bother! I forgot to keep the wing beats steady". The creature spoke as if being seen was a trivial matter, which both Bex and Tor knew it was not.

"I'm Bliss," the new arrival introduced herself, smugly, "I'm his replacement".

"His replacement?" echoed Bex, stunned. "Tor, how could you?.....why Thren's not even...."she couldn't bring herself to say the word 'dead'.

"It's not what you think Bex", Tor replied. "You should know me better than that by now. She isn't here to replace Thren himself, not exactly, but we do need reinforcements. You know we do! And Thren isn't strong enough to protect the whole city any more. I had to go to the High Council and ask for some help".

At their feet Thren stirred, restlessly, and muttered the words "Sarah....must help Sarah". He tried to sit up, but quickly slumped back down onto the floor, murmuring "Oh crap!" Within moments the angel was unconscious once more.

Tor and Bex looked at each other in horror, then Tor ran from the house. Bliss stood there for a moment, confused.

"I'll come too then, shall I?" she said, to the space where Tor had been standing, and then followed the senior angel out of the door, adding "They never mentioned any of this during training".

Paul was still sitting with the journal open on his lap. He wasn't really reading it though. He was too busy thinking about Sarah, and how she'd never want to see him again. Yet he wanted to see her. More than anything, he wanted to go and find her, and see if she was alright. Which was odd, because Paul hated conflict, any kind of conflict, and the thought of Sarah, of all people, shouting at him again, or even just refusing to speak to him, made his heart sink. He'd already decided to keep his distance, for a little while at least, but now he had a sudden urge to go to her....at once. He tried to ignore the feeling, but it was too strong for him. In the end he decided to listen to his instincts. That was something his grandmother had always recommended, and he decided to take her advice.

Leaving the journal open on his bed, and the door to his room ajar, he found himself racing along the corridors until he reached Sarah's room. The door was shut, but without even knocking Paul found himself wrenching it open. He paused, horrified by what he saw. Graham was standing there, dried blood covering the back of his head, and Sarah was struggling in his arms. She'd managed to reach out and grab a bulky text book, and was trying to batter Graham away with it, but he seemed impervious to her efforts. Graham grabbed for the pendant Sarah was wearing, the one Paul had given her on Friday, and was twisting it tight in an attempt to throttle her. After all, if he couldn't just kiss her soul-light out of her, he might as well kill her and get it anyway.

After a moment's hesitation, Paul pulled the bottle of holy water out of his pocket, and wrenched off the top.

"Let her go!" he shouted, and as Graham looked round to see who was there, Paul flung the liquid in his face, forcing the creature to release Sarah in surprise. It rounded on Paul instead.

"Two for the price of one....perfect.....you won't get away from me again. Not this time. I'm stronger than I was." Despite his words, Paul could see the demon had to pull back from the parts of Graham where the holy water had made contact with him, making it hard to control the facial muscles and eye movements in a natural way. The result was macabre, and Paul felt guilty for making even the shell of the person who had been Graham distort in such a horrid fashion.

Paul was wondering what to do next, when Sarah brought the text book down on the back of the creature's head, stunning him briefly. Tor and Bliss arrived moments later, and Dross, realising that he was at too much of a disadvantage, and that he'd lost the benefit of surprise that came with occupying a body that people in the group trusted, decided to cut his losses. He withdrew from Graham's body, leaving it to crumple to the floor, and turned back into a dark mist.....essence of demon.

    Released from captivity Graham's yellow soul-light twisted and turned in the air, though neither Tor nor Bliss could see it, and then spun upwards, and vanished. The dark cloud gathered above their heads and shot out of the doorway before they could do anything to prevent it. Dross had lost Graham's body, but retained the strength to find a new one....and he still had time to put his plan into action.

    "Well, that was easy", said Bliss. "Are they all that straightforward? We just turn up and they scurry back to hell?"

    "If only" replied Tor, "But it really isn't that simple".

Chapter Twenty-Five

Dudley was sitting quietly in one of the choir stalls in the cathedral, praying fervently for Thren, and for everyone involved in what had happened since the demon had come through, but most of all for the safety of his daughter, Bex. He knew that if Thren and Tor couldn't defeat the demon, she was in particular danger, and he didn't know how he could protect her.

He heard a soft "Ahem" nearby, and looked around to see Ernest Poole, another member of the cathedral staff, standing behind him.

"I do beg your pardon", said Poole, shyly. He was a small, plump little man a few years younger than Dudley. "I didn't wish to disturb your prayers, but I do need a favour". Dudley smiled tiredly up at his colleague. There had been a time when Poole had practically been an enemy, plotting with another clergyman, Pearson, to discredit Dudley and force him into retirement. However, at the last moment Poole had found the courage to stand up to his friend Pearson and refused to slur Dudley's good name. The dispute had been over a documentary that was being filmed about the cathedral, which the ambitious Pearson had wanted to front.

In the end the bishop had intervened and insisted that the gentler Poole should be the face of the cathedral. The poor man had found the task a daunting one, but he'd risen to the challenge, and done it well, while Pearson had chosen to transfer to another post elsewhere, away from the bishop's watchful eye. Dudley had taken the rather timid Poole under his wing, happy to advise and encourage him about the filming, without taking the limelight himself, and Poole was grateful for it. The two men had begun to form an unlikely friendship, built on a growing respect for one another.

"What do you need?" asked Dudley. "I'll help if I can".

"Nothing too difficult", replied Poole with a smile. "I was just wondering if you'd read the lesson for me in this morning's service, if you wouldn't mind. Mrs Leftwich was meant to be doing it, but she's not well". He handed Dudley a slip of paper with details of the Bible reading written on it.

"Yes, of course, what are you preaching on?"

"Forgiveness" answered Poole shyly. "I know it's a well worn theme, but it bears repeating.....and we so often think of it as being all about forgiving other people. I want to encourage everyone to forgive themselves, too. It's something I've had to learn, recently. You were so gracious with me, Dudley....forgiving what I tried to do to you, not holding it against me.....but it took me a long time to learn to forgive myself....and until I did that, I couldn't get back to doing my job well....I was so caught up in my own weaknesses that I wasn't functioning properly".

Dudley's face broke into a wide grin, as something in his friend's words struck a chord with him.

"That's it, of course! I should have realised before." He stood up and started to hurry away, calling out "Don't worry, Poole, I'll be back before the service starts".

Poole watched Dudley leave with a puzzled look on his face, then walked away to prepare for the service. Snig curled up even more tightly under the seat, wondering what the word forgiveness meant. It was one he hadn't heard much in The Darkness, and he couldn't decide what to make of it. It sounded like a comforting kind of a word, but not one that would ever apply to him. He realised too late that he'd missed a chance to ask for sanctuary. He should have tried asking one of those two soft-spoken men who'd been so close to him. Oh well, perhaps one of them would come back. He decided to stay hidden for a little while longer....being inside the cathedral felt surprisingly restful, and when Dudley had been praying, just a few feet away from him, Snig felt as if he'd been wrapped in a warm blanket. His broken bones were hurting a little less, though his shoulder blades were feeling a bit itchy.

"Snig sleepy", he whispered. "Snooze good".

Sarah and Paul stared down at Graham's lifeless body. Tor and Bliss stood in the doorway to the room. Nobody knew what to say, and the silence stretched uncomfortably around them. It was Paul who broke it.

"I'm so sorry, Sarah, I really am". "I know", whispered Sarah, "But it doesn't really help, does it? Graham's still dead". Paul stood there awkwardly, wanting to comfort Sarah, but unable to reach out to her.....knowing that she blamed him for Graham's death. Sarah stared straight at Tor, and asked "Could Thren have stopped this? If he wasn't so ill?"

"Not necessarily", the angel replied wearily. "We weren't really expecting the demon to attack Graham again....or any of you. He has no right. He had his chance with each of you last time, and failed. The only person he does have a right to go after is the person who invited him through....and for some reason, the demon has left him completely alone".

"Why?" demanded Sarah.

"We really don't know", Tor replied, "But I think it's time we started working it out". Sarah knelt down beside Graham's body, and cautiously took his hand. His face looked normal again, now that the demon had left his body, though there was some bruising around his neck. The girl flinched at the coldness of his skin, but kept her hands wrapped gently around his.

"What do we do now?" asked Bliss. "Are we supposed just stand here, achieving nothing?" Tor sighed, disappointed that her new assistant seemed to have so little understanding of what they were all feeling. Still, perhaps it was just as well.....they did have a job to do.

"I'd better phone the police", said Paul, "Though I've no idea how we're going to explain this. I just hope they don't think that we.....murdered him".

Dudley hurried from the main door of the cathedral around to his little house. Bex and Flint were sitting with Thren, but they weren't sure if he was still alive or not. His breathing was so shallow that his chest was barely moving. Dudley lowered himself down onto the floor with difficulty, then leaned forward to whisper in the angel's ear.

"Thren", said the old man, urgently. "Thren, wake up.....you've got to listen to me." There was no response. Dudley tried again, "Thren, can you hear me? This is important". When the angel still didn't respond Dudley very cautiously reached out and gave the stake sticking out of his chest a gentle tug. Thren groaned, and Bex looked at her father in horror

"You're hurting him, Dad".

"I know", said her father, "But we have to wake him up. It's the only way we might be able to save him".

"Then I'll do it", said Flint, "It seems wrong, you hurting anyone....even if it is for a good reason".

Flint moved closer to Thren, and took hold of the length of wood.

"You're sure this'll help, right?" said the young man, looking at Dudley with concern.

"I think so, but we'll only find out for sure if we try it.....we're just intending to get him to wake up enough to listen to me. Don't pull too hard. We know you can't pull it out, and we don't want to......" Dudley hesitated.

"Finish him off? No, we don't. I'll be careful". Flint gave the stake a few tugs, and Thren groaned each time he did. Gradually the pain seemed to get through to the angel, and he opened his eyes blearily.

"Leave me alone, guys....I've had enough....I wanta go Home".

"Well you can't" said Dudley gently. "Not yet. I believe you've still got a job to do".

"Not anymore, I don't....failed at that....failed at everything.....just a waste of space....that's me. Now leave me alone..." His eyes started to close again.

"No", said Bex. "We're not going to let you just slip away. Not if there's something we can do about it. ...so wake up!" She grabbed a half drunk cup of coffee, now stone cold, and flung it in Thren's face. The angel's eyes flashed open.

"Whata you doing kid?" he said weakly, "Is that any way to treat a friend?"

"Friends don't drift off 'Home' when other friends are in trouble", Bex said bluntly. "Do you want us all to be killed by that...thing?"

"Course not, but will ya look at me? I ain't no use to you guys anymore.....I can't even stand up. I've let you all down.....bad enough what happened before....but now....it's happening again, and it's all my fault. ....I couldn't save Graham....can't save none of you".

"That's enough!" Dudley cut in firmly. "You can't do your job because that ....lump of wood in your chest is causing you too much pain. It's time to get rid of it, before it kills you".

"We tried that already, remember? Nobody could pull it out. I'm a lost cause".

"That's because it's not meant to be pulled out", said Dudley. "Not by any of us.... You have to let it go.....that's the only way to get rid of it".

"What'da mean 'let it go'....I've been trying to get rid of it ever since Dross drove it into me".

"Have you?" asked Dudley, looking Thren squarely in the eyes. "Are you sure you didn't think you deserved the pain, because of what happened? Because you couldn't save all of them?" It was Thren who looked away first.

"I guess I did, kinda....why should I get to carry on as if nothing had happened. It was all my fault".

"No it wasn't", said Bex. "We all had something to do with it, me, Flint, Marty....everyone at that party. We all went along with inviting ......*it*.....in".

"You've got to try and forgive yourself, Thren" said Dudley softly. "It's the only way you can keep going".

"We need you, Thren", added Bex, "And we care about you. You're our friend. You do know that, don't you?" Thren blushed a little, and attempted, unsuccessfully, to sit up.

"Besides", added Flint, "If you feel bad about how things are now, imagine how much worse you'll feel when the demon finishes us all off, and does ....well, whatever he's planning to do to us. You don't want that to happen, do you?"

"You got that piece of wood lodged in your chest because you were trying to protect Paul during the battle", contributed Dudley. "Don't you still want to protect him....protect all of them?" Thren nodded. "Then forgive yourself, and accept that you've been forgiven by Him, by everyone, for your part in what happened before", the old man said.

"But Graham's dead", said Thren, shame-faced. "I felt it happen. I couldn't stop it, I failed. It's like the nightmare I keep having.... something evil attacks you all again, and I can't stop it....I can't save any of you.....you all die, and it's my fault."

"You felt what happened to Graham because you care", said Dudley, "but your job is to care about all of them. You can't abandon the whole group because you couldn't save one of them. They need you more than ever". Thren nodded, tears beginning to trickle down his face.

Bex caught Flint's eye and they quietly stood up and moved away into the kitchen, leaving Dudley and the angel to talk and pray together. When they entered the room a few minutes later, Thren was sitting up, the bloodied stake on the floor in front of him. He was still very pale, and bleeding from the wound in his chest, but the angel looked stronger than he had for a while.

"Help me up please, Flint, if you'd be so kind" requested Dudley. "I think I'm stuck, and if I don't get a move on, I'll be late for morning service. I'm supposed to be reading the lesson."

Chapter Twenty-Six

Dross was hovering over the city once more, trying to hold his particulate form together without a corpse to put it into. He was furious that he'd lost Graham's body so quickly, before he could use it to cause more trouble. He'd also lost the boy's tasty soul-light, and the additional power it gave him. He couldn't just step back into Lizzy's carcass, it was too far gone now, and looking slightly zombie-like was not going to help his plan.

Without a body it would be difficult to proceed, and complete the mission that he'd set himself, but where would he find a corpse on a Sunday morning, without the cover of darkness to help him? He headed for the hospital.

In The Darkness more and more demons were gathering, ready to be invited through. With each rule that got broken, each person who discovered what was really going on, the balance was shifting. The very need for the angels to warn to the students about what the demon was up to turned out to be working in his favour. Dross had to be ready to take full advantage of that opportunity, as it was his intension to give all those other demons a chance to come through into the human world just as soon as he could. That would give him power over the demons as well, which was exactly what he was after.

The main wards of the hospital were too busy for his purposes, and he ended up checking out the intensive care unit. However, all of those patients were too badly injured or too ill to be of any use, so once again he made his way down to the morgue.

He had to wait until lunchtime, before the attendants went off duty, and he could examine the available corpses. His choice was limited, but he found a body that would do temporarily, a middle-aged man who had died of a heart attack. Not too messy, or too obvious. Good fortune seemed to be on his side again.

Snig had remained under the pew in the cathedral throughout the service, letting the music and the atmosphere of worship wash over him, and finding it strangely restful. He was fairly certain that he wasn't meant to, that every moment in that holy place should repel him, but it didn't. When the service finished, and the congregation began to disperse, Snig crept along beneath the seats, darting from one to another, trying to find the men he'd seen earlier. He spotted them at last in the vestry, chatting companionably to each other. Waiting until no other humans were about, Snig slipped into the room, and hissed at them.

"'Cuse me....Snig needs help. Snig's sick". The two men turned to stare at him, Poole open mouthed and uncomprehending, Dudley merely surprised. Snig realised with amazement that these humans could see him, which had never happened to him before. But then, lots of the things Snig was going through had never happened to him before either. "Sanctuary" muttered the imp, "Snig's scared... needs... safe.... place... has to hide from horrid demon".

Poole slumped down onto a chair, speechless. Dudley took a cautious step towards the creature.

"What are you, exactly?" he asked. "I don't wish to be rude, but I haven't seen anything like you before. Are you.... supposed ...to be here, inside the cathedral?"

"Don't know, don't know lots. Snig need help so Snig here...if I'm not allowed I'll go now." The kindly old man looked more closely at Snig as the imp turned to leave, and noticed the broken bones and the bruises that were starting to show through his lumpy skin.

"Who did that to you?" he asked.

"Dross," replied the imp. "He's mean demon. He's mad at me for fighting him, so he hurt me. ...and I come to this place for help ..for sanctuary..... pleassse don't makes me go".

"You fought Dross?" said Dudley, amazed.

"Why?"

"He's hurting humans...he's not...kindly, so Snig stopped him".

"What IS that thing" whispered Poole. "How do we get rid of it?"

"I think it's an imp.....his name seems to be Snig.....and I'm not at all sure that we should get rid of him. He's here to ask for our help..... for sanctuary....and he seems to be on our side."

"Our side?" echoed Poole numbly, "Our side in what?"

Paul and Sarah were exhausted. They'd spent three hours trying to explain to the police why Graham's body was in Sarah's room. At first the detectives were convinced that they must have had something to do with Graham's death. Only the fact that the pathologist gave a time of death that agreed with the student's accounts of what had happened saved them from being arrested on the spot. That and the fact that all the other students corroborated their story of searching for Graham in the middle of the night, and seeing him on the campus after his agreed time of death. The police suspected that even if the students hadn't had a hand in Graham's death, they were still guilty of moving his body, and lying to the police, but there wasn't enough proof against any individual to make an arrest.

They couldn't decide if they were dealing with a mass hallucination, a particularly nasty student prank, or a collective attempt to deceive the police about a murder.....and Graham definitely had been murdered. The fire extinguisher had his blood on it, along with numerous prints. All the students who'd come forward were fingerprinted, much to Cath's dismay, but although some of them had touched the extinguisher none of their prints matched those around the dead boy's throat, nor did any of their hands look as if they had left the fragments of blistered skin on his neck.

The police began to search the halls of residence for more evidence, which was when they discovered the body of Lizzy Brett in one of the cleaning cupboards. When the police eventually deduced that it was she who had strangled Graham, they were even more confused, as she had been dead for even longer than he had.
Finally they had had to let the students go, though with a warning that the police would be keeping a close eye on them in the future.

"I'm sorry, Sarah", said Paul, when they were finally on their own. Sarah nodded numbly, and then looked at her friend closely.

"Why did you come? When...that thing...was here? I told you I never wanted to see you again, and then you turned up, at exactly the right time".

"I just had a feeling....I hadn't planned to come looking for you. I knew how mad at me you were, but I was reading my Gran's journal, and she was mentioning about listening to your instincts....so I did".

"Thank you" said Sarah, gratefully.

"You were doing ok anyway", said Paul. "You'd already realised who...what....you were dealing with....you were thumping him with that book.....and the angels turned up".

"I'm still glad you came looking for me though....I didn't mean what I said, earlier...about it all being your fault...about you being jealous".

"It's true" admitted Paul, "I was a little jealous, but honestly, I didn't mean to leave Graham in danger. You do know that, don't you?" Sarah, nodded, too tired to speak any more.

She was curled up on the bed in Paul's room. She couldn't face being in her own right then, not after what had happened. Paul sat on the chair beside his desk, and carried on reading his grandmother's journal, while Sarah fell into an exhausted sleep.

Tor was glaring at Thren in frustration.

"I did *not* go to get a replacement for you. Why does everybody think the worst about me? I just asked for Bliss to assist us. We need reinforcements".

"You asked for me? Personally? By name? I'm flattered!" The new angel preened herself smugly.

"No!" snapped Tor crossly, "I did not ask for you personally. I just asked for help....I told the High Council that Thren was.....that it was his time to....to...downsize".

"*Downsize?*" queried Thren, "What the heck is that supposed to mean? Find a smaller cathedral?"

"In a manner of speaking, Thren, yes", Tor replied. "We all reach this stage sooner or later. Our failures get too much for us, and we can't carry on trying to juggle everything. You're too involved in people's lives now..."

"But you used ta bawl me out for *not* caring, *not* being involved! Make up your mind, lady!"

"Well, I was wrong. I know that now, but it just makes it harder for you. The more you care, the more your failures hurt.....I've been there...so have you. Eventually we all get moved to less........ challenging......situations, and somebody else takes over our responsibilities".

"So you're telling me I got *fired*? While I was lying here...dying?"

"You didn't die, Thren", said Tor defensively.

"You didn't know that, damn it!" Thren's voice cracked. "You left me here to die, alone".

"You weren't alone!" said Bex and Tor simultaneously.

"You're not being fair, Thren" added Flint, "We were doing everything we could".

"And we didn't leave you on your own", said Bex, "Not for a moment. We wouldn't. So stop being so mean to Tor, she's doing her best". Flint blinked. He still found the sight of Bex telling Thren off a little unnerving. Even though he now counted Thren as, almost, a friend, in an awkward sort of way, he couldn't imagine ever having the confidence to put the angel in his place like that. It made him smile. Bex seemed like such a quiet girl sometimes....a good daughter, a good student...but she was no wimp. Tor smiled at the girl, proud to

127

have Bex defending her to Thren for once. Usually it was the other way round, and Tor often felt jealous of how close Bex and Thren were, but now she blushed, knowing that the girl valued her too.

"But you still had to go and get a new sidekick, Tor", complained Thren, "Am I really that useless?"

"You're not useless at all, Thren, but you are ill. It's time to reassess your duties. That's why Bliss is here. It's her job to take over protecting the city", said Tor with a glance at the new angel.

"So now I'm redundant! Terrific! Just when I was starting to feel kinda better. So where do I go now? Some kinda retirement home for tired angels".

"No such luck, I'm afraid", said Tor crisply. "You're still a guardian angel.....you just get to narrow the field a little. You get to concentrate on certain people, and leave Bliss to look after the rest of the city".

"So which people? Who am I looking after?"

"Usually you'd be allocated somewhere else, a town rather than a city, or a group of people".

"What? Ya mean I gotta leave? That sucks.....is it some find of punishment? I didn't mean to let Him down, and I guess I failed for sure.....but I don't wanta leave everyone, 'specially now, with all this trouble going on".

"I said that's what usually happens" said Tor reassuringly, "But in this case you're being allowed to stay here. You can pick a small group to look after, in the short term, and help me to deal with this demon. Bliss can look after the rest of the city".

"So I get to pick? Outta everybody?" He grinned at Bex.

"Not Bex", added Tor quickly, "Anyone but Bex.....she's still my responsibility".

"Flint then, and the rest of the students in their group, and Dudley and Amy and Luke and Harry and...." Tor interrupted him,

"That's too many, Thren. You've been in such a bad way, I've been told to limit you to just a dozen people, thirteen at the most".

"Just like the number of students at the séance? Great.....thanks for the reminder, Wonderwings.....but what about the others? I gotta look out for them too.....and the homeless shelter, and the..."

"No need to worry", said Bliss confidently. "I can look after the rest. I've done the training!" She started to flourish her clipboard about.

"Look, I took notes! Lots of notes! In fact it's time I got started".

"I'll take you up to the cathedral roof in a moment", said Tor.

"Think about who you're going to protect, Thren. Take a moment. Then we'll go up, and you can hand the rest over to Bliss!"

Thren struggled to stand up. Although the stake was out of his chest, he was still very weak, and had to be supported by Flint to get to his feet.

"If I gotta hand most of my humans over to Bliss, there's still a couple of loose ends I gotta tie up".

"Alright", said Tor, resignedly, "But you have to do it today, if you can. We need to focus on what the demon is planning, before anyone else dies. Come on, it's time for the handover".

Chapter Twenty-Seven

As the three angels stepped out onto the cathedral roof, Thren felt the panic rising again. So many soul-lights twinkled throughout the city. He was responsible for all of them, and he hadn't been doing his job properly for days. All kinds of bad things could have happened....and some of them had....and he hadn't prevented them. Guilt washed over him again. Tor came and stood calmly at his shoulder, and whispered in his ear.

"Take one last look Thren, see all those lights? They're not your problem anymore. It's Bliss's job to deal with them now. Just keep in your head the ones you want to protect, and pass the rest to her". Thren closed his eyes, images of different faces flickering across his memory, holding onto a few of them, and letting go of the rest. When he finally opened his eyes, all he could see in the city were a few familiar soul-lights, the rest had vanished.

"What the.......?" Even though he had known it was going to happen, it still came as a shock to him. He's been trying to spread himself so thinly over the city, he hadn't been able to concentrate. Now relief flooded through him. With fewer people to protect he began to feel he might just be able to do his job properly and look after them. He turned to speak to Bliss.....she was staring down at a city full of soul-lights in horror.

"All of these?" she was muttering. "I'm supposed to look after all of these?"

"Yes," said Tor. "So I suggest you get started. You know what to look out for, don't you?"

"Yes," said Bliss, her voice sounding suddenly small and scared. "I took notes during Guardianship Training.....and I made charts, to remind myself what the different colours of soul-lights meant, but I wasn't expecting......" she looked down over the city of Chester, feeling completely overwhelmed.

"Colour charts? You made colour charts?" Thren chuckled weakly. "I *so* could have done with some of those when I started". Tor glared at him, again.

"What you could have done with was paying attention in class....which is exactly what Bliss has done". She turned to the new angel, "I'm sure you'll be fine, dear." Bliss gulped, as all three angels stared down over the city. Tor, of course, could only see Bex's soul-light, Thren could see the other students in that group, and Dudley's.

He'd hung onto Poole's too, for some reason, though he wasn't quite sure why, but he'd grown fond of the old guy, who'd tried so hard to turn himself around after his mean behaviour the term before....plus he was a friend of Dudley's. Apart from that, he'd kept responsibility for Duncan, naturally, who was likely to be in the greatest danger, after inviting the demon through, and the other student who was playing a lead in the same show, Munroe. Thren hadn't noticed him much up to now, but figured anyone close to Duncan could be dragged into danger too. It meant handing over the safety of Amy, and Luke, but he reckoned he could still help them that day, without being able to see their soul-lights.

As he turned his back on the city, he saw Dudley coming through the door that opened onto the roof.

"I'm sorry to disturb you", said the old man, "but there's something I think you ought to see".

***

The students had gathered in Nesta's room. They felt the need to be together, to grieve over Graham's death, and talk through what was going on. Most of them were still struggling to believe any of it had actually happened.

"It feels as if the last few months have been.....unreal", said Cath. "If I'd known what had really happened I'd have coped with it better".

"I'm not sure I would," protested Debbie. "I rather not know about any of it, even now". Sarah looked round at the others, questioningly, "We all knew that what went on was a bit strange though, didn't we? It started straight after the séance at Marty's party. We couldn't pretend it was a coincidence?"

"I did", muttered Marty, sheepishly, "but I guess that's because I didn't want to believe what I'd started.....if I'd known....it was only meant to be a bit of fun...." He was twisting a cigarette packet in his hand, longing to go outside for a smoke, but for once Debbie didn't nag him about it. Instead she said, "We know that, Marty, nobody's blaming you now".

"Besides" Flint chipped in, "it was Bex and I who actually invited him in that time....and we had to un-invite him in the end, to get rid of him".

"By which time Mark was already dead", whispered Sam.

"You can't keep blaming yourself for that, Sam" Bex answered, putting an arm around his shoulders. "He wouldn't have wanted you to.....and I'm sorry we couldn't tell you all what really happened, but we didn't want to start more trouble by breaking the rules".

"But ....." Tim couldn't bring himself to say the word demon,

".....trouble came back anyway. None of us asked it in this time, but it's coming for us again. It's killed Graham....and I honestly think it would have tried to kill you this morning Marty, if I hadn't interrupted".

"And me", added Sarah.

"So what can we do?" asked Nesta. "We can't just pretend that this isn't happening."

"I've been thinking about that", said Paul, "We can do the obvious stuff, of course, stick together, go out in group or pairs, be on the alert.... but there are a few other things too....."

Dudley led Thren and Tor into the vestry, where Poole was waiting with Snig. When the angels entered the room, Snig cowered away from them, trying to hide behind Poole's clerical robes. Poole, who could see the imp's reaction, but not the angels themselves, found the whole situation a little strange, but he trusted Dudley implicitly, so he tried not to panic. Faced with an imp, Dudley had realised he'd have to explain at least some of what was going on to Poole, and had gone to get the angels' advice on the matter. He had also needed to tell them that the demon they were dealing with was definitely Dross.

They had concluded that Poole would have to be put in the picture, at least to some extent, but that they didn't want to appear to him, and break even more rules. The number of humans who knew what was going on seemed to be getting out of hand. Poole however, was no fool. Faced with an actual imp, which was begging for protection from a demon, it was not a big stretch to believe that if creatures of darkness existed, creatures of light could also. It was even scriptural, which he found rather reassuring.

"Snig", Dudley spoke softly, "It's alright, you can come out now. They won't hurt you". The imp continued to hide behind Poole.

"When you say 'they'," Poole asked gently, "Just what exactly are you talking about Dudley? If you don't mind me asking?" His friend hesitated before replying.

"Angels". It was Snig who answered, "Scary great angels. Seen them before" He pointed at Thren, "That one kicked me back into The Darkness".

"Nobody's going to kick you now", said Tor, trying to sound reassuring. The imp was not convinced, and tried to crawl under a chair.

"Am I hearing voices?" asked Poole tentatively. "Is it just my imagination?"

"I'm afraid not..... you really can hear an angel", his friend replied.

"Two", added Snig, "Two nasty angels. Scary".

"It's ok, little fella", said Thren, crouching down, to seem less threatening. "You needn't be afraid of us now. We're on the same side, from what I've heard, so I guess that makes us your friends now".

"Only in 'the enemy of my enemy is my friend' sort of a way" said Tor, under her breath. The imp gave her the creeps. "What is that thing doing here, and why is he visible to humans anyway? Imps aren't supposed to be seen", she muttered.

"Hey, lighten up Tor. We gotta help him. Look at the state he's in". Thren peered more closely at the creature, to study his injuries, and realised exactly which imp they were dealing with. "Now Tor," he said, "You gotta stay real calm, cos you and this little guy....you got history".

"You?" hissed Tor, as she realised what Thren meant. "You're the one who glued me to the roof....the reason why I had to have all my hair cut off. You little...." she tried to lunge forward, but Thren held her back.

"Play nice, lady....the poor little guy has come to us for help....you can't turn on him now....'sides, I like your hair cut....it suits you....so let it go". He knelt down beside the quivering imp. "Now, what can we do for you, buddy?"

Tim and Nesta were arguing, which was rare. They had planned to go to the zoo that afternoon, a trip which Tim thought they should cancel, but Nesta had done a placement there, as part of the biology course, observing the behaviour of the coatimundi. She'd borrowed some books off one of the keepers on that section, and had arranged to return them that afternoon.

"It can wait, Nesta", growled Tim. "There are more important things going on just now".

"I know that", she replied, "But I need to do stuff that feels normal, besides, if anything... happens, I'd hate to think I hadn't returned those books, while I had the chance."

"If anything happens, borrowed books will be the least of our problems". "I know, but going to the zoo feels better than just hanging around here waiting for something else terrible to happen. As long as we go together, we should be alright".

"Ok" Tim conceded, "We'll go, but we stick together, and we don't trust anyone we meet, not even our friends at the zoo. Alright?"

"I suppose so, but it does seem horrid", sighed Nesta. "Not as horrid as if anything happened to either of us. I couldn't bear it if I lost you, Nesta". She reached out and took his hand, squeezing it gently.

"We'll be alright, Tim".

Duncan texted Cath, yet again. And yet again, he got no reply. She couldn't work out how to answer his requests to meet up for a coffee. She knew so much that he was unaware of. She was sure if she spent any time with him at the moment, she'd let things slip. Things she was certain the angels would say she should keep to herself. So she just avoided answering him all together. Taking the coward's way out. She was beginning to understand how her friends had felt, when they couldn't explain what had happened to her in the spring term.

Duncan gave up, and sent a text to Munroe instead. They were the leads in the production the students were performing, it might be good to meet up for a coffee before that evening's rehearsal, and talk about the play. Somehow Duncan wasn't feeling comfortable anymore, sitting in his empty flat, studying the script. The book itself repelled him and attracted him in equal measure. He decided to take it with him to the rehearsal and return it to the director. After all, he knew his lines now. He didn't need it anymore. His phone pinged. It was a message from Munroe, arranging when and where to meet. Duncan put the manuscript, with its strange leathery cover, into his rucksack, along with everything else he'd need for that evening's dress rehearsal, and set off to meet up with his friend.

He didn't notice an older man standing across the road from the house, watching him. Dross had got hold of some clothes that made him look rather like an old-fashioned professor, and was planning to follow Duncan to his rehearsal, and see what he could do to get the most benefit out of the play.

Chapter Twenty-Eight

Duncan and Munroe were sitting chatting in a coffee shop, trying to make their drinks last until it was time to go to the dress rehearsal. Dross, in his tweedy disguise, sat nearby, un-noticed, listening to their conversation.

"And another thing", Duncan was saying. "You're getting some of the lines wrong, during the summoning section. Look!" He pulled the script out of his bag and opened the relevant page, holding the book out to Munroe.

"I changed them on purpose", Munroe admitted, embarrassed.

"Why?" asked Duncan. "It's not on. You don't have the right to go around changing the script. You should perform it as it's written."

"I know", agreed Munroe, uncomfortably. "And I do, with the rest of the play, but that speech, where I'm meant to summon the devil. It makes me feel ....there's something bad about it."

"Oh, so you know more about how to write a scene than the author?" said Duncan. "That's just arrogant".

"I don't mean it's badly written", Munroe protested. "I mean it's bad....there's something creepy about it."

"It's supposed to be creepy", groaned Duncan. "That's the point. And you're making that sign wrong.....the Sigil".

"I know". Munroe said guiltily. "I'm doing that on purpose too. The whole thing... it just feels wrong. I wish I'd never got this part...the more we rehearse it the less happy I am about it".

"Why?" asked Duncan, "It's just a play".

"I know that", said Munroe, "And I can't explain why it bothers me but it does. I'm not usually superstitious, and I don't exactly believe in stuff, heaven and hell and all that...but this play.....it really feels as if we're messing with things we don't understand."

"Well, I wish you'd take it seriously", said Duncan, getting annoyed, "You can't just change the lines 'cos you don't like them. Here, have another look. I need you to say the words as they're written....and what about the tech crew? How can they get it right if you're changing the cues?" He thrust the book at Munroe, who took it reluctantly, and glanced at the open page.

"Hang on," said Munroe, "This isn't the original speech. It's been changed. I may not be saying it as it's written, but I do know it. This scene has been altered!"

"What does it matter?" Duncan was starting to get annoyed, "The way it's written here is the way you should say it, this is the original script", he glared at his friend, as the determination Dross had fed into his mind came to the fore. The play had to be done as it was written.....as it was **now** written.

Munroe looked at his friend nervously.

"Hey, Dunc, keep your hair on....You can't expect me to relearn this before tonight's dress rehearsal, can you?....Anyway, nobody else will know these lines either. The tech crew will have no chance".

"I need you to do the speech this way". Duncan was adamant, leaning in towards his friend aggressively.

"Back off", said Munroe, pushing his chair back and standing up to leave. "Don't tell me what to do!" He grabbed his bag, and left the coffee shop, calling out "I'll see you at the dress", as he left. Dross waited a moment, then stood up and followed him. A change of plan was in order.

Outside the coffee shop Thren was waiting. With fewer soul-lights to watch over, he had picked up on Munroe's agitation, as his light blue soul-light flickered in alarm. The angel saw the young man walk swiftly away from his friend, and he noticed the older man following him, but of course, he couldn't tell that this man had no soul-light. He just looked like hundreds of other people milling around the city, whose soul-lights Thren could no longer see.

Both the young men's soul-lights were tinged with red, after their argument, but Munroe seemed distressed as well as angry, so in the end, Thren started to follow him, leaving Duncan alone. Dross groaned. He could see Thren, even if the angel hadn't spotted him. He wouldn't be able to kill the young man and take over his body, not with a Guardian Angel watching. His rage started to boil. He would not let Thren and the others beat him a second time. He needed a distraction, something to draw the angel away from Munroe, so that demon could come back and attack him later.

Tim and Nesta were wandering round the zoo. They'd returned the books that Nesta had been worried about, and watched her beloved coatimundi for a while. Nesta could recognise and name every single one of them, having spent so much time observing them. Tim had to admit that it was good to be strolling around in the sunshine for a while, and to see how friendly the some of the keepers were with Nesta. He was proud of how much she'd grown in confidence in the last few months, not letting her disability get in the way of her goals. She was determined to complete her biology degree, and go on to find a job that would make use of her skills. Tim had to admit that she was much more focused than he was. Although they were both on the same course, and he was keeping up with his studies, Nesta was far ahead of him academically, and in terms of knowing what she wanted to do when she graduated. If any of them survived to graduate, that is.

He looked around, wondering if the angels were watching him. He knew that they would know he and Nesta were at the zoo. At Paul's suggestion they'd all agreed it made sense, while the demon was after them, to give the angels a heads up if any of them were going far off campus, by calling Bex, and asking her to pass the information on.

It all felt a little silly and surreal....but Graham was dead, and that was very real indeed. Tor watched them from a distance. There was a display of almost life sized dinosaur models at the zoo for the summer, and Tim and Nesta were heading towards them.

Tim nipped off to go to the toilet, and when he returned Nesta looked at him closely.

"Password?" she demanded.

"Do we really have to do this?" asked Tim exasperated. "It's me!"

"Password?" Nesta said firmly.

"Alright. Hippopotamus. Happy now?"

"Yes," grinned Nesta. "I just needed to hear you say it. Paul's right. It seems far too easy for... that thing....to attack one of us, and then pretend to be that person. We need to keep checking that we're with who we think we're with".

Tor smiled. It was good to see the students taking the situation seriously. The angel approved of Paul's password idea too, so that they would know if anyone wasn't....themselves anymore. Nearby, Dross grinned. The password idea was good....and now he knew the word, he could use it!

Thren had left Munroe to his own devices, since he seemed to have calmed down, and was not in any danger. The angel had an appointment to keep, and it was important to him. He was still feeling weak and exhausted, but he managed to struggle across the city to the children's home where Luke was waiting impatiently. Outside a car drew up. Amy leapt out as soon as Harriet stopped the engine, and a moment later, Jay and his wife climbed out and stood beside the girl. Jay looked at Harriet.

"Are you sure we should sit in on this?" he asked, nervously.

"Definitely", his wife replied. "Otherwise how can we help Amy if the meeting is a disaster?" Thren followed them into the home. Luke and Amy hugged each other, then looked awkwardly at Jay and Harriet. Amy stepped forward to make the introductions.

"This is my big brother Luke.....and these are Harriet and Jay, who are looking after me.....at the moment. I hope you like each other, you're all nice, so you should do!" There was a pause, and then Luke stepped forward to shake hands.

"Thank you for taking care of Amy for me. I hope she's been behaving herself".

"Luke", said Amy indignantly, "I always behave myself! Don't I?" She turned to her foster parents for confirmation. They nodded. Amy was always good, too good sometimes. It was the behaviour of a child who knew she must never be naughty, in case she got sent away. "Play with me, Luke, pleaseeeee!" She was tugging at her brother's arm. Luke started a game with her, chasing her round the common room, and teasing her, and suddenly Jay and Harriet saw Amy laughing and playing and messing about with her brother, and acting like any other little girl. Thren slipped up behind them and whispered, "Look at that. See how close these two are? They need each other, you gotta be able to understand that. They oughta be together. It's obvious. Surely you got room for one more?" He couldn't tell if they were hearing him or not, but Harriet slipped her arm through Jay's and rested her head on his shoulder as they watched the children play. Luke did look like a child, briefly, as he played with his sister. He was only fifteen, but he so rarely got the chance to feel like a kid. Life had been serious for such a long time.

Thren noticed that the boy was a little taller than the last time he'd seen him. He was still scrawny though, and his dark blond hair never looked tidy. Thren couldn't see the boy's fiery yellow soul-light any more, but the last time he had checked up on Luke, it had seemed a little dimmer, which Thren had put down to worry. He wished he could have kept these two children under his care, but all he could do now was try to make the most of this final afternoon doing his best for them.

The doorbell rang, and a couple of minutes later, one of the staff from the home came in.

"Your visitor is here....Harry ??? Are you ready to see him? I'll sit in on the meeting with you". She ushered Jay and Harriet over to a sofa on the far side of the room, saying softly that it would be best if they just observed, without joining in the conversation to start with. Then she went to fetch Harry.

Thren nodded his approval when Harry entered the room. He'd been keeping an eye on the guy over the last few months, and so he wasn't as surprised as the children to see Harry smartly dressed, and looking healthy. He'd beaten his problem with alcohol, which he'd turned to when the children's mother had died, and he couldn't cope with the consequences. Thren was delighted with how much progress the man had made, and the way he was learning to control his temper.

"Harry!" squealed Amy, "You look like you again...the old you. The one we moved in with!" She went flying across the room to wrap her arms around the man, who was standing there with a nervous smile on his face.

"Amy sweetheart, you've grown! How are you doing?" Amy was still clinging to him.

"You don't have to hug me, Amy, I know I was a rubbish dad to you....to both of you". He looked hesitantly over at Luke. Luke, who he had lashed out at, who he had driven into running away. The boy made the first move, stepping towards the man and holding his hand out.

"You did your best, Harry, we know that now...and we weren't really your problem. Not after mum died".

Harry smiled gratefully.

"I've been worried about you both though. I know I couldn't cope with looking after you, but that didn't mean......are you ok? Is this where you live now?"

"I live here", Luke replied, "But Amy doesn't, she's being fostered by...." The boy gestured towards the couple sitting on the sofa.

"They're very nice" Amy said, trying to reassure Harry. The man was horrified.

"You mean you're not together? I thought you'd be kept together,....you were always so close". Luke hesitated, and dropped his voice as he spoke to the older man.

"Nobody wants teenage boys Harry, but it's better for Amy to have a proper foster home. That's why we're apart."

Harry looked stricken by guilt.

"If I'd managed better, over the past few months.....if I'd known how to cope....it's my fault you're been separated".

"It's alright, Harry", said Amy, holding his hand. "We understand....and we haven't forgotten you. I got your letters. We don't live with you anymore, but you are still family.....sort of".

"You're all the family we've got", added Luke. "It's good to see you". Harry's eyes were wet with tears. He'd been longing to see the children again, and check that they were alright, but he'd been dreading it too. He'd expected anger, resentment, blame, but he should have known better. There had been a point, when they and their mother had first moved in with Harry, when they really had felt like a close little family. The children seemed able to remember that part of their time with him, and not just the grief and the anger and the drinking.

"I'm glad you're getting better Harry" Amy said, giving him another hug. "And I still want to get your letters. I'll write back too.....if that's ok?"

"I'd love that, sweetheart".

Thren stood behind Harry, and whispered to him.

"See, it's going ok. I told ya it would. They don't hate you, they're better than that. You're doing ok, Harry". The angel patted the man on the back, and even though Harry couldn't feel it, somehow he still felt better.

Thren moved towards Harriet and Jay, and spent the rest of the visit whispering in their ears, trying to influence them, pointing out what a lovely boy Luke was, and how close he and Amy were, and how much better it would be for them both to be together, permanently, in Amy's foster home. He didn't know if he was having any effect, but he'd done his best. Now it was time to leave them to think about it, and get back to protecting the people who were still his responsibility, before it was too late.

Chapter Twenty-Nine

Dross was trying to think of a way to attack Tim and Nesta without confronting Tor, who he could see was keeping an eye on them. He hoped that she would move on when she saw that they weren't in any apparent danger, but she seemed to be sticking to them like glue. As they wandered through the dinosaur display, he caught up with the young couple, and got into a conversation with them about the creatures they were viewing.

"Of course, some of these models are not full sized you know", he said, putting his fuddy-duddy professor look to good use. "Oh no, some of them would have been much bigger."

Nesta peered up at the huge dinosaur model towering over them, before she replied.

"It's still big enough to give you an idea of the scale of them though".

"I wouldn't have wanted to meet a live one" agreed Tim, "Even at this size, they're pretty daunting", he grinned at Nesta. "I know we're both really keen on conservation, but I'm not sorry these guys went extinct".

"Oh, I don't know", said Nesta, as they moved towards another model in the display. "They are amazing, and some of them are beautiful". Tim grinned at her.

"You only think that cos you were hooked on 'Primeval' when you were younger!"

"Who wouldn't be," Nesta grinned back at him, "Though I think I fancied Connor more than the dinosaurs". Seeing Dross's puzzled face Tim explained apologetically.

"It was a TV show....with dinosaurs".

"And a couple of cute actors", added Nesta, with a grin.

Dross ran out of patience. He reached out to take hold of the handles of Nesta's wheelchair, wondering if he could subtly steer her away from Tim. At that moment the dinosaur they were approaching turned its head and spat out a jet of water, which caught Dross full in the face. He leapt back, alarmed. He hadn't realised that some of the models were animated. Perched up on top of the head of a nearby Brontosaurus, which gave her an excellent view of that part of the zoo, Tor saw the man who'd been talking to Tim and Nesta jump when the animatronic dinosaur spat at him. Tim and Nesta waved the man a hasty goodbye and hurried on, anxious to lose the chatty

141

stranger. While they weren't exactly on a date, they didn't want some strange gatecrasher either. Besides, they needed to get out of his sight before they burst out laughing.

"Did you see his face?" Tim chuckled, when they'd rounded a bend in the path, and were hidden from the man's view. "Somehow I don't think he was expecting that".

"He did get soaked, didn't he?" Nesta agreed, giggling. They both stopped laughing at the same time, looking guiltily at each other. It wasn't really the time to be laughing.....not after what had happened to Graham. "Let's go home", said Nesta, solemnly. Tim nodded, and they hurried through the remainder of the dinosaur display and made their way back towards the campus.

Dross shook his head, and dragged his hands across his wet face, then turned on his heel and left. There had to be easier targets than those two. Seeing the students leaving the zoo, Tor glanced around to check that anyone who could see her, such as Thren or Bliss, weren't around, and then slid down the length of the Brontosaurus's neck.

"Wheeeeee!" she cried, joyfully, loving the sensation of speed. When she reached the ground she was grinning, but then put on a straight face, and strolled towards the exit. She loved the zoo, almost as much as Thren did, though she'd never admit it to him. Nonetheless, she was glad her fellow angel hadn't seen her "mad moment" sliding down the creature's neck. It was just the kind of thing Thren would enjoy doing himself, but it wouldn't do to let him know his mentor could be just as silly as him sometimes.

After scouring the places that the students tended to hang out, Dross came across Marty and Debbie, sitting in a coffee shop on Northgate Street. They were huddled up close, Marty's arm around Debbie's shoulders. Dross bought himself a coffee, and took a seat at table near to them.

"Do you think it's really happening?" Debbie was asking. "Everything the others were talking about this morning".

"I don't want to believe it", said Marty, rubbing his eyes with the back of his hand, "But it does make sense of what happened before ....and of Graham's....death". Marty's face suddenly crumpled as he cried, "I started all this!" Dross could see the boy's hands were shaking. "Me and my stupid séance idea.......if I hadn't had that party..........and that....thing...it poisoned me.....tried to steal my soul. I can't bear to think about it."

"Then don't", said Debbie, reassuringly. "Try not to, at any rate. The others aren't blaming you, you know".

"They should be!" snapped Marty. "And while I'm accepting responsibility for that, there's something else I need to tell you. You might as well know the worst, then you can decide if you want to dump me".

"Why would I?" asked Debbie, puzzled.

Marty sighed, then took a deep breath, and told her everything.... about the debts he'd built up trying to impress her, and her parents, about the fact that he wouldn't be able to visit her over the summer, because he'd be too busy working to try and pay them off, if he could get work, and about how worried he was that he couldn't ever treat her the way she'd like to be treated...not in terms of paying for dates and buying her fancy presents, anyway.

Having got it all off his chest, Marty was nervous. He wanted to look at Debbie and see how she'd taken his admission, but he didn't dare. Instead he fumbled in his pocket for a packet of cigarettes.

"I need a fag, I'll be back in a bit", Debbie looked at him with concern. "It's alright", said Marty. "I'm only stepping outside for a couple of minutes....I'll be careful".

"Do you want me to go with you?" Debbie asked. "We could leave the coffees....I'm not that thirsty anyway". Marty shook his head. "I just need a moment alone....I won't be long".

Marty made his way out of the coffee shop. Debbie could see him though the open doorway, lighting a cigarette with trembling hands. She was feeling dreadful about what Marty had told her....not so much about him being in debt, though that was worrying, but because it was her fault. She'd never had to worry about money, and it just hadn't occurred to her that any of her friends, especially Marty, who was usually so sensible, could get into such a mess. The thought that he'd done it to try and make a good impression on her, and her parents......it was terrible. The very idea of it made her feel guilty, and slightly queasy. She remembered how she'd sulked the day before, about Marty not buying tickets to the races.... to the point where he'd taken her out to the cinema in the evening to apologise. More money he couldn't afford to spend.

She stood up to nip to the ladies, and spotted Dross watching her.

"Can you keep an eye on our coffees please?" she said to the pleasant looking older gentleman sitting nearby. "Don't let anyone clear them. We'll be back in a minute". Dross nodded, and Debbie made her way to the corridor at the back of the shop, where the customer toilets were. When she came out a couple of minutes later, Dross was standing in the corridor waiting for her.

Debbie smiled politely and tried to step round him, but the man started shoving her down the corridor towards a fire exit. Distracted by what Marty had just told her, Debbie wasn't really paying attention at first. She just thought the man must be confused, or clumsy. By the time she realised what was really going on, she was trapped. She turned to push on the release bar of the fire exit. The door opened, but Dross simply propelled her out into a back yard. Debbie's pink and orange soul-light turned blue with fear, as the man lunged forward and put his hands around her throat, gripping it tightly. Up on the cathedral roof, where he'd gone after the meeting at the children's home, Thren saw Debbie's soul-light flare, and, still being too weak to fly, he hurried on foot towards the coffee shop. He saw Marty stub out his cigarette and step inside, heading for the table where Debbie was waiting for him. He sat down beside her, and gave her a weak grin.

"Red Bull", he whispered, putting on a silly accent to try and sound like a spy. The password idea did feel a bit ridiculous.

"Hippopotamus", she replied, smiling brightly at him.

"That's not your password," said Marty, suddenly alarmed. "You've got to give me your own password". Debbie opened her mouth again, looking confused, but just repeated the word "Hippopotamus". Marty froze, horrified, as Thren hurried unseen towards them.

Dross had been too eager to pick off both students at one go, and had rushed the transfer into Debbie's body. Thren could see her soul-light battering against the inside of her frame, trying to free itself from the creature that had taken her over. The angel realised with a strange mixture of horror and relief that Dross must have made a mistake. Debbie had passed out, but she wasn't dead. She was aware of Dross inhabiting her, controlling her, which was sickening, but at least it meant that there was still a chance to save her. Marty was reaching into his pocket again.

"This sure ain't no time for another cigarette, Marty, gotta get your priorities right". The boy looked round puzzled, but continued to search his pockets, finally pulling out a small bottle filled with clear liquid.

"*Right*", Marty heard the voice saying in his ear. "Great idea, kid.....if that's what I think it is, go for it." Marty twisted the lid off the bottle and flung the contents in Debbie's face. Dross tried to twist her body out of reach, but found Thren's arms pinioning him in place so that the full force of the holy water hit him in the face. Repelled by the pain that caused him, and knowing that getting into a showdown with an angel at that point would ruin his more ambitious plan, Dross decided to retreat again, and his essence slid out of Debbie's body, and after twisting itself tightly around Thren's face for a moment, causing him to cough and splutter, swirled down the corridor and out through the open fire door.

Thren wanted to follow the demon, but couldn't let go of Debbie, who'd passed out in his arms.

"It's ok, Debbie, you're gonna be ok" he muttered, hoping it was true.

"You did well, kid" he said to Marty, quietly. "Good call, carrying holy water, having passwords.....geeky, but good".

"It was Paul's idea", whispered Marty, trying to overcome the sheer weirdness of having a conversation with what had to be an angel, even if he couldn't see who he was talking to.

"That figures" replied Thren, "He's gotta have been a boy scout when he was a kid. Always prepared."

Out in the back yard Dross slipped back into shell of the middle-aged man whose corpse had been abandoned on the ground when he took over Debbie. Hauling the body back onto its feet, Dross left the back yard through a gate that led into an alleyway. He was burning with rage that his plans weren't working. The students seemed much better prepared this time. Still, at least he had caused a distraction. With a little luck the angels would be too busy with protecting the original group of students, to notice what he was up to with Duncan and Munroe. All he needed was a little more time, and then he could release the gathering demons in to the world.

Chapter Thirty

Debbie stirred in Thren's arms, and opened her eyes to see Marty's concerned face staring at her. She reached up a hand to rub her bruised throat, and realised that somebody was supporting her, holding her up....and she knew it wasn't Marty, because he was in front of her.

"Don't panic, kid," Thren whispered in her ear. "I'm one of the good guys. Dross has gone now".

Debbie tried to speak, but her throat hurt too much, and she was weak with shock.

"Do you want me to get a doctor?" Marty was asking. "I should call an ambulance, you've been hurt". Debbie shook her head, wearily.

"Just get me out of here", she croaked.

With Thren supporting her on one side, and Marty on the other, Debbie was helped out of the coffee shop. It was too far to walk her back to the campus, so they turned towards the cathedral instead, Debbie struggling not to throw up in the street as waves of nausea swept over her at the thought of what had just happened.

In Dudley's little house, Bex and Flint were curled up together on the sofa, while Paul and Sarah sat on the floor, with Paul's grandmother's journal open in front of them.

"All this time", Paul was saying, "And I never realised that she could see angels too.....I wish I could ask her about it all."

"Too late now", said Flint, sympathetically, "But at least she left you her journal." Sarah reached out and turned a page, "She must have known you'd need to know what she'd learned. She wanted to help you".

"Is there anything in there to help us?" Bex asked. "Anything we can use against Dross?"

"I think so," Paul replied. "There's a lot of stuff in here about the rules....the ones we shouldn't break, because it alters the balance of power, and lets ....things....through into our world.....but the rules work both ways. We've been too busy to think about it.....but I'm pretty sure the demon is breaking the rules too....going after some of us when we didn't invite him through this time. Maybe there's something in that that will help us".

"So who should the demon be going after?" asked Cath, as she walked in from the kitchen carrying a tray of coffee mugs. Sam followed her, and moved a small table into the middle of the room so that she had somewhere to put the tray down.

"Whoever invited him through, for a start", said Paul, sadly, "Though I wouldn't wish that on anybody".

"That would be Duncan then", said Tor, suddenly becoming visible in the room. Sam dropped his mug in surprise, spilling coffee everywhere, and Bex hurried to the kitchen to fetch a cloth and clean up the mess.

"I do wish you wouldn't do that, Tor", said Bex, as she knelt on the floor mopping up coffee. "Sneaking up on us, it's not fair".

"It's my job" muttered Tor, offended. "I'm supposed to look after you".

"Well, learn to knock, or something". Seeing Tor's hurt expression Bex quickly added "Not that I'm not grateful, Tor. We all are....it's just......disturbing when you appear out of nowhere".

"I shouldn't be appearing at all, really," said Tor guiltily, "But as you've all seen me already, it hardly seems worth using the energy it takes to keep myself invisible all the time. I might need it later". The students looked at each other nervously.

"What do you mean, Tor?" asked Flint cautiously. "What do you think is going to happen later?"

"I'm not exactly sure, but Paul's right, Dross should be going after Duncan, not the rest of you". The angel turned the idea round in her mind, "Which must mean he's planning something.....something big enough that he's willing to leave Duncan alone for the moment".

"So he's planning something worse?" asked Flint.

"Worse than killing him or stealing his soul?" added Sarah. "What could be worse than that?" The thought of what had happened to Graham almost overwhelmed her, but she struggled not to burst into tears again. Everyone in the room had had some experience of the demon, some of them considerably worse than her own. She had to try and be strong, to help with....whatever they had to do. She felt Paul's hand on top of hers, grasping it reassuringly. She squeezed his hand in return. That was the thing with Paul. He always seemed to understand how she was feeling. She turned her head and gave him a watery smile.

There was a hammering at the front door, and Flint hurried to answer it. He returned to the sitting room followed by Marty, and a still invisible Thren, supporting Debbie. They settled her on the sofa and looked around at the roomful of serious faces. Seeing Tor was visible, Thren adjusted his wing beats too, so both the angels could be seen. Debbie's eyes widened and Marty swore under his breath as they took in the impressive sight.....well, fairly impressive. Thren's white robe was still bloodstained and Tor, with her short hair and clothes borrowed from Bex's wardrobe was not what either of them were expecting.

Over in the cathedral Dudley and Poole were staring at Snig, or to be precise, at Snig's back. The itchy lumps on his shoulders were starting to crack open and the little creature's skin was peeling off that part of his body.

"Hurts", the imp was wailing. "Hurts.....make it stop. Make it stop".

"Poor thing", said Poole compassionately. "It does seem to be in a lot pain. Isn't there anything we can do, Dudley?"

"We could try and put some cold water on its back. That might take the sting out of it, anyway", replied Dudley.

"I'll go and get some", offered Poole, helpfully.

"Thanks, Ernest, but it might be easier to look after him at mine. The house is close enough, and at least nobody else will see him there".

"Mmmm", agreed Poole, "He would be a little hard to explain. I don't quite understand it myself yet".

"Noooooo!" howled the imp. "Sanctuary. Safe here. Stay here. You said I could stay here.....even nasty angels say I could stay....keep safe". Dudley knelt down beside him and spoke gently.

"We'll keep you safe Snig, I give you my word. ....but we need to try and help you too. We can do that better at my house.... it's right beside the cathedral, so you could run back here if you needed to. So, will you trust us?" Snig nodded, and thrust his clawed hand into Dudley's.

"Suppose so", the imp whispered. Poole pulled off the clerical robes he was wearing over his suit, and they wrapped the shivering imp up in them. It was Poole who gently lifted the creature up, walked out of the cathedral beside his friend, and round to Dudley's house.

When the two men entered Dudley's sitting room everybody was talking at once, so nobody heard them coming in through the front door. Everyone's attention was focused on Debbie. Poole stopped in amazement, staring at the angels, who hadn't had time to make themselves invisible. Marty was crouched on the floor beside the sofa, holding Debbie's hand, as she tried to explain what had happened to her.

"It was terrifying", she croaked, her voice still rasping. "This man....he looked perfectly normal, but then he started....started choking me. I couldn't breathe.....I thought that was it....that I was going to die. When I ....came to....it was disgusting....it was like he was in my body....beside me.... squeezing me out. He was controlling what I said....what I did. It was like being kidnapped, from the inside out...and he felt.....vile...pure evil". Nobody spoke. They were all too shocked, trying to imagine the horror of it.

"Is that what it was like for Graham?" whispered Sarah. "Is that what that thing did to him? How could you let that happen?" She turned her rage and fear on Thren, and ran at him, beating her fists against his chest. Thren flinched with pain, his chest still sore even though the shaft of wood was no longer impaled there, but he stood his ground and let Sarah take out her anger and grief on him. He figured it was the least he deserved. Eventually she stopped attacking him, and began to shake with dry rasping sobs.

"I couldn't save him, Sarah," said Thren gently, "I'm real sorry, but there wasn't anything I could do. I was too darn sick to help him when he needed me, but you gotta know it wouldn't have been like it was for Debbie. Graham was dead. Dross killed him first, and then took over his body... He wouldn't have felt it the same way, I give you my word....and the demon didn't have another body to transfer straight into when he left Graham's, so your friend's soul-light won't be trapped".

"Thren, please", Debbie spoke softly, "Don't let this happen to anyone else. You have to find a way to stop it".

At the mention of the demon's name, the bundle in Poole's arms began to wriggle in fear, and a moment later Snig dropped onto the carpet. The students stared at it in revulsion. Looking round the room, and seeing so many human eyes looking back at him, Snig was horrified too. He scrambled up onto Dudley's shoulders, and clung there shivering and whining, his face tucked into Dudley's neck, his back towards the centre of the room. Thren glanced at the creature, then took a closer look at its back, and gave a low whistle.

"Will ya look at that.....wing buds! Who'd have thought it!" Sure enough, pushing out through the cracked skin on the imp's back, were two tiny white lumps, covered in downy feathers.

"Scared", cried Snig. "Snig's scared .... what's happening to Snig?"

Chapter Thirty-One

Bex had taken Debbie upstairs to get a hot shower, and a change of clothing. The usually elegant young woman was a wreck, desperate to get rid of any trace of contact with the demon who had taken her over. She felt contaminated by him, and had already decided to destroy the clothes she'd been wearing that day, since she'd never be able to put them on again without remembering his disgusting presence.

Downstairs the others were talking about what they could do next, while Poole was trying hard not to stare at the angels. He'd never expected to be in this position.....not just seeing angels, but having a conversation with them about how to defeat a demon. He felt humbled that some of the students seemed to have a much clearer idea about the situation, and how to handle it, than he did. He cleared his throat and made a tentative suggestion.

"Perhaps we should tell the Bishop what's going on?"

"Perhaps we should" said Dudley, smiling encouragingly at his friend, "When we have a clearer idea ourselves. At the moment it would be rather hard to know what to tell him".

"It all comes down to what Dross is planning", said Tor, "And why he's breaking the rules by going after all of you. He had his chance to destroy each of you last time. He doesn't have the right to attack you all again".

"So he is breaking the rules, then?" asked Paul.

"He sure is," agreed Thren, "But I don't get why he can get away with it like this. It don't seem fair that for every little slip-up we make, more and more bad things happen....but there's Dross breaking the rules every which way.....and he's still here".

"What do you mean?" asked Flint.

"Well," Thren answered, "He's gotta stick to the rules too....by rights he oughta be sucked back into the invisible realm for going after people who didn't call him through.....not this time, anyhow".

"What have I missed?" asked Bex, as she came back in and settled down on the floor next to Flint. Dudley looked around the crowded room, wondering if he should borrow some extra chairs, before dragging his mind back to the matter in hand.

"We're trying to figure out how Dross is managing to get away with going after us, when he doesn't have the right to", said Sarah, answering Bex's question. She was calmer now, and felt sorry for how she'd reacted, attacking Thren that way. It was Dross who was their enemy, not Thren, and if she wanted to help defeat the demon, she'd have to stay focused on what they needed to do next. Thren noticed that her usually fuzzy pink soul-light was glowing more strongly as she pulled herself together. Knowing how grief stricken she was, he admired her fighting spirit.

"Saltings." It was Snig who answered Sarah's question. He crawled out from behind Dudley's chair, where he'd been hiding to avoid everyone staring at him. "It's saltings".

"What do you mean, Snig?" Dudley asked gently. "What's a salting?" Snig looked bashful when everybody turned to look at him. "Saltings keeps him here".

"Of course", said Tor. "I should have realised. That book, the one in Duncan's room, the one made from.....human skin....it's a salting".

"I still don't get it, what's a salting?" asked Thren, puzzled.

"We imps bring saltings through, plants them places. See what happens. When people find them, saltings make trouble.....I'm good at salting, me....was. Not no more! Don't wants to help demons no more.....demons cruel.....peoples kindly". He crept over to Bex and curled up next to her. She reached out a hand and gently stroked the creature's head.

"So if a 'salting' is used to invite a demon through into our world....?" Paul asked.

"Then it anchors him here," Tor answered. "Stops him being sucked back into The Darkness, even if he does break the rules".

"So we gotta get hold of that book", announced Thren.

The book was still in Duncan's rucksack. When he reached the theatre on campus, where the dress rehearsal was due to take place, he started chatting to a couple of the other members of the cast, and forgot his plan to pass the script back to the director. He'd arrived early and was frustrated to see that most of his fellow actors hadn't turned up yet. An older gentleman, dressed in a tweed jacket, was sitting in one of the seats in the back row. Duncan assumed the man was a friend of the director, there to watch the dress rehearsal, or even someone who'd come along to review the play.

The young man strolled over to talk to the stage manager, and was soon caught up in a discussion about the technical aspects of the production. Dross sat quietly, turning his plans over in his head. It had been his intention to wait until the first night, when there would be an audience in the building, before putting his plan into action, but now he was considering bringing the event forward, before the angels found a way to throw a spanner in the works. There seemed to be plenty of students about already, back stage. With the cast, when the rest of them got there, and anybody else who happened to pop in, there should be enough people for the other demons to take over, the demons who had gathered in The Darkness, more and more of them with every human who discovered what was going on. Dross licked his lips, which were going dry and papery. Without a soul-light to delay the rate of decay, his body was already beginning to decompose.....another reason to put his plan into action more quickly.

Bex had brought a bowl of warm soapy water into the sitting room, and was using a cloth to wash the sore, itchy flesh around Snig's wing buds. The cracked skin at their bases began to slough away as the water softened it, and more of the creature's feathery wings began to appear.

"What do ya think's going on with the little fella, Tor?" Thren asked his fellow angel, softly.

"I have no idea", Tor replied stiffly. "If he's turning into.....well, it seems most unfair. Especially after what he did to me... he should be punished, not rewarded".

"I'm guessing he's had years of being punished", said Thren, thoughtfully. "Trapped in The Darkness.....being pushed around by demons like Dross. Look at the poor little guy....you can see how beat up he is....Dross did that to him. 'Sides, seems like he's changed...he's on our side now. He even got into a fight with Dross to save a human. Guess that's why this....whatever it is....is happening to him".

"Be kind, Tor" added Bex. "He probably can't help what he is.....was....and if he's changing....well, that's a good thing, isn't it?"

"I suppose so," Tor agreed reluctantly. Dudley looked at the imp, and noticed it seemed to be getting paler. "It's definitely changing", he said. "I wonder what it'll turn into?"

"Never mind that creature!" snapped Tor. "What matters at the moment is stopping the demon, and getting hold of that book. I wish I knew what he was up too".

"It's obvious", said Flint, suddenly putting all the pieces together. "The book isn't just 'a book', is it? It's a script.....that's why Dross hasn't gone after Duncan....because he needs him....or the play will get cancelled.....Dross wants to use the play somehow".

"When does it open?" Poole asked nervously.

"Tomorrow night", said Cath, "It's due to run all week".

"But the dress rehearsal is tonight," Flint added. He glanced at his watch "I'm due there soon, I'd better head off". Flint stood up to leave, but Dudley called out to him.

"Wait a minute. Before you go, we need a plan.... and if Dross is planning something big, we have to be ready for it....all of us. We can't fight him if we've got anything holding us back, any guilty secret Dross can use against us". Flint groaned, then muttered gloomily.

"Oh, well, it was bound to come out sometime, I suppose".

Munroe wandered into the theatre and glanced around, hoping to avoid another argument with Duncan about the play. He could see his friend's point of view....usually he would perform a speech as it was written but there was something about this script.....something that completely freaked him out. If he could have dropped out of this production he would have done, but it was part of their course work....plus, like all actors, he felt 'the show must go on'. He just wished he wasn't in it. He couldn't even put into words why it bothered him so much. He didn't have any particular faith, in anything.....but that didn't mean he couldn't consider the possibility of there being things in the world that he didn't understand.....and didn't particularly want to come into contact with. Duncan was helping one of the stage crew to position some of the props, so Munroe took the opportunity to slip out of the auditorium without getting into another disagreement, and headed for the dressing rooms. Dross, unnoticed, stood up and followed him.

"You wanted to know why I'm a couple of years older than the rest of you?" Flint said, glancing around the room. "Prison, that's where I was for two years, well, a young offenders institution anyway". While Bex and Paul and Dudley made the connection with what they already knew of Flint's past, the others looked blank.

"I stole my parent's car", Flint explained wearily. "Took it for a joy ride...my little brother came with me. The roads were icy and I crashed the car.....he was killed, and I walked away in one piece. How unfair was that?" Bex stood up and took his hand.

"You told us about this last year, it's alright".

"No, it isn't," Flint cried bitterly. "I didn't tell you I was sent down for it. I didn't tell you my parents hated me so much that they insisted I was prosecuted for it. The police didn't want to....it was a first offence, and it was the family car I borrowed, not some stranger's ....but Jamie was killed, and my parents wanted to punish me". Flint voice softened. "The judge was kind really. He saw I was devastated by what had happened. He could have sent me away for much longer...ten years........ fourteen even. Instead I got two. Two years in a young offenders place....I deserved a lot worse....I still do".

"Quite!" said Tor, in a smug voice. "I knew there was a reason why I didn't think you were good enough for Bex".

"Shut it, Tor", growled Thren. "Cut the kid some slack, will you".

"I don't see why I should", Tor replied sulkily.

"Cos we all deserve second chances.... Flint, me, that little guy over there", Thren pointed to the imp, "Even you, Wonderwings, even you. It's not like you've never made a mistake now, is it?"

"I suppose not" conceded Tor, so stiffly that it was obvious she didn't really agree that her mistakes were anything like as bad as anyone else's.

"Well", said Dudley calmly, "I'll tell you what I told Thren this morning.....what my good friend Poole here helped me realise", Poole blushed at the description, as Dudley carried on speaking, "That you have to forgive yourself, Flint. You can't keep on hating yourself for your mistake....if you cling on to your guilt, it will limit you....and Dross will use it against you, to make you weaker. You've admitted what you did, and how bad it made you feel, but you can't let it haunt you forever, or it'll ruin your life".

"It already has", said Flint, "Bye Bex." He hurried out of the room, avoiding making eye contact with any of his friends....if that's what they still were.

Chapter Thirty-Two

Munroe entered the men's dressing room. The rest of the cast were beginning to arrive, and most of them had already claimed a chair and some dressing table space in front of the mirrors. Munroe picked somewhere to sit, and began to lay out his make-up. Dross, glancing in through the open door, was annoyed to see his target surrounded by other students. The demon had been hoping that the boy would have a dressing room to himself...a nice quiet place where Dross could kill him and take over the young man's body before the dress rehearsal began. Obviously he'd have to rethink his plan.

Duncan came into the room and saw an empty space at the dressing table beside Munroe, but after their earlier argument he chose to tuck himself into a cramped corner rather than sit beside his friend. He pulled his stage shoes and a couple of pieces of costume out of his rucksack, and kicked the bag under his chair. In the corridor outside the dressing rooms, Dross seethed. Now he couldn't get at either of the young men. As he was standing there, Flint came hurrying along the corridor, and brushed past him. The young man seemed anxious and distracted, as he too rushed into the dressing room to prepare for the dress rehearsal. Dross still longed to get his hands on the young man's guilt tinged grey soul-light, but that would come later. First he needed to get hold of Munroe.

Bex had called Tim and Nesta and suggested that they meet the rest of the group outside the theatre on the campus, Dudley dispatched Poole to tell the bishop what they thought might be about to happen, and Tor went to fetch Bliss. Paul and Dudley returned Snig to the cathedral, where he curled up under a seat in the choir stalls, whimpering, then they collected anything from the cathedral that they thought might be useful if they were going up against Dross.

"It feels as if we're preparing to go into battle", said Paul, nervously.

"I'm very much afraid we are", Dudley replied. "Of course, it might not be tonight. Dross might decide to wait until later in the week, but we have to be ready, just in case".

It was a sombre group that left Bex's home and walked down towards the campus. Up on the roof Tor was arguing with Bliss.

"I don't see why I should get drawn into this" the new angel was saying, sulkily. "I'm here to look after the rest of the city, which is quite enough to cope with. Surely this other business is your and Thren's problem, not mine".

"Oh, really", said Tor sarcastically. "You think this demon is sticking to the rules? That he's only going to attack the humans Thren and I are protecting? That nobody else is going to get caught in the cross-fire? That wouldn't look very good on your record would it? A major incident on your first day on the job, and you refused to attend?" Bliss began to look nervous.

"Do you really need me there?" she asked. "Yes", said Tor firmly. "We need all the help we can get. Plus we can only see the soul-lights of the people under our protection. You can see everyone else's".

"Why does that matter?" the younger angel asked, querulously.

"Because between us" Tor explained patiently, "We might be able to work out who hasn't got a soul-light at all".

Dross was trying to be inconspicuous, and succeeding. It was surprising how little notice the cast and crew were taking of a middle-aged, tweedy-looking professor type hanging about the theatre. Perhaps because it was part of the university everyone took it for granted that there might be a few extra academic types around. Dross also thought that it might be partly because the age of his new body made him seem like less of a threat. Whatever the reason, it was very helpful. The students were too polite to ask him what he was doing there, simply because he looked as if he belonged at the university. The cast started to emerge from the dressing rooms, and make their way to the wings. Flint hung back for a moment, hoping to look in Duncan's rucksack, and see if the book was there, but Duncan reappeared at the dressing-room door, and grabbed the bag himself, pulling the book out of it.

"I'd better give this back to the director", he muttered to Flint, as he left the room, the book tucked under his arm.

"Shit", said Flint under his breath, as he followed Duncan towards the wings.

The girls in the cast were standing in the shadows, checking that each other's hair and costumes were looking exactly right. It might only be the dress rehearsal, but everyone wanted it to go well, plus they knew the production photos were being taken that night, and nobody wanted to look less than their best. Dross smiled to himself. It really didn't matter to him what they looked like, by the end of the night they'd be just so much demon fodder.

Outside the theatre Bex and Paul were explaining to Tim and Nesta what they thought was going on. Once they'd been brought up to speed Dudley glanced round at all the students, who were looking nervous and awkward.

"None of you have to be here, you know". Dudley said, "You didn't ask this creature through into the world, not this time, and it shouldn't be your problem getting rid of it. If you choose to leave, that's quite understandable. I'm sure no-one will think any less of you if you want to go home". Nobody moved. Thren, who was currently invisible, felt he too ought to encourage them to back out if they wanted to.

"Look guys, some of you have had a real shock, what with Graham dying, and all....and Debbie, what you've been through today, that was real bad. Dudley's right. This ain't your problem, and you shouldn't have to sort it out."

"But you could do with the help, right?" asked Paul.

"Yeah", Thren conceded. "We sure could. If Dross is up to something big, we'll need all the help we can get to stop him".

"Then count me in", said Paul, "I'm ready".

"Me too", said Sarah, quietly determined. She was scared, Thren could tell, from the way her soul-light was flickering, but she wasn't going to let that stop her. Thren admired her courage. The others all nodded their agreement.

"I'd rather go in and face it than wait for it to pick us off one by one", said Sam. "Besides, I've got a score to settle. That thing killed Mark, and Graham, and we can't just leave it for the police to deal with. They'd never believe us if we told them what's really going on".

Dudley looked fondly at his daughter.

"I don't suppose I can convince you to go home, can I? You could be the one in the greatest danger, you know. It's your blood he's after". Bex shook her head, and slipped her hand into her father's.

"I'm going in with you, and that's that. If this is our best chance of stopping him, I need to be part of it".

"Very well" said Dudley. "Those of you who feel you can pray, get ready to do so.....Paul, can you make sure everyone has something to use against the demon, if it comes to it? I don't want any of you going in unprotected".

"Why is the demon more interested in Bex's blood, especially?" asked Cath.

"Oh I know, I know," said Bliss, appearing suddenly and waving one arm in the air like an over-enthusiastic schoolgirl. "It's because she has angel blood in her....from way back. Isn't that exciting?" Tor materialized and gave Bliss a withering look.

"Oh yes, terribly", said Tor, infuriated, "And telling the world about it is just what we didn't need you to do. Didn't they teach you not to break the rules during your guardianship training?"

"Training?" Sam grinned as he whispered to Cath, "They have training?"

"Obviously not enough", Cath whispered back. Tor shushed them both like naughty children.

"True," Tor snapped, "Not enough training, Bliss, or you'd know not to break the rules. Every time you mention something you shouldn't, you're shifting the balance of power in favour of The Darkness".

"Oh no," said the new angel, conscience-stricken, "I didn't mean too....I'm terribly sorry".

"Don't worry, kid" said Thren kindly, "We've all done it.....even Wonderwings over there. She sure hates to admit it, but she's not perfect either".

"Perhaps not", said Tor proudly, "But I'm certainly better at not breaking the rules than either of you! And I'm better at focusing on the task in hand. So come along, it's time to get started."

Dudley, Bex and the rest of the group of friends slipped into the auditorium just as the houselights were going down. Dross didn't see them come in, since he was still lurking backstage, and all three angels made sure that they kept themselves invisible as they spread out through the building. They'd agreed that Bliss should point to anyone she noticed didn't have a soul-light. If that turned out to be someone who wasn't under Thren's or Tor's protection, then they'd know which body the demon was hiding in.

Debbie grabbed Marty's hand as they entered the darkened space.

"Marty" she whispered. "Before everything gets even ....scarier, there's something I have to say to you". Marty hung his head, miserably. Debbie was going to dump him, he was sure of it. Not only was he up to his eyeballs in debt, but he'd failed to prevent the demon from attacking her earlier. "About the money thing", Debbie continued. "I'm so sorry. I've been completely selfish....not even thinking about how much I was expecting from you....and I've decided....I want to help. I think we should try and clear your debts together". Marty pulled away, embarrassed.

"I don't want a handout from your dad, Debbie. I'll sort it out myself".

"No, Marty", replied Debbie. "That's not what I meant. What I'm saying....well, trying to say, is...we're a team. We'll both get any work we can this summer....that way we can clear the debts much more quickly....before they get any worse".

"Really?" said Marty amazed. "You'd do that?"

"Of course", she smiled at him. "I love you, don't I? Mind you, it does all depend on what happens tonight. If things go badly with that....demon, your money issues will be the least of our troubles".

"At least we'll be fighting him together", said Marty confidently, snatching a quick kiss, before they moved further into the theatre. If Debbie still loved him, he felt ready to tackle anything....even a demon.

The play began, and the cast moved through their scenes. The students nudged each other as Flint came on. He played his part well, though his mind wasn't really on it, but he only had a few lines, in the first and third acts. The production was really meant to be a showcase for the third year students like Duncan and Munroe. The first years like Flint were just taking the smaller parts, and filling in the gaps, while the second years had slightly meatier roles. Being a dress rehearsal, there wasn't a full interval between the first and second act. As soon as any scene changes were complete, the second act would begin.

Dross had been waiting quietly in the wings, but now his patience was exhausted. He saw Munroe leave the stage and head for the dressing room, and followed him. The young man was having a swig of water from the bottle on the dressing table, before going back on stage. Dross stepped into the room, relieved to find that Munroe was the only person in it this time. The rest of the cast were helping the crew with the scene change. Knowing he didn't have much time, Dross shut the dressing room door behind him, stepped up to Munroe, and started to throttle him. The young man's eyes began to widen as the air was choked out of him, and spittle appeared at the corner of his mouth. Thren, seeing the icy fear-tinged flickering of

Munroe's soul-light, even through the walls of the theatre, headed for the dressing room, but by the time he reached it, the student was stepping out of the room into the corridor, and heading for the stage. He looked unhurt, and his soul-light had stopped flickering, so Thren wondered if what he'd noticed was just a touch of stage fright. He didn't realise that on this occasion Dross had *chosen* to co-habit a body, briefly, and was concentrating all his energy on shielding the soul-light of the terrified actor, and keeping it quiet and still, so as not to attract the angel's attention. If Thren had looked into the dressing room, he would have seen the abandoned dead body of a middle - aged man in a tweed suit, shoved behind the door, and he might have guessed what was going on, but the angel didn't open the door.

Chapter Thirty-Three

As the second act was about to start Dross, wearing Munroe's body, prepared to step onto the stage. This was the run up to his big scene, the one where his character, Redwood, summons the devil. At first Dross had been disappointed when he realised that he wouldn't have time to kill Munroe, and do a proper transfer into his body, but so long as he could keep the boy's soul-light steady, it shouldn't make much difference. He only needed to get to the end of this scene, and then he could destroy Munroe, and Duncan and anybody else he could get his hands on. Most importantly, he could go after Bex, and drag her into The Darkness with him.

He glanced around the stage from the wings and was pleased with what he saw. Under Dross's subconscious influence, Duncan had persuaded the back stage team to set up the pentagram correctly, complete with its circle of salt, and place black candles at the five points. All the other props were in place, and atmospheric music began to play. Originally Dross had assumed that Duncan was playing Redwood, the man who summoned the devil, which would have been perfect, rather than playing the role of the devil himself, but the boy had still been useful in making sure that all the paraphernalia for the summoning was ready.

In the shadows back stage Dross could see Duncan, in his demon costume, preparing for his own entrance. Dross permitted himself a little smile. Although Duncan had refused to take a traditional "red tights and tail" approach to his character, his choice of a cross between plain black cloths and some "horror type" prosthetics weren't a patch on what a real demon should look like, and Dross should know. He sidled up to Duncan, whom he noticed was still clutching the book, and held out his hand for it. Duncan had intended to pass the original script back to the director, but he felt strangely reluctant to part with it.

"You do want me to get the lines right, don't you?" asked Munroe in a hushed voice, and Duncan handed it over.

A moment later the second act began and Dross stepped onto the stage. With the book open in his hand, he stood in the centre of the pentagram and began to read out the amended speech. Bex noticed the director, seated in the auditorium, scribbling a hasty note on his pad of paper..... presumably to remind himself to say something to Munroe later about taking the script onstage with him.

Bex thought Munroe was acting rather oddly. She'd seen him in a couple of plays before, when she'd been to watch Flint in them, and he'd always struck her as a very natural actor, with smooth movements, and a soft but powerful voice. Now however, he seemed a little jerky. When he raised his hand to make a series of big gestures during the speech, he seemed to be almost forcing his body against its will. His voice, too, seemed harsher, which could just be how he was choosing to play the character....but he hadn't sounded like that in the first act. Bex glanced around the auditorium, trying to see if she could spot Thren, or Tor. She was sure something was wrong.

"Thren", she whispered, "Thren?"

In the wings, Flint was puzzled too. Although he wasn't on in this act, he tended to watch from the wings, willing his fellow cast members on, but Munroe was definitely off his game. Flint had heard him deliver this speech dozens of times, usually very powerfully. Now the voice was huskier, and some of the lines had changed. Flint, too, started looking round for the angels, but then felt foolish. Why should he think they'd be anywhere near him? Even if they had come down to the theatre to see what Dross was up to, they'd hardly be keeping an eye out for an ex-gaol bird. He'd seen the disgusted look Tor had given him when he'd confessed, and he wasn't surprised that Bex's guardian angel didn't think he was good enough for her charge. Flint had hoped to get hold of the book, to prove that he was good for something, but he'd failed at that too. Duncan had been hanging onto it for ages, until he handed it over to Munroe, which was odd in itself. Munroe knew his lines, why take the script on with him? Flint's flesh began to creep, as he listened to Munroe's big speech, and realised that some more of the words had been changed subtly.

"Mighty Masters of Dark Realms", Munroe intoned, "Come before me now, summoned by my terrible power, by fire and flame, by cold earth and warm air and smooth water.....and by the eternal power of each of your own true names, the sigils used to bring you into my world. Come Dark Ones....I conjure you to appear before me. Come Dark Lords Come! Veni, Veni, Domini Tenebrarum . Come and assist me. Come and devour! " Duncan made his entrance as the devil, in a flash of light and a puff of theatrical smoke, but before he could begin his big speech in response to being summoned, other creatures began to appear on the stage beside him.

One by one, the demons who had been gathering with each rule that got broken, began to appear, as swirls of dark, choking mist. Eight separate twisting demons, called forcefully into the world by one of their own, empowered in turn by the horrific book. The strength of Dross's summoning gave the creatures more shape than Dross had had when he was first invited through. It was as if the smoky shapes were shadows of themselves as they truly appeared in the darkness. Some had spines and claws and slavering mouths, translucent, but terrible. Some looked more human, but their vicious eyes and the way they licked their opaque lips suggested that their appetites were far from natural. All of them were hungry, and one of them, the most disgusting looking, cried out through drooling lips.

"Who called us here? Who can we devour?"

"It was I who called you....but you can feast on anyone!" Dross replied, complacently, "The book will hold you here, however many rules you break.....but first a favour.....in return for my invitation. I need your help. There is one human here.....well guarded, but of angel blood...." There was a strange slobbering sound as the newly arrived demons grasped the possibilities. Their teeth chattered against each other, and their claws rattled on the floor. Bex sat shaking in her seat, thankful that the auditorium was still in darkness, and then tried to slide silently down into the foot well between the rows of seating.

This was what the demons really wanted.....her blood...the blood of the descendant of an angel.....but to be effective, and set the demons free, it had to be shed in The Darkness, not in the human world. She reached down into her bulky shoulder bag and got out a bottle filled with holy water, a heavy metal cross that Paul had fetched from the cathedral for her, and a kitchen knife. This time she was prepared. Stranded in the centre of the stage, surrounded by terrible shadowy shapes, Duncan quaked. The play wasn't a play anymore. It had turned horribly real, and he wished he was anywhere but stuck in the middle of it. It was Cath who moved first, to help her friend. She felt guilty about not warning Duncan of the danger he was in, although she had she understood why she wasn't allowed to. Every demon on the stage represented a rule that had been broken, a secret that had been told, some of them by her. Now she was determined to help her friend, any way she could. She ran onto the stage and grabbed Duncan by the hand, pulling him out of the circle of demons before they turned on him, as the nearest, easiest victim. Once she had broken his "rabbit in the headlights" state of shock, he was more than willing to run with her. They tore down the corridor behind the stage and ran into the dressing room, where Duncan hastily ripped off his demon disguise, fully aware now of how pathetic it looked compared to the real creatures. The last thing he wanted was to look remotely like the ....things.... on the stage.

"Here," said Cath, "Take this". She handed him a large metal cross.

"Are you mad?" asked Duncan, "What am I meant to do with this?"

"Anything you can!" Cath replied quickly. "Anything to protect yourself! The demon has a right to come after you, because you invited him in, so you have to be ready". In any other circumstances he would have suspected his friend of being unexpectedly high on drugs, or drunk.....but he had just stood on a stage, surrounded by demons.....actual, terrifying demons, and triggered by what Cath had said, his memories of the night he'd summoned the creature began to come back. He stared at her, wide eyed.

"He's after me?"

"He's after all of us, but we're going to fight him. I'm not letting him anywhere near me again". She looked seriously into her friend's eyes and said "I'd rather be dead". She glanced back towards the door and for the first time noticed that there was a dead body lying on the floor behind it, the corpse of a middle aged man in a tweed jacket. Cath flinched, but there was no time to get hysterical.
The dressing room door burst open and Sam charged in.

"I saw you running this way. Are you ok?" he asked.

"I guess so", Cath replied, shakily. Duncan just nodded, still struggling to come to terms with what was going on. "What's happening out there?" Cath asked.

"Not sure," Sam replied. "Those things seem to be spreading out. I'm going back to see if I can help". He spun out of the door.

"Going back?" questioned Duncan, amazed.

"It's what we have to do", said Cath, "To fight it...them. We know how bad it can get if we don't", she followed Sam out of the room and towards the stage. Duncan glanced down at the dead body on the floor. He hoped he wasn't going to end up like that.

Out on the stage the angels had surrounded the demons, but since there were nine demons, and only three angels, surrounded was a bit of an over optimistic description. Bliss was pointing at the swirling demons in horror.

"They don't have soul-lights. None of them do!"

"Thank you, Bliss", said Tor stiffly, "but I think we know where Dross is hiding", and she pointed at Munroe. Dross had stopped wasting his energy trying to control the boy's soul-light, now that he'd achieved his objective and brought the waiting demons through. Thren could see Munroe's light blue soul-light, now icy with fear, battering against the inside of the boy's own body, trying to escape, to put some distance between himself, and the terrible demon who was occupying him.

"Get that thing out of him" cried Debbie running towards the stage, Thren nodded, his chest hurting, not from the spike this time, but from an awareness that many of his charges were in danger, Munroe most of all. Thren leapt forward, grabbing the young man's body, trying to free him from the demon's control. If there had only been one demon present, Dross, it would have been more manageable. Dudley had hurried forward, praying, which was having an effect on Dross, making his hold over Munroe a little weaker. Debbie and Marty, along with Nesta and Tim, were approaching Munroe with liquid spray bottles, washed out and filled with holy water. That had been Paul's idea. He thought it might be more efficient than normal water bottles, allowing them to spray the liquid over a larger area. Flint dashed over and tried to grab the book out of Munroe's hands but the demon wasn't prepared to give it up so easily. Paul and Sarah hurried to help Flint, but in the tussle, the book left Munroe's fingers and flew through the air towards one of the other demons, which managed to make itself just solid enough to catch it, enveloping the book in its dark essence and holding it in mid-air. Another of the demon shapes was trying to wrap itself around Dudley, seeing him as the leader of the group, and the strongest spiritually. The old man's pure white soul-light burned brightly, making it difficult for the demon to touch him. Every contact hurt the creature from The Darkness more than it hurt Dudley, However, it was managing to distract him and interrupt his prayers, enabling Dross to battle to free himself from Thren's grip. Seeing her father enshrouded by one of the disgusting creatures, Bex ran towards him, adding her prayers to his and spraying holy water over the demon, making it flinch away from Dudley, and contract briefly. Dross raised Munroe's arm and pointed towards her, shouting out to the other demons.

"That's her. Get her". The smoky shapes whisked through the air and began to twist themselves around her body, their smell almost choking her, their touch repellent. Thren and Tor looked over at her in horror, as three of the demons began to drag her towards the pentagram on the stage.

Chapter Thirty-Four

Tor dived towards Bex trying to free her from the grasp of the demons, who were planning to use the pentagram and all the other props that Dross had had Duncan set up, as a mechanism to drag her down into The Darkness while she was still alive.

"So kind of you to come to me", Dross said to Bex, his undisguised voice sounding strange coming through Munroe's lips. "I thought I'd have to send these creatures after you, and here you are, right on the spot. So very convenient.....and how foolish of your guardians to let you come. Not that it matters; I'd have got hold of you one way or another". Dross grinned, but Munroe was still trying to battle with him from the inside, so the smile came out twisted and creepy looking.

"And Thren", Dross continued, "My dear old friend, Threnody. What a pleasure to see you again....a little past your best, perhaps, but still battling on I see. I could have saved you all these struggles you know, if you'd only chosen more wisely the last time we met. You should have come with me, your old friend Temporalus... though the name Dross suits me better, don't you think?...You chose the wrong side, you must see that now, and soon you'll be begging me for mercy.....not that it'll do you any good. You do know He's lost, don't you? And I've won.... my Master will be delighted....until he realises that I've made myself more powerful than he is".

Bliss was trying to get the rest of the cast and crew out of the building before the creatures turned on them. At first everyone had frozen in fear or confusion when the terrible demons had appeared on the stage. Now Bliss was whispering in the director's ear, trying to influence him into taking control, and getting his students out of the theatre. Her words got through to him, breaking into his fear-fed paralysis and he edged around the stage, after signalling to the team in the lighting box to get out, and made his way into the wings. The man did what he could to silently guide the other students away from the back stage area and out of the building before the demons attacked them.

Two of the creatures, hungry for soul-lights, noticed that some of their potential prey were leaving, and started to chase after them, but Bliss held them off, using a combination of prayer, and beating the insubstantial demons around the head with her clip board, until the other humans had escaped. The demons didn't put up much of a fight, since there were still a lot of possible victims left in the building.....and if they could help Dross capture the power of angel blood, they would soon be free to feast on as many human soul-lights as they chose. Thren was ignoring Dross's taunts, too busy trying to free Munroe from Dross's control to answer, but the demon was causing the boy's body to thrash around so violently that the angel feared the student would get seriously injured.

"I sure could do with a little help here", Thren called. Dudley resumed his praying and Debbie, Marty, Tim & Nesta began to spray holy water all over Munroe. Dross reluctantly wrenched himself out of Munroe's body, twisting as he did so, deliberately snapping the bones in the arm Thren was gripping. The young man slumped to the ground exhausted and in pain, but nonetheless grateful to be free of the disgusting creature that had taken over his body. Debbie and Nesta took up positions beside Munroe, waving their spray bottles around like guns, determined to protect him so that none of the other demons could grab him and feast on his soul-light while he was vulnerable. Tim and Marty turned their attention and weapons on the creature that was attacking Dudley, squirting that too with holy water and driving it back towards the pentagram.

Bex had run out of holy water and was fighting the demons who had grabbed her with the heavy metal cross, using it to beat them. The creatures would cringe back when it made contact with them but then leap in to attack again as soon as she turned the cross on a different one. Tor was trying to pull the demons away from her charge, but with little success.

"Nine demons against three angels....this ain't gonna end well", muttered Thren as he launched himself at the creatures surrounding Bex. Dudley was staring at Bex in horror, feeling powerless to rescue his daughter. Suddenly he had an idea.

"If it's soul-lights you're after", he shouted to the demons, "Take mine in exchange for Bex".

Snig stirred in his sleep, then sat bolt upright, wide awake and startled. He was needed somewhere, he could sense it, but he didn't know why, or by who, which was rather alarming. He'd never felt summoned before....and hoped it wasn't Dross, or some other demon, dragging him into doing its bidding. He stared up at the misericord above his head. All the choir stalls had strange creatures carved into the underside of the ancient wooden folding seats. These 'mercy seats' were like little shelves for people to lean against when they were standing up for long periods during services. The one he was looking at was some type of avenging angel armed with a spear.....he found it alarming, and hoped it wasn't a bad omen. He scrambled to his feet, which seemed less twisted than they had been before, and hurried towards the great doors of the cathedral. He hesitated in the doorway. He felt safe and peaceful inside the building, and he was afraid that if he stepped outside, Dross would attack him again. Once more he felt something tugging him on, out into the city, and down towards the campus. He took a deep breath, and stepped out onto the street.

The demons were all turned to face Dudley. Nobody ever offered up their soul-light.... they had to be wrenched, or cheated out of them, or the person was killed, and the soul-light captured before it escaped. The offer was tempting....so tempting that some of the demons began to scuttle towards Bex's father, drooling. They had a dilemma....since none of them were occupying a human body, no one demon had quite enough physical strength to kill Dudley and take his soul-light. If they worked together, they could undoubtedly forge their nebulous forms into one substantial one, with the ability to strangle the old man, but co-operation was not one of their strong points. None of them wanted to risk helping another, and have that demon get the soul-light rather than themselves, so they circled Dudley like a pack of dogs, snarling at each other.

"No", cried Dross, "Ignore him. You can have him later. First we have to deal with the girl." Dudley's soul-light glowed almost white ....the sign of a pure spirit....surely it would taste wonderful, the demons were thinking, and give the one that devoured it great power. Although they heard Dross, most of the creatures continued to circle around the old clergyman, leaving only the demon who was protecting the book, and two others who were helping Dross with Bex. Thren and Tor were trying to wrench those two off the girl, so that they could move her away from the pentagram, but the very fact that the demons were disembodied made it harder to fight them. They slithered out between the angels' fingers like so much mist, while having just enough strength to hold Bex in place.

"No, Dad," Bex was shouting, "Don't do it! Flint! Where are you?"

"Here," he replied, trying to duck past one of the demons to reach her.

"Take the knife", she ordered, throwing the kitchen knife she carried towards him. Flint picked it up as she added, "You've got to stop them hurting my dad. They want me alive....they have to kill me in The Darkness. That way my blood will set them all free. ...so, you've got to....", she gulped, terrified, then carried on "You've got to kill me now....here". Flint stared at her in horror.

"Perfect", said Dross, sarcastically. "Give the boy some more guilt to deal with.....his soul-light's going to taste delicious by the time I get to swallow it....again". Inside, the demon was alarmed. Bex's plan had a grisly logic to it. If she died in this world, she would be just one more dead human. He might get to enjoy devouring her pretty silver soul-light, but it wouldn't free the demons from The Darkness forever....or raise him to supreme status, as the one who had made it all happen. Somewhere in the building he heard a door slamming open, but he was too preoccupied to worry about it. He had to try and regain control.

Flint was clutching the knife, staring at Bex in shock. Surely she didn't really mean him to kill her?

"Thren?" Flint shouted in desperation, "What am I meant to do.....I can't kill her".

"I should hope not", Tor replied, wrestling with one of the demons. "Or you'll have me to deal with".

"Nothing new there then", murmured Thren, as another demon tried to wrap itself round his face. "You give the guy a hard time whatever he does.....but seriously, killing Bex? Don't go there Flint!"

"He's got to", Bex cried. "It's the only thing that can stop this".

"Then someone had sure better come up with a different solution, 'cos we ain't going down that route". Thren found himself flat on the ground as another demon tackled him, knocking his legs out from beneath him.

"We must!" called Bex, as Dross himself grabbed hold of her, and tried to position her exactly where he wanted her.

"I can't do it", Flint called out "I can't kill you".

"Why not?" Dross asked, trying to manipulate him. "You've killed before.....your poor brother, wasn't it?....and you went to prison for it...I bet he kept that secret, didn't he?" Dross looked round at the students, smirking. "You see, he's not even worthy of killing his girlfriend, that would be the act of a hero....and he's a coward, he just doesn't want to go back to prison. I bet none of you want anything to do with him, now you know the truth". Flint hung his head in shame, knowing it was true. He wasn't sure whether he couldn't kill Bex because he loved her, or because he was terrified of being responsible for another death....but whatever the reason, he couldn't do it. The knife dropped from his fingers, and landed, blade down, on the inner circle of the pentagram, cutting through the circle of salt. Some of the demons twitched.

"You're wrong" said Sarah, finding the courage to step forward, "We know all about Flint's past, and we're still proud to call him our friend". She reached out and took Flint's hand, supportively. "If he can't kill Bex, it's because he's a good person. We know what he did in the past, but that was then. It's not who he is now. You're just trying to stop him killing her by making him feel ashamed."

"Anyway" said Cath, stepping up nervously to stand on Flint's other side, "What makes you think we're going to take any notice of what you say? We know what you're like, what you did to Graham".

"And to Mark, last time", added Sam, moving in closer to join Flint and the girls. "How can you try and make *him* feel guilty? *You're* evil". Dross glared at them all.

"Way to go, Sam," said Thren, from inside the coils of one of the demons. "You tell him".

"How sweet!" said Dross, dripping sarcasm. "A little show of solidarity. Don't feel too encouraged, Flint.....they don't mean what they're saying about you. They're just doing it to annoy me....but it won't work. Nothing you can do will work....Like you!" the demon sneered, turning on Dudley, "Do you think a sacrificial gesture and the prayers of one good man can work against all this?" Dross gestured to the other demons, still circling around Dudley, each of them desperate to get hold of his soul-light for themselves.

"What about the prayers of three good men?" asked the bishop, stepping onto the stage to stand on Dudley's right hand side. "Need a hand, Dudley?" said Poole, tentatively, taking his place on his friend's left.

The three men prayed together, with and for each other, and the demons drew back. The bishop's golden soul-light pulsed beside Dudley's pure white one, while Poole's purple soul-light glowed brighter with each passing moment. Dross snarled.

"It doesn't change anything," he croaked. "We can still win. Once we drag the girl into The Darkness it's over....for all of you".

At that moment Paul sprang towards the demon which was protecting the book. He was sure that getting hold of that, and destroying it, was the key to winning the battle. He sprayed holy water onto the creature, while at the same time thrusting a bible into its core. The creature dropped the book, as it sprang back trying to fend off Paul's assault. Paul lunged forward to grab the book, but Dross saw what he was trying to do. The demon made a strange gesture, and the candles that had been placed at the five points of the pentagram flared brightly, then the flames from them seemed to leap through the air towards the book......but instead of burning it, they formed a dome of flames around and above it, to protect it from anyone who tried to reach for it.

Paul tried anyway, as did Flint, but the flames burned their hands, and they couldn't snatch the book out from within them. Dross laughed.... a dry, humourless sound that echoed around the theatre.

"Losers" he sniggered, "But do keep trying, it's so entertaining to watch, and I do love the smell of burning humans! Just like a barbeque. It's whetting my appetite for what's to come".

"Throw a coat over it or something", called Bex, still pinned in place by demons. Sam grabbed a cloth that was draped over a piece of furniture on the stage, and flung it on top the fire, expecting the lack of oxygen to put out the flames. Instead they flared even more brightly, as they burnt the cloth to ashes in seconds. Dross laughed again, louder this time, and the other demons began to join in, creating an eerie sinister sound that boomed around the empty auditorium.

"Check Mate", said Dross, "Game Over".

Chapter Thirty-Five

Dudley, Poole and the Bishop were still praying, their conjoined power weakening the demons' grip on Bex, and forcing the ones prowling around Dudley to back off a little, unnerved by the circle of pale light that seemed to spread out from the three godly men. Dross, however, had a point. It was a stale mate while the demons had control of the book that was holding them all in the human world, but none of them had a human body to work through. Thren and Tor were becoming exhausted as they battled the demons, but didn't seem to be making any progress.

"Not sure how much longer I can keep this up, guys", Thren's voice was getting weaker. He was tiring more quickly than Tor, because he wasn't fully recovered from the events of the last few days.

Dross moved towards Flint, expanding his presence to tower over the young man.

"Your soul-light really is going to taste delightful......all that guilt. The simplest thing would be for you to kill yourself now, and save me the bother. Remove your sorry presence from the world. You do know it would be a relief for everybody, don't you? They're just all too polite to say it. Why, your girlfriend even gave you the knife. Think of it...you could be free of all this guilt and pain, just like that".

"Don't let him play you, kid", Thren called out. "Ya can't allow him to use how you feel as a weapon against you".

Flint glanced down at the knife, as tendrils of Dross's disgusting essence tried to push itself into his ears and mouth, pumping him full of self loathing. It would be a relief, Flint admitted to himself, not to feel overwhelmed by guilt all the time, but tempting as it was at that moment, under the influence of Dross's unrelenting pressure, he knew that wasn't the way to do it. He glanced around at his friends, amazed that they still seemed ready to stand by him, even though they all now knew the worst about him. They seemed able to forgive him, and see past what he'd done. He realised that Dudley was right. He was the one who needed forgiveness, and he was the one who had to do the forgiving, and let himself move on, but he wasn't sure if he could do it. Suddenly he reached down to grab the knife from the floor.

Bliss had been patrolling the building, checking for "non-combatants", as she thought of all the humans in her care, the ones who were not directly involved in what was happening on the stage. While she wasn't sure of the exact protocol for a demon incursion into the human world, she thought it seemed to be a professional approach to take to the situation. She didn't want to admit, even to herself, that making sure everyone else was out of the building was an excellent excuse for not going back to join the other angels in battle. It was only her first day, for heaven's sake, and she wasn't even sure she liked them. Thren seemed totally unprofessional, an emotional wreck, and Tor was much too bossy. Bliss decided to check the entire building one more time before going to find out how the others were getting on.

"Can't be too careful", she said to herself, crisply. She couldn't see any soul-lights in the building, apart from a bright golden one in the area of the stage. She decided that even if its owner was her responsibility, they didn't seem in need of her assistance, and carried on with her patrol. She was passing the door to the dressing room when she heard sobbing. She couldn't see a soul-light, so she tried to tell herself that whoever was inside wasn't really her responsibility, but the person sounded so distressed that she felt compelled to go and check on whoever it was. Especially as she had to concede that the other angels were probably a tiny bit busy battling with the demons .....without her assistance. She pushed open the door and saw Duncan, hunched up on the floor, weeping, his arms wrapped around a cross, clutching it to himself like a security blanket.

"It's my fault" he was saying to himself. "I invited it in....I didn't mean too, I didn't".

As the student had seen the demons already, Bliss didn't see the point of remaining invisible herself. She appeared in front of him and spoke firmly.

"Pull yourself together, young man.....and if you invited one of those creatures in, you should come and help deal with it! Come along!" She thought guiltily of her own mistake, casually letting slip about Bex having angel blood.....that might, just possibly, have increased the power of the demons that the others were fighting at that moment. "Let's go and correct our mistakes, shall we?" she said brightly, trying to pretend that she wasn't as nervous as Duncan. In his terror he took rather a lot of convincing, but eventually she got him on his feet and started to lead him towards the stage.

Flint was brandishing the knife, but he wasn't about to use it on himself. He pulled away from the snaky tendrils that Dross was using to try to influence him, and shook his head to clear his thoughts. Then he turned on the demon.

"You just want me to finish myself off, so that you can take over my body! That's it, isn't it? You've not strong enough to kill me yourself at the moment, so you want to force me to do it for you. Well, I won't do it....I won't let you manipulate me. I've made some mistakes in the past, but I'm not that stupid". He thrust the knife at the demon, but it passed right through the creature, without having any effect.

"It was worth a try", said Dross sounding casually dismissive. Inside he was raging. Flint's body would have been so useful to inflict some serious damage on the others and bring the struggle to a close. He glanced around the stage, wondering if there was another student he could pick on. Bex was far too strong spiritually and emotionally...... Cath, perhaps? She seemed rather fragile. He glanced towards the three men who were praying, but they were beginning to glow too brightly for him to be able to look at them directly. The circle of light around them seemed to be expanding too, forcing the demons to back off and away from it. Already that meant that Munroe and Debbie and Nesta, who were now encompassed by it, were beyond his reach. Realising this themselves, they beckoned Tim and Marty over to join them. The other students were still focused on Bex, and what was happening in the centre of the pentagram. The demon noticed that there was another flicker of light, this one around Sarah, who was praying as well, and there was a faint glow surrounding Paul, too. Dross felt he needed to move quickly, before the battle shifted in favour of his enemies. He was furious that all of the students seemed to be working together, alongside the angels, to defeat him. He hadn't expected that, since loyalty and teamwork were outside his experience.

The three praying men tried to move towards the pentagram, hoping to bring it into the circle of their prayer light, and protect Bex that way, but some of the demons formed themselves into a barrier, pushing back against the light, and although it seemed to cause the creatures some pain, the men found that they couldn't move any nearer. When one set of demons found the contact with the light too painful, another set replaced them, and so it went on, neither side being able to make any progress.

Dross reached out towards the book, realising that its dark power it might give him the additional strength he needed to win the fight. He put his hand into the flames, though of course he didn't get burnt by them. Just as his fingers touched the cover of the script, something small and pale charged into the theatre and leapt into the fire. The little figure was scorched as it entered the flames, but it wrapped itself around the book anyway and pulled it backwards out of the burning circle that protected it, flinging it into the bright light around Dudley, Poole and the bishop. Dross cursed, knowing it would be almost impossible for him to retrieve it from within the circle of prayer powered light. The creature that had wrenched the book away from him dropped to the floor, its skin burnt and blistered, its wing buds frazzled off. Snig's body lay unmoving on the stage. Dross formed his substance into a foot and kicked at it angrily.

"Leave the little fella alone", gasped Thren in the silence that followed. The demon he was struggling with was wearing him out, and now the ones that had first been forced backward by prayer were turning to join their companions, fighting with Thren and Tor and holding Bex in position.

"Yes," added Tor, surprising herself, "Don't hurt it!"

"What do you care about some stupid imp?" sneered Dross. "It's probably dead, anyway". The demon concentrated on making his foot even more substantial, and brought it down hard on the little imp's skull, crushing it. "There", said the demon, "Problem solved". He gazed around at the horrified faces. "Ahhh! Did I upset you? That's nothing to what'll happen when hell breaks loose". He glared at the other demons. "Get that girl out of here and into The Darkness, **now**. There are only two angels. You can easily defeat them!" Slowly the demon turned his head. He forced himself to stare into the bright light, the dark pits in his misty face looking into Dudley's eyes. "I've just remembered", the demon said silkily, "You offered us your soul-light. Time to hand it over!" Dudley hesitated for a moment, knowing the full implications of what he was agreeing to, then stood up straighter and spoke solemnly.

"It's yours. I give it to you....so long as you set Bex free."
Dross spun round, making his hand solid enough to grab the knife off Flint, and aimed it at Dudley's chest. With a rare burst of courage Poole tried to step forward and shield his friend with his own body, but his portly frame wasn't built for heroics, he was too slow, and Dudley brought his own arm up to brush his friend aside, as Dross threw the knife straight at Dudley's chest. The old man gasped, and crumpled to the floor.

"In exchange... for .... Bex...."

Poole and the bishop knelt beside Dudley, trying to stop the blood flowing out of his chest. The circle of light began to dim. Thren watched in horror as Dudley's pure white soul-light floated above the old man's body. Dross reached out his hand, pulled the soul-light nearer then wrapped himself around it. Even though he didn't have a corporeal body to trap it in, he managed to hold onto the glowing globe, and could feel the power of it flowing through his essence. Bex cried out in despair, struggling so fiercely to free herself that she managed to pull away from the demons that were holding her while they were still distracted, though she ripped the muscles in her shoulder doing it. She ran into the fading circle of light to wrap her arms around her father's body, and wept. Thren felt such a violent pain in his chest that he thought for a moment that the spike was back....but it was grief he was feeling. Grief for a beloved friend.

Chapter Thirty-Six

The students had watched in horrified silence. They all knew Dudley and liked him, Thren and Tor had been proud to count him as their friend, and now he was dead. Bliss, unmoved by the tragedy, stepped onto the stage.

"You're wrong, you know", she spoke nervously. "There aren't two angels, there are three!"

"What does it matter?" said Dross, sarcasm dripping from every word. "You don't count....you ran away as soon as the battle began". Bliss blushed uncomfortably, but replied in a firm voice.

"Perhaps, but I'm back now, and I've brought help!" She shoved a trembling Duncan forward.

"That's not help", said Dross, licking his lips, "That's dessert". Duncan looked at Bliss, horrified that she seemed to be serving him up to the demon, practically on a plate. Bliss smiled at the boy reassuringly.

"He has something to say to you", she added.

"I do?" squeaked Duncan,

"Yes," said Bliss serenely. "He's the one who invited you here, so he has to un-invite you".

"I do?" repeated Duncan.

"Yes" she said firmly, "So get on with it". Duncan gulped.

"I didn't mean to invite you here.", he whispered, "I wish I hadn't done it .....and I'm....withdrawing my invitation....as of now". Dross slid towards him, feeling his grip on the human world loosen a little, but refusing to admit it. He wasn't about to fail now!

"You think it's that simple do you?" said the demon. "You think I'm just going to vanish before your eyes and everything will be just how it was before? Don't be so simplistic! I'm here now, and I'm not going anywhere, ever". Dross turned to shout at the other demons again.

"Now get that girl and put her back in place". The demons hesitated, and Dross realised that Poole and the Bishop were praying again, the circle of light, though smaller, was still powerful.....and Bex was in the middle of it, cradling her father's body in her arms.

As Tor and Thren continued to battle with some of the demons, the others were moving towards Bex, circling the light. Paul stepped forward and faced Dross.

"You can't take her now......you know you can't. Dudley gave up his soul-light in exchange for Bex. You accepted the deal. You can't cheat, there are rules!"

"My dear boy", said Dross, drooling in Paul's face. "I am a demon, in case you hadn't noticed. I cheat......it's what demons do......and the rules are about to be blown apart, by that girl's blood".

"First you have to get her into The Darkness", said Paul, defiantly, "And that plan's not going great, is it? You can't even get her back to the pentagram".

"And even if you could", added Duncan, realising what Dross was planning, "You'd need the pentagram to work, wouldn't you?" He reached down with the large metal cross he was clutching and dragged it through the circle of salt, and the demons twitched again. Paul caught on at once, and called out to the other students.

"Break it up, blow out the candles, anything to stop it working!" The students all leapt into action, scattering props, rubbing out the markings on the floor, and using some of the holy water they had left to douse the candles. The demons began to mill about restlessly, waiting for Dross the give them more orders, but he was looking round in horror as his plan began to fall apart.

"I'll manage without the trimmings, then", growled Dross and began to move towards Bex himself, but something seemed to be happening to him. The soul-light that had felt so empowering at first was now beginning to burn uncomfortably within him.

"Why are they still here?" cried Flint. "We wrecked the pentagram, Duncan has un-invited Dross, and they've broken the rules. Shouldn't they be sucked back into The Darkness now?"

"It's that damn book", Thren's voice was barely audible. "Snig said that's what's keeping Dross here. Somebody's gotta deal with it..." the angel collapsed under the pressure of three demons battling with him. Even in their present insubstantial form he couldn't fight them any longer. Tor tried to move towards him, to stop the demons that were beginning to rip at the open wound in his chest, but she too was worn down by the battle, and lacked the strength to reach him. It was Bliss who suddenly sprang forward and started to pull the creatures away. Having avoided the start of the struggle, she was feeling fresh and strong, just as the other angels, and the demons they were fighting, were beginning to tire.

Flint jumped into the circle of light, and grabbed the book. Its covering felt so revolting, it made him cringe, but the sense of peace within the circle helped him not to freak out completely.

"How do we destroy it, Paul? What can we do?"

"Try burning it?" Paul answered, and Marty pulled some matches out of his pocket and handed them to Flint. He grinned ruefully at Debbie, adding "Bet you're glad I didn't quit smoking now". She answered him with a glare.

Flint held a flickering match to the script and the dry pages began to burn, but the cover seemed more resistant to the flames. Dross howled when he saw the salting that was holding him in the human realm beginning to go up in smoke, and tried to reach into the circle of light to grab it, but the light itself repelled him, and the more he tried to enter it, the more he could feel himself being destroyed from the inside. The very prayer light that was damaging him seemed to be strengthening the power of Dudley's pure soul-light to burn up the demon's essence from within. Bex was still crouched inside the circle weeping, just out of Dross's reach, and the cover of the book was finally beginning to catch fire. It burned with a horrid scorching smell, the flames searing Flint's fingers, forcing him to drop it onto the floor. There it slowly liquefied, forming a stinking, fatty puddle on the stage. The last of the sparks fizzled out, and Dross howled again. The other demons turned away from the angels and focused on Dross. They had all tried to attack people who hadn't invited them into the world, the rules had been broken, and they could feel the tug of The Darkness, dragging at them. They only had the right to destroy one creature....Dross, who *had* invited them....and Dross had a soul-light, a powerful treasure to take back into The Darkness. Suddenly the demons attacked their leader, ripping into his essence, each trying to extract and capture the soul-light for itself, before they were forced out of the human realm. Dross tried to defend himself, but at the same time, he dived towards Duncan, determined to claim the boy's dark blue soul-light. He'd been imagining how it would taste for days. Now he wished he'd collected it sooner. He couldn't bear to return to The Darkness without the soul-light of the human who'd invited him into the world, not for a second time.

Bliss placed herself in front of Duncan, to protect him from the demon, but she needn't have bothered, for Dross was disappearing in a melee of demons, all tearing and pinching at him as he tried to hang on to the only soul-light he had gained....the very thing that was too pure for him, or any demon, to contain. Soon there was nothing left of Dross....the other demons had been so ferocious in their struggle for Dudley's soul-light that their leader's essence was scattered, drifting away in harmless threads, not even worth sucking back into The

Darkness. Soon those demons were tugged away themselves, cursing and swearing as The Darkness claimed them, before they had had a chance to benefit from their time in the human realm. Their struggle for Dudley's soul-light had merely freed it from Dross's control, but none of the demons could hold onto it for long enough to claim it for themselves. As the creatures were sucked back to where they belonged, Dudley's soul-light spun free, glowing so brightly that everyone, not just Thren, could briefly see a faint shimmer of its light.

It hovered for a moment, starting to rise upwards, but then changed direction. It moved back into the circle of light, not to re-enter Dudley's body, but to brush comfortingly against Bex's cheek. It moved again to touch Flint's forehead, the nearest the old man could come to giving them his blessing. The light spun towards Thren and Tor, circling them too, before drifting down to touch Snig's broken corpse. That done, the pure white light shot up into the air and vanished.

Chapter Thirty-Seven

There was a shocked silence, broken only by Bex's sobs. Flint stumbled over to crouch beside her on the stage. He tried to put his arms around her, but he couldn't hold her tightly, because his hands were burnt and blistered. He felt tears rolling down his cheeks, and didn't even try to hide them. Dudley had become family to him, and he wasn't ashamed to show how much the old man's death had hurt him. At the same time, the nature of Dudley's farewell left him with a sense of peace. As the circle of prayer light began to fade Flint finally let go of his guilt about his brother...he'd never forget what he did, or cease to regret it, but the guilt that had been crippling him for years, holding him back from trusting people because he was afraid of their rejection, that was gone. Dudley had wanted better for him, Flint knew that, and he couldn't let the old man down. If he was going to take care of Bex, he'd need to be as strong, as steady as he could be, for her sake, as well as his own.

Bex leaned against Flint's shoulder, her sobs subsiding. Her own shoulder throbbed where she'd torn the muscles, but that was nothing compared to the pain, the sense of loss, she felt inside. Tor reached down and helped Thren up off the floor. He could barely stand, and his chest was bleeding again from where the demons had ripped at the wound, but that was the least of his worries. Tears were running down his face too, and Tor, who was feeling Bex's pain even more directly, looked broken.

"We let him down, Tor. We shoulda been able to save him, and we couldn't". Tor just nodded, miserably, unable to speak.

"No, you didn't let him down", said the bishop, gently. "Between you, you fought off the demons, protected the students and stopped all hell breaking loose. Dudley chose to let that thing take him. He'd have done anything to save Bex, and he did it willingly......and nothing anyone could have done would have stopped him". He stopped, embarrassed, wondering what right he had to be lecturing the angels.

When Poole had explained what was happening and dragged him down to the campus he had been amazed at the sight that confronted him. He'd never expected to see angels, or terrible creatures like Dross, or have been part of diving demons away. He crouched down beside Dudley's body, taking hold of Bex's hand diffidently.

"I'm so sorry, Bex," he said, "I really am. I... we..... everyone at the cathedral that is, we'll all help, with the practical stuff. We'll do everything we can......." Bex squeezed his hand, in acknowledgement, still too distressed to say anything. After a moment she glanced up at Poole, and managed a watery smile of thanks. She had seen him trying to step in front of Dudley, even though he wasn't quick enough, and was grateful. Poole himself was numb, having watched his friend and mentor die. He was torn between relief at having survived the battle, and a sense that the world would have been a better place if Dudley had lived instead of him. Then again, he was pretty sure his soul-light, assuming he had one, would not have had the same powerful effect on the demon that Dudley's had had.

Munroe sat up, clutching his broken arm, confused by the battle that had raged around him. Like Debbie, having his body taken over by Dross had sickened him, and he was thankful it was over, and aware that he owed his survival to his fellow students, and to Thren and Tor.....who were angels. Not quite what he might have imagined, but definitely angels. He was still trying to process that information. Duncan nervously moved over to speak to his friend.

"I'm sorry, you were right about not performing that scene as it was written. There was something wrong about it. I shouldn't have been such a bloody diva!"

"That's ok" replied Munroe. "In the end, I didn't have a choice about how I played the scene....that....thing....just took over. It was gross". Duncan nodded, and reached down to help his friend to his feet. The other students milled around, uncertain what to do next. Tim and Nesta were holding hands, thankful to have survived.

"It makes me realise just how lucky we were, last term", Nesta said.

"Lucky? I had a broken arm, that...thing almost killed me", replied Tim.

"But it didn't, did it?" Nesta continued. "Thren saved both of us. I thought I saw him you, know, at the time. Then I told myself I was just being silly, but I wasn't. If anything had happened to you...then or now..." Nesta's face crumpled a little.

"Well it didn't", said Tim reassuringly, "And I'm hoping it never will.....but whatever happens, at least we'll face it together".
Sam and Cath caught each others' eyes. They were both staring at the angels.

"It's such a relief to know I'm not going crazy", said Cath, "Though the thought of my....of part of me....being carried around inside that ghastly creature for days....it's disgusting".

"I don't feel quite so bad about Mark either" Sam admitted. "Seeing that.....thing.....I don't think anything I could have done would have saved him".

"I suppose we can both move on then" said Cath, "Try to put the past behind us and get back to being ourselves".

"Yes," said Sam, looking over at Bex sadly. "But what about the present? Bex is going to have to deal with that".

"I admit I'm glad you had some matches," Debbie whispered to Marty, "But I still want you to quit smoking. I don't want you to die on me!" Marty grinned.

"After what we've just been through, you're worried about me dying from cancer? That would take years to kill me. We could have died right here."

"Well since we didn't, I'd rather you lived a long, healthy life, with me. I want us to grow old together". Marty kissed her, partly to change the subject, admittedly, but partly because knowing how easily any of them could have died made him value her all the more.

"I could go along with that plan", he murmured.

"Besides", she added with a grin, "You can't afford to smoke anymore".

Sarah found she had grabbed onto Paul's arm tightly towards the end of the battle, and let it go, feeling embarrassed.

"I'm sorry, did I hurt you? I was hanging on pretty hard".

"That's ok", he replied trying to appear nonchalant, as if he had the girl he really liked clinging onto him every day........ If only.

"Your hands," said Sarah concerned. "They're burned".

"Not as badly as Flint's", Paul said, staring over at his friend. "I suppose we'll both need to go to the hospital, later". He turned to Sarah and added, "That was terrifying. We could all have died......and Flint was expecting me to know what to do!"

"You did know", relied Sarah, reassuringly. "You were the most prepared of any of us".

"I guess that's what comes of being a geek", Paul smiled ruefully.

"Nothing wrong with geeks" grinned Sarah, "After today, I may become one myself.....I'd rather be prepared, next time."

"Who says there's going to be a next time?" asked Paul surprised, as Sarah went and picked up an abandoned coat from the wings and laid it gently over Snig's body.

Thren and Tor exchanged worried looks.

"What's the matter?" asked Bliss airily, hoping nobody would ask why she took so long to come and join in the battle. Tor lowered her voice and said "Those demons, the ones who went back into The Darkness....they know who Bex is....and what's special about her".

"And where to find her", added Thren, "We sure gotta do something about that".

"Not yet," Tor's voice was gentle. "Let her grieve first". Thren put a comforting arm around Tor's shoulder, and she leaned against him, allowing herself a moment of weakness before she had to be strong again, for Bex's sake.

Bex and Flint stood up, moving away from Dudley's body. The bishop and Poole had agreed that they should be the ones to call the police, and come up with a believable explanation for the events that had occurred. A theatrical effect that had gone horribly wrong seemed to be the most likely and acceptable explanation.....though it was Thren who knelt down and wiped Flint and Bex's prints off the handle of the knife.

"They sure got enough to deal with, without the cops thinking they're murderers." The angel gently swept his hands over Dudley's face, closing his eyes. "Goodbye, old friend", he whispered. "Guess I'll see you again, one day. Thanks.... for everything".

Flint moved over to Paul, trying to find a way to put into words how grateful he was. He'd realised during the battle that he'd come to rely on Paul. Other people might see the Art History student as a bit nerdy and isolated, but Flint knew that it was Paul who took their situation seriously and prepared for it, Paul who he depended on to come up with the solutions. Unable to find the right words, Flint just gave his friend a hug. For Flint, who was not a huggy person, and who'd always kept himself a little detached from people, that was a big deal.

Sarah glanced over to where she'd thrown the coat down to cover Snig's body, and thought she saw it move. She nudged Paul, and pointed. The coat was definitely wriggling. Soon everyone was staring at the heap on the floor. Tor moved across to it and whisked the coat away. There, curled up on the stage, was Snig, no longer burnt and broken, no longer an imp, but transformed. His skin was pale and smooth, and free from bruises, and from his shoulders sprouted a proper set of white, feathery wings. He was the same size that he had been before, and his face was still a little impish, but he was definitely something other, something new. He stared round at everybody, shyly.

"Well, what'da you know?" grinned Thren. "It's some kind of a cherub".

"Cherubs don't exist, they're fictional" said Tor, as determined to be precise as ever, "And it's certainly not one of the cherubim".

"Well, whatever the heck it is.....I guess it's supposed to be here. It sure earned the right, after everything it did to help. And I figure it's what Dudley woulda wanted". He reached down to help the little creature to its feet.

"Snig's strange", said the little creature, its voice softer than it was before.

"You can say that again, Buddy" Thren replied.

Dudley had had a splendid funeral in the cathedral, with everyone paying tribute to him. Not just the bishop, and Poole, and the other members of the clergy team, but old friends and people from around the city, and from the homeless shelter where he'd helped out. They all came to pay their respects. There were so many people whose lives he had touched. Even Luke was there, Thren noticed, remembering how Dudley had helped the boy when he was a runaway. Amy was sitting beside him, along with Harriet and Jay, who had brought them both, which Thren hoped was an encouraging sign.

All of the students who were Bex's friends had come, of course, and she appreciated it, but the only people she was really aware of as her father's coffin was carried into the cathedral, were Flint, with his bandaged hands, supporting her on one side, and Tor, invisible on the other. She could see Thren too, standing to attention beside the coffin, though nobody else in the cathedral was aware of Dudley's heavenly sentinel.

Chapter Thirty-Eight

Once the funeral was over, and Bex had had time to recover a little, Tor decided it was time to act. Leaving Bliss watching over the city, she insisted that Thren accompany her to Bex's house to have a proper discussion.

"It's too soon, Tor", Thren was saying as she practically dragged him along with her. "The kid ain't ready yet".

"She probably never will be", growled Tor, "But we've left it long enough already. She's in danger here."

"She's in danger anywhere", said Thren as they reached the door, and Tor rang the bell, making an effort to try and respect Bex's privacy. It was Flint who came to let them in. He showed the angels into the sitting room, where Bex, Paul and Sarah were chatting, in a subdued kind of way.

"We need to talk" said Tor, briskly. "You're not going to like what I have to say, but I do need you to listen to me, and consider the matter seriously."

"It's alright", said Bex solemnly, her arm still in a sling to protect her injured shoulder. "I think I know what you're going to say".

"You do?" asked Tor, surprised. "You think I should go away, don't you?" asked Bex. "Leave Chester? Leave everyone?"

"Well, yes," replied Tor awkwardly, "It would be safer. The next chance they get, those creatures will be back. They know exactly what you are now... and where to find you".

"I'm not sure I care," answered Bex, wearily, "Not without Dad".

"Now look here", said Tor, crossly, "Your father gave up his life trying to protect you, and I'm not going to let you throw that away".

"I know", said Bex, "I know he did.....and I know I have to leave, too....but does it have to be now? Dad wouldn't have wanted me to abandon my chance of getting a degree".

"So don't" said Flint. "I saw this coming, as well, and I've been looking into courses at other universities. You can transfer to somewhere else. There's a biology degree course at Cardiff. It looks as if you could go straight into the second year there, it's a similar structure to the one you're doing here. ....and it's a good course." Tor looked at Flint with surprised approval.

"But how can I leave everyone?" said Bex, "I don't want to go down there on my own....I wouldn't even have a home to come back to in the holidays..... though this doesn't feel exactly like my home anymore.... not without Dad. The house wasn't even his really, it belongs to the cathedral..... though the bishop says I can stay on for as long as I want to." She looked round sadly, "It's the only place I've ever lived...even if it does feel different now".

"I'd still be there", said Tor. "You know I would be". Bex tried to look delighted, but even though she was fond of Tor, stepping out into a whole new life with only her guardian angel for company was rather daunting.

"You wouldn't be on your own", Flint added. "I've checked, and I can transfer too... to the Royal Welsh College of Music & Drama. It's not as if I have any family to hang around here for....they'd be happy to see the back of me. It's only my sister who keeps in touch, and she's moved away from home herself. We could complete our exams, get all your stuff packed up and arrange to move after I've finished in the Mystery Plays". Flint looked at Thren, nervously, and asked "I can still be in that, can't I? I'd hate to let everyone down at this stage".

Tor sniffed disapprovingly before answering.

"I really think Bex should move away as soon as possible...and your role in a production is hardly relevant".

"It sure is relevant to Flint", said Thren, "And to a load of other people".

"And to me", added Bex, firmly. "I expect it'll take ages to organise everything anyway and we could still be down there and ready to start our new courses by September".

"Alright", Tor agreed, "We'll just have to be extra vigilant until then....but you leave as soon as the production is over". Secretly she was rather pleased. The angel had been looking forward to watching the spectacular stories unfold, but she wasn't about to admit that to anyone.

"Two of us against the world then!" said Bex, sounding more positive. She squeezed Flint's hand, and he flinched. The bandages were off, but he still had dressings on the burns on his hands.

"So long as you promise to stop doing that", muttered Flint. "What happens to you now, Thren?" Bex looked anxious. "If Flint moves away, and everyone else you have to protect stays here? I guess you stay here too?"

"I'm kinda fuzzy on that one", Thren admitted. "I just hope I'm not sent somewhere completely different, protecting a new group of people. I've gotten kinda fond of the folks I've got". He grinned ruefully, "I wouldn't have figured on that happening a few months ago".

"Well," said Tor, "I've spoken to the High Council, and due to your ....extraordinary level of commitment, and the toll it's already taken on you, they've decided that you can move straight to being a personal guardian....like me!"

"Yeah, but who of.....I mean, you didn't know Bex before you were assigned to her, did you? Am I just gonna get sent to some random? Someone I don't even care about?"

"You'd learn to care, Thren, you know you would. That's your problem entirely.....but no. Out of the group you've already narrowed it down to.....you're allowed to choose whoever you think needs you most. The rest will become Bliss's responsibility".

"Really? My pick? Hey, that's pretty cool". He thought for a moment. "I guess if Bex is moving away, most of the students here will be ok, they won't be targets anymore, so their lives will go back to normal....and Poole, he ain't gonna need me". He looked at the others. He figured Paul could get into trouble...the whole being able to see angels thing....there could be a down side to that, alright. Sarah was a tough little warrior too, despite the soft fuzzy pink soul-light....though Thren had noticed that these days it had an edgier glint to it. Flint, he was bound to be in danger, just by being with Bex. "I guess it's between you three. I figure you're the ones who might need my help".

"You'll have to choose", said Tor. "Bex and Flint are going to be miles away, and Paul and Sarah are here! Besides, I can look after Flint for you!" Thren wasn't convinced that Tor had warmed to Flint sufficiently to look after him properly. Despite everything, she still didn't seem to think he was good enough for Bex.

Flint spoke up, looking in Thren's eyes.

"You know I don't deserve any special treatment, you should stay here, with the others".

"Hey, if we all got what we deserved, kid, I'd sure be in trouble right now. You deserve anything good that's coming your way. Dudley knew that, and so do I". He hesitated, still unsure who to choose. The temptation was to choose Flint to stay close to Bex, who felt like family, but he knew he ought to decide based on who'd need his help the most.

"I can make it easier for you", said Paul, shyly. "I figure I'm part of the team anyhow. If there is any more trouble, I sort of think I should be there, with Bex and Flint. Is there an Art History course at Cardiff?"

"You'd do that?" asked Bex, amazed. Flint stared at Paul.

"You'd jack everything in to come with us?" he asked his friend.

"I might be needed", said Paul, simply. "And if I am, I want to be there".

"Me too" added Sarah, suddenly. Thren whistled in surprise.

"Hey, since when did you two become an item?" Paul stared at Sarah, stunned.

"We're not!" said Sarah quickly. "We're just friends, Paul and I.....but being best friends....that's pretty special too. I don't want to lose that.....and even if I can't do anything remarkable, like Paul ....I still want to be there".

"Are you sure?" asked Tor, in full nanny mode, "It's a big decision."

"I'm sure", said Sarah, "It may seem crazy, and I've no idea how to explain it to my parents, but I'm sure. This is the team I'm meant to be part of".

"That's it then", said Thren, relieved. "Decision made! Can I be responsible for three people, Tor?"

"I suppose so", she said, uncertainly, "I'll have to check. You always do seem to get away with breaking all the rules".

"What can I say?" replied Thren, with a grin, "Somebody up there likes me!"

"It seems He does", replied Tor curtly.

"You're all going away?" asked a small voice, and Snig crawled out from behind the sofa. "Don't want you to go". He'd stolen one of Bex's t-shirts to wear, which on him was long enough to be a robe. If he'd picked something white it would have looked about right, but he'd chosen an old blue one with a conservation message on it which read "Keep Calm and Save the World". With his wings sticking out through holes he'd ripped in the back of it, he looked decidedly odd. "I'm not staying here with Bliss angel. She doesn't like me".

"Neither do I!" said Tor indignantly, "So go away!"

"Lighten up, Tor", laughed Thren, "Why shouldn't the little fella come with us? I figure Dudley woulda liked that idea".

"We don't even know what he is!" Tor protested.

"I'm with you....that's what I am", replied Snig, grinning.

Tor's face fell.

"What's up Wonderwings?" asked Thren.

Tor leaned forward and whispered in Thren's ear, "I've just realised, if you're protecting Flint, and I'm protecting Bex, then as long as they stay together........"

Thren finished the sentence "…..we're stuck together too…….. maybe for years…….what did I do to deserve that, for heaven's sake? You, breathing down my neck….forever…."

"And you", Tor added, "Breaking every rule in the book".

"I *so* didn't sign up for this", grumbled Thren.

"Too late now" said Flint overhearing.

"You're stuck with each other" added Bex, smiling for the first time in days. Thren looked around the room, with a rueful grin on his face. "I guess it could be worse, at that".

About the Author

Fiona was born and brought up on the Wirral Peninsula and has been addicted to books, animals and theatre since she was a child. This has led to a rather varied career. She did a Zoology degree at Liverpool University, followed by drama training, and has since juggled acting, writing, directing, theatre administration, and being a bat worker and environmental educationalist, as well as working as a zookeeper/presenter at Chester Zoo for a couple of years. She's written a number of plays and musicals for the theatre companies she's worked with, as well as 'Manx Folk Tales' (Published by The History Press in 2015) and 'Soul-lights' (Published by Prior Press in 2012). Due to her previous publisher's retirement, and the difficulty of placing a sequel with a new publisher, she made the decision to bring this book out herself.

Fiona performs across the country as a storyteller and puppeteer, working as The Yarn Spinner (www.theyarnspinner.com), and is a member of The Society for Storytelling. She also builds puppets, for her own work and for other people, as Touchstone Puppets. (www.touchstonepuppets.com). Fiona is currently involved in creating touring productions with Off Book Theatre, alongside her storytelling work.

Fiona's been married for over 35 years....which gives you some indication of just how patient her husband is.....he has put up with years of her being so focused on writing that nothing else gets done, and filling the house with animals, props, costumes, actors and puppets in various stages of construction. (The realistic dinosaur puppets took up a lot of room!) They moved down to South Wales in 2013, settling in a beautiful valley about 12 miles away from Abergavenny, and soon got involved in a lovely new church and a terrific theatre group. At the moment Fiona's learning to play the harp, and trying to manage a rather large garden and an unruly dog, alongside her performance and writing work.

If you want to follow her work you can find her on Facebook listed as Fiona Angwin - Writer.

Final Note

If you have enjoyed reading this book, Fiona would really appreciate a little help. As a self-published author she needs a lot more reviews to get people to hear about her work. Please take a couple of minutes to go to the Soul-Scars page on Amazon and leave an honest review. That way she gets to sell - and hopefully therefore write - more books! Thanks!

Printed in Great Britain
by Amazon